Adventurer, you whose weight is borne by your winged soul! The mystical world of Theldesia is home to dragons and giants, magical beasts, and demihumans. Fragrant green winds blow across this new yet ancient land that opens before you like a blank page. Fill it with your life.

LOG HORIZON

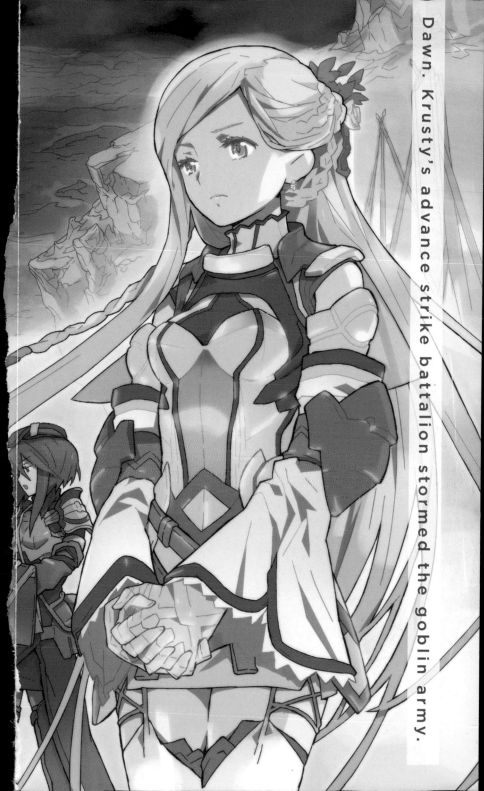

Dawn. Krusty's advance strike battalion stormed the gobliin army.

LOG HORIZON

LOG HORIZON CHARACTER POPULARITY POLL

LOG HORIZON HAS A BIG CAST OF CHARACTERS, FROM WOMENS' UNDERWEAR ENTHUSIASTS TO DASHING CAT GENTLEMEN, FROM ASSASSINS TO POLITICIANS TO SHIROE HIMSELF! WHO'S YOUR FAVORITE?

▶▶▶ **GO TO**
WWW.YENPRESS.COM/
LOG-HORIZON-EXTRAS/
AND VOTE FOR YOUR
FAVORITE!

1

▶ **SHIROE**
Our Machiavellian liege with hermit tendencies

2

▶ **NAOTSUGU**
Loves panties! A completely reliable vanguard

3

▶ **AKATSUKI**
This taciturn, petite beauty is a master assassin

4

▶ **MARIELLE**
Soft skin! Everyone's big sister! Akiba's Sunflower

5

▶ **NYANTA**
Cook, swordsman, dandy, and reliable retiree

6

▶ **TOUYA**
A samurai boy who heads straight for the goal once he's in motion

▶ **MINOR**
An ear
schoo
class

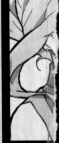

▶ **HENR**
A shre
she's
a pas

▶ **KRUS**
An al
type
"Bers

Adventurer, you whose weight is borne by your winged soul! The mystical world of Theldesia is home to dragons and giants, magical beasts, and demihumans. Fragrant green winds blow across this new yet ancient land that opens before you like a blank page. Fill it with your life.

LOG HORIZON

4 GAME'S END 【PART 2】

MAMARE TOUNO   ILLUSTRATION BY **KAZUHIRO HARA**

YEN ON

NEW YORK

CONTENTS

176

▸BOY SAMURAI

TOUYA

▸LOVELY ASSASSIN

AKATSUKI

▸MACHIAVELLI-WITH-GLASSES

SHIROE

HE GOT CAUGHT UP IN THE CATASTROPHE RIGHT AFTER HE BEGAN PLAYING *ELDER TALES*. UNTIL BEING RESCUED BY SHIROE, HE WAS ABUSED BY A BRUTAL GUILD, BUT HE HAS ALWAYS BEEN A KID WITH A STRONG CORE. HE'S MINORI'S YOUNGER TWIN BROTHER.

ALTHOUGH SHE FORMERLY HID THE FACT THAT SHE WAS FEMALE AND PLAYED AS A SILENT MAN, AFTER BEING SWALLOWED UP BY THE GAME, SHE CHANGED HER BODY TO MATCH HER REAL-WORLD SELF AND BEGAN PLAYING AS A SLENDER, BRILLIANT ASSASSIN.

AN INTELLECTUAL ENCHANTER WHO ONCE ACTED AS COUNSELOR FOR THE LEGENDARY BAND OF PLAYERS, THE DEBAUCHERY TEA PARTY. HE MAY BE A VETERAN PLAYER, BUT INSIDE HE'S A UNIVERSITY STUDENT AND HARD-CORE GAMER WITH HERMIT TENDENCIES.

▼ PLOT

IN ANOTHER WORLD, THREE MONTHS AFTER IMPRISONMENT: IN *ELDER TALES*, TOO, THE SEASONS HAVE TURNED TO SUMMER. AT MARI'S SUGGESTION, A SUMMER CAMP TO TRAIN NEWBIES IS BEING HELD ON THE COAST.

LOG HORIZON SENT ITS NEWBIE MEMBERS, TOUYA AND MINORI, WHILE NAOTSU-GU AND NYANTA WENT ALONG AS INSTRUCTORS. AS THE NEW PLAYERS LOCKED HORNS AND GOT THROUGH TROUBLE AND HARSH TRIALS ALIKE, THEY GRADUALLY LEARNED THE TEAMWORK NEEDED FOR COMBAT.

MEANWHILE, THE ROUND TABLE COUNCIL—AKIBA'S ORGANIZATION OF SELF-GOVERNMENT—RECEIVED A LETTER. AS A RESULT, SHIROE AND SEVERAL OTHER ROUND TABLE COUNCIL MEMBERS WERE DISPATCHED FROM AKIBA AS REPRESENTATIVES TO NEGOTIATE WITH EASTAL, THE LEAGUE OF FREE CITIES—AN ORGANIZATION BY AND FOR THE PEOPLE OF THE EARTH.

MINORI

▶MIDDLE SCHOOL MIKO

SHE'S A VERY RESPONSIBLE GIRL, AND SHE ACTIVELY LOOKS AFTER HER ENERGETIC, RECKLESS LITTLE BROTHER, TOUYA. AS TWINS, TOUYA THE WARRIOR AND MINORI THE HEALER ARE ABLE TO EXECUTE WELL-SYNCED COMBINATION PLAYS.

ISUZU

▶PIGTAILED HIGH SCHOOLER

SHE ISN'T GOOD AT TALKING TO BOYS, BUT FOR SOME REASON, SHE'S ABLE TO JOKE AROUND WITH RUNDEL-HAUS. UNUSUALLY FOR A BARD, SHE USES A TWO-HANDED SPEAR BECAUSE—IN CLASSIC NEWBIE STYLE—SHE CHOSE IT FOR ITS LOOKS.

RUNDEL

▶PUPPY-DOG PRINCE

HE'S EXTREMELY PROUD AND SOME OF THE THINGS HE SAYS SOUND ARROGANT, BUT THERE'S NO MALICE IN HIM. A HOT-BLOODED TYPE WHO TAKES GREAT PRIDE IN HIS CLASS OF SORCERER. HIS GOOD LOOKS ARE STRAIGHT OUT OF A CLASSIC GIRLS' MANGA.

ALTHOUGH BOTH GROUPS KNEW THAT ADVENTURERS AND PEOPLE OF THE EARTH NEEDED TO COEXIST, THE NEGOTIATIONS TOWARD ALLIANCE MOVED AT A SNAIL'S PACE AS EACH SIDE TRIED TO READ THE OTHER'S TRUE INTENTIONS. THEN, DURING THE NEWBIE CAMP, MARI SPOTTED A HOARD OF SAHUAGINS SO VAST THEY COVERED THE BEACH. IT WAS THE HARBINGER OF A LOOMING CRISIS UNLIKE ANYTHING *ELDER TALES* HAD SEEN BEFORE...

CHAPTER.
1

THE RETURN OF
THE GOBLIN KING

▶ NAME: KRUSTY

▶ LEVEL: 90

▶ RACE: HUMAN

▶ CLASS: GUARDIAN

▶ HP: 13871

▶ MP: 6847

▶ ITEM 1:

[FRESH BLOOD DEMON AX]

A TWO-HANDED, FANTASY-CLASS AX THAT CAN BE EQUIPPED AT LEVEL 90. IT COMPENSATES FOR HATE VALUES INCREASED BY ATTACKS, DRAWING MONSTERS TO ITSELF. IT BOASTS THE MOST DAMAGE OF ALL CURRENTLY IDENTIFIED EQUIPMENT, AND IT'S AN ITEM MANY ADVENTURERS ASPIRE TO OWN.

▶ ITEM 2:

[EINHERJAR'S ARMOR]

FULL-BODY, FANTASY-CLASS ARMOR MADE OF EBONY STEEL. IT'S SAID IT MAY BE WORN ONLY BY THOSE BRAVE WARRIORS WHO ARE BOUND FOR RAGNARÖK GUIDED BY VALKYRIES. IT GREATLY INCREASES ITS WEARER'S PHYSICAL STRENGTH AND STAMINA, AND IT WEAKENS ATTRIBUTE ATTACKS FROM GIANTS AND IMMORTALS.

▶ ITEM 3:

[RAGAIN]

AN ARMLET FASHIONED OF STONE THAT CANCELS THE RECAST TIME RESTRICTIONS FOR BERSERKER SPECIAL SKILLS AND MAKES IT POSSIBLE TO REUSE THE ABILITIES. IT PROVIDES A PERMANENTLY ACTIVE EFFECT THAT WORKS TO PROLONG LIFE FOR ABOUT TEN SECONDS IN A FRENZIED STATE WHEN THE CHARACTER DIES. ITS ABBREVIATED NAME COMES FROM THE WORDS "RAGE AGAIN."

\<Comb and Hand Mirror\>
Tools to help you look nice.
Can also be used to look around corners.

► 1

While Marielle shielded the newbie Adventurers and Shouryuu kicked up waves, bellowing a challenge to the sahuagins, another battle was beginning in the mountains at the center of the Zantleaf Peninsula.

The enemy was goblins.

There was no telling where they'd sprung from, but a significant number of small, squad-sized groups seemed to be prowling through the forest.

Naotsugu's group was in the square outside Forest Ragranda, and by now they'd beaten back a dozen or so attacks. There were thirteen players gathered in the square: the five members of Minori's party and the six members of the advanced party, plus Naotsugu and Lezarik, the Cleric sent by the Knights of the Black Sword.

They had thought the first attack was an accidental encounter with rogue goblins.

After a few more skirmishes, however, Naotsugu had changed his mind, deciding their party must have stumbled into the path of a small traveling tribe. However, when the number of encounters reached six, the doubt had grown too large to ignore.

At that point, Nyanta had gone into the mountains to reconnoiter.

While awaiting his return, thirteen people had broken camp and were keeping a wary eye on the surrounding area.

As far as enemies went, in terms of fighting power, a single goblin wasn't much of a threat. Of course, the race had prodigious strength in numbers and plentiful troop variations, so when considered as an army, they were formidable. However, goblins' core level range was only 10 to 20. In other words, when viewed as individuals, even Minori and the other newbies—whose levels were only around 25— could easily handle them.

As a result, the newbies were relatively calm as they worked the campsite, even though the situation was potentially murky. Leaving items earmarked for the big tent to Naotsugu and Lezarik (who had mass-reducing bags), the newbies began to pack the sundry items around them into ready-made rucksacks.

"Something smells fishy."

"Hm?"

Naotsugu had spoken as he was taking down the tent, and Lezarik, right next to him, responded with a question.

"I don't like this. Not one bit. Vague bad-feeling city."

"But they're just goblins."

From Lezarik's expression, he thought he was making a big deal over nothing. Even Lezarik, a healer, could put down ten or twenty goblins on his own.

"Yeah, but the goblin encounter rate out here in the mountains shouldn't be this high, should it?"

"Well..."

Naotsugu shot a glance at the newbs to check on them. They'd split up, putting saddlebags on the horses and extinguishing the fire. "Plus, we've got those guys with us now. If something happens, I've got the feeling it's gonna blow up big-time."

"Hmm..."

Lezarik was also a veteran player—sent from the Knights of the Black Sword, one of Akiba's distinguished large guilds—and he didn't laugh off Naotsugu's words. He seemed to be considering something.

The bushes rustled, ejecting a thin shadow into the square.

A green corduroy jacket. A too-thin, cat-headed gentleman wearing a necktie: It was Nyanta. His eyes were narrowed, as usual, but the somewhat hard expression on his face wasn't usual at all. He went over to Naotsugu and Lezarik.

"What's up?"

"Mm."

Nyanta's attitude naturally drew Naotsugu and Lezarik—the leaders—to him.

The newbies were continuing to strike the camp as instructed, and they didn't seem to have noticed that Nyanta was back yet.

"Things don't feel good. It's a large-scale march: An army of at least several thousand goblins is passing through one ridge over. It's impossible to tell just how many of them there really are."

At Nyanta's words, all at once, Lezarik's face grew tense.

There had been cases of goblins conducting military operations in the past. In fact, goblins were one of the varieties of demihuman that enjoyed military action, and they plundered repeatedly in groups. However, goblins rarely marched by the thousands over long distances.

Goblin intelligence was low, and their basic approach consisted of spreading a ring of plunder over nearby towns and villages like the plague.

Something was odd here. Something wasn't right. The instincts of the three veteran players had picked up on this accurately, and as a result, their expressions were tense.

"Tch! Well, there's no help for it."

Naotsugu nodded once, as though he'd vaguely suspected this. "Did you call it in?" he asked Nyanta.

"I reported it to Shiroecchi. However, I can't reach Miss Marielle or Shouryuu."

"You can't?"

"They may be napping, or busy fighting, or perhaps they're both involved in other telechats at the moment. I don't know which it is."

Nyanta's words were calm, but much of his usual composure was missing.

He had been joking about the napping, and although that might have been possible with Marielle, it was hard to imagine with Shouryuu. Upon hearing his concerns, Lezarik's gaze suddenly went distant, as if he was looking at something far away. It was the expression unique to telechats.

Noticing this, Naotsugu and Nyanta stopped talking and waited, but Lezarik's response was also, "No, it's no good. There should be Knights of the Black Sword at the coast as well, but I can't reach them."

Neither Naotsugu nor Nyanta had any other Crescent Moon League members registered to their friend lists. ...Or rather, Serara was on Nyanta's list, but she was right there with them, working to dismantle the camp.

Naotsugu and the others had gone out with the junior members many times before, but the only one they'd needed to be able to contact had been Shouryuu, and after that they'd been able to handle everything through regular conversation. This might have been carelessness on their part.

The three of them let their imaginations run.

There were all sorts of possibilities, and they had reason to assume the worst. However, whatever the case, they couldn't rush headlong to the coast. Doing that would mean leaving their own newbies behind.

Even if each individual goblin was low level, apparently there was a horde of at least several thousand out there, just one peak away. Even if they didn't cross the ridge, no doubt there were squads of goblins lurking in the nearby forest.

They didn't dare leave new players here in the mountains.

"So how did the goblins look?"

"The ones mewving through the valley are a large-scale plunder tribe. It looked as if the woods themselves had begun to walk. I've never seen an army of that size before. I saw hobgoblins and trolls as well—it looked like a full-fledged invasion brigade, complete with magical beast mewnits. They seemed to be traveling west-southwest, but that isn't certain, so I can't say..."

"Then the ones we've been encountering are advance scout squads?"

Abruptly, Minori's voice spoke.

When Naotsugu turned, there stood Touya, Minori, and the other three members of the beginner party. All wore rigid, tense expressions: Apparently they'd overheard the conversation.

"Several thousand... One ridge over?"

Rundelhaus lifted his eyes, as if he were looking through the trees of the forest. His face held not fear, but determination.

During the brief moment when the three leaders were speechless, Serara began to speak in a clear voice.

"I took care of the newbies at the Crescent Moon League. So, um, you see... I have all of them registered to my friend list. Right? You do, too, don't you, Isuzu?"

"Y-yes. Of course."

"Do you think you could contact them and find out what the situation is?"

Before Naotsugu could speak, the two had agreed to Minori's request and opened their friend lists. Seeing this, Naotsugu scratched at his head, laughing at his own carelessness. He'd forgotten that Serara and Isuzu, members of the Crescent Moon League themselves, would have an easier time making contact with others in it.

When he thought about it, it was completely obvious.

And now that things had come to this, there was no point in hiding anything: If they were returning to the camp, they'd have to tell everyone about it in any case. Naotsugu and Lezarik called over the remaining six members of the advance party and briefly explained the situation.

Anyway, they'd been planning to strike camp and return to the abandoned school after noon; they couldn't very well work on capturing the dungeon when they were surrounded by an army of goblins. Their current issues were choosing a route to travel by, and discovering the state of the other training units that were scattered across the area.

Serara and Isuzu added their voices to the conversation.

According to the information the two of them had gathered, a fierce running battle was in progress along the coast. Blue Goblins had come up out of the sea, and their group was heading toward the abandoned school in a traveling formation, with the high-level leaders bringing up the rear.

"Blue gobs? ...Tch! Wait, sahuagins?! What the heck?!" Naotsugu exclaimed.

Sahuagins were minor monsters, and he'd never heard of any being sighted on the peninsula. That particular monster appeared in the warmer areas farther south.

"A coincidence...perhaps?"

Naturally, Lezarik was asking about the connection between the goblins and the sahuagins. Since none of the members had the answer to that question, it was met with silence. However, it was probably too optimistic to explain away the two armies' almost simultaneous appearance as coincidence.

At present, it didn't seem as though heading for the abandoned school was necessarily the best choice. If worse came to worst, they might find themselves surrounded by goblins and sahuagins.

Still, yeah, I guess if it comes right down to it, we can all just use Call of Home, Naotsugu thought, steadfastly convinced.

Chanting Call of Home would get them back to Akiba easily, but once they were back, getting to Zantleaf again would require a journey of several days. That made it an option best kept as a last resort.

He also thought it would be dangerous to carelessly take Minori and the other newbies back to the abandoned school.

However, if Marielle's group was heading back to the school, the most important thing was to meet up with them somehow, call roll, and make sure all the summer camp participants were safe.

Nyanta and Lezarik agreed with that plan.

Once the assembled had made up their minds, the rest happened quickly.

Since there was no telling when the goblin army might turn up, it was pointless to wait around where they were.

According to what Nyanta had said, there were small detachments of goblin scouts scattered through the surrounding forest over a fairly wide range. As that was the case, they'd probably find themselves in a few battles, but it would probably be safer to just go ahead and force their way through.

"Okay then, we're about to head back to the abandoned school camp. Nyanta, Lezarik, and I will be in the lead as a party of three. Yes, I said 'three,' but we're not about to let a bunch of newbies like you show us up, so don't you worry. Got it? Awright! The advanced party's gonna bring up the rear. Do a good, solid job, guys. Keep a close eye on what's behind you, but don't let the distance between us get too big. The beginner party is at the center of the formation. If we get into a battle up at the front, you're in charge of providing backup. Don't let your guard down just because you're in the middle!!"

The group mounted their horses, just as Naotsugu had instructed.

They were planning to cut across the hilly area at the center of the Zantleaf region.

This'll probably be a bit of a war, Naotsugu thought to himself, uneasily.

Zantleaf, surrounded by goblins and sahuagins.

If that was in fact the case, his dependable friends would take steps to cope with the enemy's movements. He had his own job to do.

Naotsugu put his hand on his mount's neck and started down the road through the forest.

▶ **2**

Go back in time slightly.

Shiroe had learned of the ominous presence that had begun to blanket the Zantleaf Peninsula when Naotsugu had contacted him, but the Lords' Council, which was composed of People of the Earth, had received news of the goblin attack even earlier.

Adventurers were able to use the telechat function to communicate with distant companions instantly, but the People of the Earth also had a means of long-distance communication only they could use.

It was a long-distance conversation spell that used crystal balls.

When *Elder Tales* was a game, the People of the Earth had been non-player characters, known colloquially as NPCs. They'd only been part of the game's background, and so, unlike the Adventurers, they hadn't had any combat abilities or convenient functions supported by the game system.

However, on the other hand, *Elder Tales* was a story, and in order to render their side of it, it had been stated that the People of the Earth could use various types of magic.

These included, for example, secret arts used to make magic

items, and teleportation spells to allow them to escape from the player-protagonists.

It had been mere background information, with no kind of in-depth clarification of their abilities whatsoever, but ever since the Catastrophe, in this other world, such information had morphed into a proper system of magic.

One such type of this magic was a long-distance communication spell that utilized crystal balls.

In certain instances, this sort of communication technique could be a far more powerful weapon than a band of knights. The lords of the League of Free Cities understood this, and each kept a dedicated magician in his territory at all times.

The plundering goblin tribe was traveling through the mountains, and it didn't invade the fortified cities where the lords lived. The only casualties were unlucky travelers and extremely tiny settlements in the mountains.

The first one to register the existence of the goblin army was Marquis Kilivar, the governor of Tsukuba. However, since the goblins were marching through the mountains, their discovery was delayed, and he got the message about the time the goblins' advance units reached Zantleaf.

The information had been brought to him the previous evening.

The magician who had been left in charge of the town of Tsukuba during his lord's absence had decided that this was a state of emergency, and had contacted Marquis Kilivar immediately. After a moment's hesitation, Marquis Kilivar sounded out Duke Sergiad about convening an extraordinary Lords' Council. Kilivar's personal pride as a marquis was a small thing in comparison with this incident, and he sought help from the rest of the lords.

That was how the People of the Earth's conference had begun, but naturally, it grew complicated. A terrifyingly large army of goblins... It was an incident serious enough to endanger their respective rules.

The lords were at their wits' end, and the conference continued all through the night.

Why weren't Krusty and the other Adventurers called to this conference? There were several reasons.

First, Krusty and the Round Table Council weren't yet formal members of the Lords' Council of Eastal.

Of course they'd determined to hold a decoration ceremony at some point during the conference period and had set a course of accepting them as formal members. However, because each lord hoped to conduct plenty of negotiations beforehand, the award ceremony was scheduled to be held during the last half of the period. Since the ceremony hadn't yet been held, at present they weren't formal members.

Second, some members of the Lords' Council hadn't managed to resolve their unease regarding the Round Table Council, and the emotional discomfort remained. A few of them even pointed out, absurdly, that the goblin invasion itself might be an Adventurer conspiracy.

Behind such statements lay the fact that, although the goblin tribes of the Ouu Mountains had been a source of headaches for the people who lived in those mountains for a very long time, they hadn't launched an invasion that had taken them outside the mountains in the past eighty years. They were one of the mountains' dangers, true, and local residents found them inconvenient, but they weren't a serious problem for those who lived down in the foothills.

The goblins had been "sealed" in the Mountains of Ouu this way because the Adventurers regularly attacked them, paring away their fighting strength.

Because the lords of the areas near the Ouu Mountains understood the importance of letting the Adventurers strip the goblins of their military power, they paid significant sums in bounties every year.

When *Elder Tales* was a game, quest requests such as "Eradicate the goblins," "Attack a goblin settlement," and "Take back goods from the goblin tribe" had been made through the town's taverns, and Adventurers had headed into the mountains, drawn by the rewards.

However, that hadn't happened this year. The Adventurers hadn't touched a single one of the requests involving the goblin tribes of the Ouu Mountains. Consequently, the League of Free Cities—and in particular the lords whose territories bordered the Ouu Mountains—had started to advance their conspiracy theory: That the invasion itself was a plot by the Adventurers.

Of course, the reality was different.

Since the event the People of the Earth called the May Incident and the Adventurers called the Catastrophe, the world had been going through inexorable changes. The Adventurers had been pressed to the limit in their efforts to adapt to these changes, and they hadn't had time for other things. In the process, it was no wonder that various quests had been left relatively untouched compared to when this had been a game.

The explanation that the Adventurers had left the goblins to their own devices not out of malice but because they'd prioritized coping with some sort of trouble, was widely shared even among the People of the Earth. However, it was also true that lords whose territories were being assaulted by a horde were emotionally unable to let this explanation satisfy them.

And so—

"It really is true, then?"

"Yes. The Knights of Izumo…are gone."

"They don't exist? Do you mean to say they've been annihilated?!"

"We don't even know whether they've been annihilated or not. No corpses or traces of battle have been found. They've simply disappeared. 'Spirited away' might be the best way to describe it."

This was an affirmed fact.

They were still waiting impatiently for additional information regarding the Knights of Izumo, however.

The Knights were one of the Thirteen Global Chivalric Orders. They were the guardians of the world, the ultimate military force created by the good human races. They were Ancients, mysterious superhumans that had been created through an old magic now lost; they lay dormant in the bloodlines of the People of the Earth, and their births, when they occurred, seemed miraculous.

The Thirteen Global Chivalric Orders were bands of heroes composed entirely of these Ancients.

Because they were the guardians of mankind, they took no part in conflicts between lords or other People of the Earth. They also wouldn't put in appearances for incidents along the lines of demihumans attacking a village. However, during large-scale disasters or mass invasions by demihumans, they'd sally forth as they always had, nearly without exception, protecting the human world.

It was these heroes, the Knights of Izumo, who had vanished.

The fact had come to light a month after the May Incident, but because the matter was so serious, information about it had been strictly regulated in the League of Free Cities. At first, a conspiracy of the Ancient Dynasty of Westlande had been suspected in the Knights' disappearance, but the miniscule amount of information that trickled in from their spies had made it clear that the Ancient Dynasty also seemed upset by the incident.

The Knights of Izumo were the only one of the Thirteen Global Chivalric Orders specifically known to the lords. No doubt the other twelve Orders were acting as guardians of the world in other countries, but at the very least, none of them had ever appeared in Yamato.

And now, the Knights of Izumo were gone.

All of the several fortresses they'd used as their bases of operation were deserted. The scouts had reported that they'd found no sign of combat, and that it hadn't felt as if there'd been preparations for a hasty expedition, either.

They'd simply stepped out for a walk one fine day and had failed to return.

That was the impression they'd been given by the sense of casual, everyday routine that had remained there, crystallized.

"But...then...in that case..."

"Hmm..."

Several lords clawed at their heads.

Goblin demihumans. A huge tribe, well over ten thousand strong. Of course, these numbers wouldn't be impossible to beat back, provided they camped on the plains, and all the armies of the League of Free Cities went into battle against them.

However, the Goblins were currently heading south through the mountains, and there was no telling where they'd strike. It might be the town of Hitachi or the town of Fourbridge, or they might turn back and mount an attack on the castle town of Urumiya.

Like many other towns belonging to Eastal, these were fortified cities with high castle walls that guarded the lords' mansions and the city streets alike. While it depended on the number of soldiers and townspeople, if they thoroughly concentrated on defense, they could probably protect themselves from most enemies. However, that said, when asked whether a city could defend itself from more than ten thousand goblins on its own, they had no ready answer. In the first place, there was the problem of supplies, and more than anything, their spirits would probably be broken.

They'd been counting on the Knights of Izumo.

The town that was currently in the most painful position was Tsukuba.

The goblin plunder tribe that had been sighted was believed to be in the mountains just a few dozen kilometers away from Tsukuba, as the crow flies.

The other human towns that were likely goblin destinations were, as stated earlier, Hitachi, Fourbridge, the castle town of Urumiya, and an unfortified fishing town with no lord: the village of Choushi.

Or perhaps—

"Or perhaps Maihama, hm?" Duke Sergiad muttered, putting a strong, bony hand to his chin.

From where they were, in the Ancient Court of Eternal Ice, Maihama was located beyond the ruined city of Eastal, toward Zantleaf. In the worst-case scenario, from the position where they'd been sighted, the goblins would be able to attack it in two or three days' time.

The upshot was that the goblin army's invasion was cutting deep into the throat of the League of Free Cities.

No, from the League of Free Cities' perspective, they'd actually *allowed* them to invade that far.

The thorn was already in a place where it would be impossible to remove without bloodshed. The poison was on the verge of rotting the areas close to the League's heart.

A stifled hush hung over the Council.

It was a very bitter silence.

The conference had begun late at night, and as they exchanged heavy words, it continued into the small hours. Considered rationally, it was already far too late to be holding conferences. The enemy was a few days away from a large number of cities.

Now that it had come to this, there was nothing for it: The lords of Eastal, the League of Free Cities, would have to join forces, send their troops out together, and surround and destroy the goblin army.

However, doing so would require an astronomical number of

sacrifices. Cavalry units would be nearly useless in the mountains and forests, where visibility was bad. Moreover, the heavy cavalry, whose main combat method was charging, would be powerless.

It would also be difficult to fight as a large group. The lords' allied forces would be fragmented, and many of their troops would be lost in battle with the goblin tribe. The mountains were perfect for lurking and hiding, and it was possible that, even after all that, they'd still let the goblin tribe escape. There was no guarantee that the lords' forces would be able to annihilate them.

In that case, would it be all right if all the lords simply returned to their territories and confined themselves to their castles? The answer was no.

Of course, most of the cities would be able to withstand sieges that lasted several months. However, the goblins could attack nearby villages and settlements and burn the fields while keeping the fortified city surrounded and under attack, and then hide in the mountains before reinforcements arrived. Their goal wasn't the occupation of the city; they were after food and property. In that sense, they were more like a band of armed refugees than an army.

It was as if the problems of the mountainous northeastern Yamato Archipelago had been laid bare. With topography like this, it would be extremely difficult for a huge organization like an army to work together in a coordinated fashion.

As he rubbed his aching temples, Sergiad thought to himself.

I suppose the conclusion reached by the Lords' Council will be an encircling operation, with the consent of all lords... There's nothing for it but to prepare to lose many soldiers and adopt a strategy of defeating the enemy no matter the cost to ourselves. ...In that case, though, the problem will be determining which lord will fire the first arrow...

"Fire the first arrow" sounded good, but the role was incredibly close to that of a sacrificial pawn.

First, a fortified city, somewhere, would be surrounded. That city would shore up its defenses and resist the goblins. The goblins would wear themselves out trying to conquer this stronghold. The lords' alliance would then encircle the goblin army and annihilate it.

From a military standpoint, this was the correct strategy.

It was nearly the only feasible way for them to wipe out the goblin army. However, the strategy required the sacrifice of a fortified city.

The most likely candidates for the sacrifice were, first and foremost, the town of Tsukuba, and then the city of Maihama, which Duke Sergiad governed.

All of the lords were aware of this.

However, they were hesitant to say it.

It was easy to say "be surrounded," but it was equivalent to telling them to accept the fact that the nearby villages, and the fields and orchards they'd cultivated so desperately, would be reduced to dust and ashes. In addition, there was a good possibility that many of their citizens would lose their lives. "Sacrifice yourself" wasn't the sort of thing they could say easily.

"...I-in accordance with the charter of the League of Free Cities, we seek the aid of the Lords' Council."

Marquis Kilivar of Tsukuba's voice was nearly a shriek.

However, even at that voice, most of the lords responded by wordlessly averting their eyes.

"Th-that's it! Akiba! We have the town of Akiba! Let's make them use their forces to annihilate the goblins. We must! After all, aren't they the cause of all this?!"

Marquis Kilivar, half-despairing, screamed as if to prevent the silence from crushing him. At these words, several of the lords seemed to show interest.

Hmm...

Sergiad's expression also remained stern, but he closed his eyes and thought.

Marquis was right.

His thoughts up until now had been bound by the existing framework of the League of Free Cities. However, at present, there was a new element in the picture: the town of Akiba and its Adventurers. They might be able to find some effective way to cope with the situation.

That said—

Although their existence was a powerful weapon for the League, at the same time, it was a double-edged sword. No one could guarantee that the Adventurers themselves were a controllable force.

Was it all right to ask beings like them for help? If they asked for aid, they'd have to tell them everything. ...Including the fact that their deterrent, the Knights of Izumo, was absent.

Adventurers were powerful, after all.

If they felt so inclined and decided to declare war on Eastal, the goblin uprising would be nothing compared to the disaster they would trigger. The circumstances were too unclear for them to tell the Adventurers that the Knights of Izumo, who should have been able to restrain them, had disappeared.

Personally, Sergiad didn't think it would be a bad idea to trust the three young men who had come to them as delegates.

Michitaka had the air of a wealthy merchant. He seemed to be the sort of person who was big enough to absorb short-term loss for the sake of a good cause and his own merchant's code.

The youth who had called himself Shiroe seemed scholarly, but his essence was like a well-tempered sword. No matter the difficulty, once that sword was drawn, no doubt he'd slice clean through his obstacle.

Then there was Krusty. The young man who organized the Round Table Council was no knight. Heaven had blessed him with more talents than could be expressed by the word *knight*. On the other hand, however, the depth of light and darkness to the young man called Krusty had a density that even Sergiad, at the age of sixty, could not see through.

Of course, he had to draw a firm line between his own personal goodwill and his decision as Sergiad Cowen, Leading Lord of Eastal, the League of Free Cities, Ruler of the City of Maihama, and the greatest noble in the East. In addition, it wouldn't do to mistake the three representatives' personal good faith for the political decisions of the town of Akiba.

To say nothing of the fact that the Ancient Dynasty of Westlande is undoubtedly keeping an eye on this situation...

Several lords were with Marquis Kilivar, who was loudly insisting that the Adventurers be sent into battle. A smaller number of lords argued against it, bringing up the matter of the Knights of Izumo and saying that it would be a bad idea for reasons of secrecy.

However, the majority of the lords expressed doubts regarding realistic means: It would be a fine thing if the Adventurers went into battle, but how were they to actually draw them onto the battlefield? They didn't have any reward or power of coercion that could make it happen.

All in all, the council buzzed like a prodded wasps' nest.

The confusion did not die down until the next day, when Shiroe and the others received the report from Nyanta, who was away at summer camp.

▶ 3

The morning after the lords' conference:

A telechat from Zantleaf informed Shiroe and the others of the emergency outside the Eastal convention.

It wasn't clear whether Nyanta's report had been the first. At roughly the same time as Shiroe, Michitaka and Krusty were also contacted by their own guild members.

The Zantleaf Peninsula was under a large-scale attack by demihuman tribes.

At this, Shiroe and his companions had returned to the living room to hold an emergency measures meeting. The only people present were Shiroe, Michitaka, Krusty, and a few other Adventurer representatives—their attendants were either on duty guarding the conference room or out gathering intel.

Simultaneously, an emergency Round Table Council had been convened in the Round Table Room on the top floor of the guild center in Akiba. In this way, even though there was a great distance between them, and although it was slightly inconvenient, they were able to hold a jury-rigged Round Table Council by using telechat relays.

"Situation first."

In response to Michitaka's demand, Shiroe read off notes he'd made regarding the information they had at present.

"Attacks by multiple demihuman species have been confirmed on the Zantleaf Peninsula, beginning this morning. Sixty-seven players from the town of Akiba, including new players, are currently there for a summer training camp. The invading forces from the sea are sahuagins. Although their total numbers are unclear, there are several hundred at the very least. There is a large-scale plunder tribe composed mainly of goblins in the hilly, forested area at the peninsula's center. This one is at least ten thousand strong."

"Ten thousand" was easy enough to say, but it was a preposterous number, a number that would give even ordinary players vertigo.

The basic unit for group battles in *Elder Tales* was the party. This was a tactical unit used when fellow Adventurers pooled their strength and worked together in a coordinated manner, and its upper limit was six members. When leaving on an ordinary adventure or tackling a dungeon, the Adventurers of *Elder Tales* coped by forming such parties.

However, sometimes, events or quests that couldn't be handled by six-member parties came up. For times like these, *Elder Tales* had a system known as "raids."

There were several levels of raid, but the most typical was a "full raid," made up of four small, six-person units—in other words, parties—joined into a group of twenty-four players. Almost all heroic battles in *Elder Tales* had been fought in this configuration.

When the Debauchery Tea Party had won their griffins in Hades' Breath, it had been the result of a twenty-four-member raid.

There was another unit that surpassed even full raids: "legion raids," in which four of these twenty-four-player companies were joined together. Very few examples existed in the history of *Elder Tales*. It was a group unit intended for ultra-large-scale live events, for extreme difficulties, or to respond to national crises.

It was hard for a total of ninety-six people to cooperate, and it was impossible for a normal player to even grasp the general state of the battle. Commanding took enormous courage and great tactical sense.

Goblin levels were by no means high, however.

They were mob monsters, and a level-90 player could easily handle several dozen of them on their own. However, no one had even heard of a group whose total numbers were a hundred times that of a ninety-six-member legion raid.

"Not only that, but these numbers are mere estimates. I believe the actual numbers are even greater."

"What do you mean?" Krusty said, responding to Shiroe.

"It's about the cause of this invasion."

'The cause? You have an idea about what that might be?'

One of the present attendants was relaying the exchange via telechat.

The question had probably come from Soujirou of the West Wind Brigade. Shiroe prefaced his response with: "This is only my conjecture, not verified fact," then began to speak:

"It's likely that the Return of the Goblin King is behind this invasion."

At Shiroe's words, not only the room in which the three guild masters were conversing, but the Round Table Council in Akiba, and Marielle—who was participating from central Zantleaf via telechat—fell silent.

The Return of the Goblin King had been a regularly occurring game event, back when *Elder Tales* was a game.

Seventh Fall, the Goblin tribes' castle, was located in the deepest part of the Black Forest, a deep, dark forest in the Ouu region.

Once every two years, the coronation of the Goblin King was held at this castle. The individual crowned was the strongest leader among the six local goblin tribes.

Explained in game terms, it was an event that occurred once every two months in Earth time. During this event, the entrance to the Seventh Fall zone was opened for just one week, and any player who was able to sneak in and subjugate the Goblin King within that period would acquire a powerful item.

The event had been extraordinarily popular, for two reasons: First, the items dropped by the Goblin King were fairly powerful ones. They weren't magic items that a player from a major guild with an ultra-high level would want badly enough to kill for, but within the range of items that the average player was able to obtain, their performance made them highly sought after.

A second point, one that couldn't be overlooked, was that the castle guard and the Goblin King's strength were variable.

According to the game's backstory, "Goblin King" was a position taken by the strongest Goblin of the surrounding tribes. In other words, if players attacked the Goblin strongholds scattered across the Ouu region beforehand and chipped away at their power, the strength of the Goblins in the Seventh Fall zone would be significantly reduced. In addition, the level and strength of the Goblin King would be weakened.

Due to these peculiarities, the Return of the Goblin King had grown popular as a fulfilling quest that players could challenge even if they didn't belong to a major combat guild.

"—That's right. The Return of the Goblin King, the one with which you're all familiar. There's an important element to that event which we're forgetting, since it almost never actually happened."

The subjugation of the Goblin King required a raid, but as long as you'd cut back the goblins' power beforehand, the difficulty wasn't high at all, to the point where it might as well have been designed for midsized guilds. For that reason, even Shiroe didn't know of any cases where the Goblin King went unsubjugated within that one-week period.

However, if memory served him right, there had been an additional note in the event description.

"I see… You mean the bit about how, if the Goblin King doesn't get subjugated within that one week, he'll unite the surrounding goblin tribes and form an army dozens of times bigger?"

Michitaka had put his finger on it, and Shiroe nodded.

It was just as he'd said.

Once successfully crowned, the Goblin King would become the hero of the goblin tribes, and his forces would increase dramatically.

Ever since the Catastrophe, Shiroe and the other Adventurers had been desperate to create a livable environment for themselves in this other world. So desperate, in fact, that although the Return of the Goblin King had been a popular event when *Elder Tales* was a game, they'd let it slip by without a thought.

"'Do you think the goblins have managed to hold on to all their power as well?'" one of the attendants asked, conveying a messaged received via telechat.

Shiroe thought a little, then nodded. "Yes. Absolutely no attacks were launched against the six surrounding tribes this time around, and no successive attacks were mounted on Seventh Fall, the Goblin King's main castle. It's probably best to assume that the levels of the Goblin King's royal guard and combat units are the highest they've ever been. Of course, the King is probably formidable as well. …What makes me more uneasy is the question of how large the united goblin tribes actually are."

A subdued silence filled the conference room.

Every one of them was mute, not because they wanted to be, but because they didn't know what to say.

That said, it didn't turn into a panic, most likely because they'd been granted a certain sense of security. They'd received a report that the summer camp group had safely evacuated to the abandoned school, and Marielle of the Crescent Moon League was currently taking part in this conference by telechat *from* that very school.

Since the telechat function could only be used one-on-one, Henrietta was in the conference room, in communication with Marielle and acting as her proxy.

In addition, even if powerful monsters surrounded the abandoned school in which the group had barricaded itself, the group could use Call of Home to find shelter in Akiba, and they wouldn't take any damage.

The fact that there was a large goblin army on the move near the root of the Zantleaf Peninsula meant it was probably heading west or south, razing nearby villages and settlements as it went, but there was still some distance left between it and the town of Akiba. Besides, even if the army did attempt to invade, Akiba had enough manpower to engage it.

And while the Goblin King was more powerful than he'd ever been, they could guess his approximate level. Subjugating the Goblin King required a full raid—twenty-four Adventurers—and there were more than five hundred times that in Akiba.

Still, this time is…

The town of Akiba was fine. However, Eastal, the League of Free Cities, couldn't afford to sit by idly, as Akiba's Round Table Council could. If the army of ten thousand stayed the size it was currently, it would have enough power to capture a weaker fortified city.

Unfortunately, Shiroe didn't have much military knowledge, so he couldn't say for certain, but he suspected that quite a few of the League of Free Cities' lords were turning pale.

"What about the Knights of Izumo?"

Henrietta spoke hesitantly, addressing the whole group.

At her words, a murmur of something like agreement went up: "Oho," "Now that you mention it…"

The Knights of Izumo.

They were a chivalric order on the Japanese server, composed of Ancients.

Ancients were heroic beings born from among the People of the

Earth. They had combat abilities that surpassed even Adventurers' abilities, and they were the good human races' trump card. The Adventurers' overwhelming numbers meant they'd practically monopolized demihuman subjugation and quests ever since they'd first appeared in this world, but during battles where the fate of the world hung in the balance, chivalric orders of Ancients always stepped in.

There were twelve servers around the world, and thirteen chivalric orders. One of these, the Knights of Izumo, held a position equivalent to guardian deity for the Japanese server, or rather, for the Yamato Archipelago.

When *Elder Tales* was a game, Shiroe had frequently heard stories of these knights. It wasn't just him, either; the higher players' levels got, the more often they heard tales of the legendary chivalric orders. On quite a few quests, they fought alongside them or followed in their footsteps.

Because they were the guardians of all the good human races in this world, they didn't involve themselves in political conflicts between lords, but they'd probably bestir themselves for a demihuman invasion.

From the atmosphere in the conference room, everyone seemed to feel as if there was no need for them to do anything, but Shiroe was skeptical. For example, they hadn't confirmed whether the Knights of Izumo were still functional at this point.

He was irritated with himself for being overly critical as usual, but it seemed strange to him that the goblin tribes would head south in the first place. All the official site had said about it was, "If left alone, the Goblin King will unite the nearby forces and build a great kingdom."

…Is this really all right?

However, it wasn't as though Shiroe had a clear answer, either. Besides, now that the Spirit Theory issue was on the table, he was hesitant about conducting a large-scale battle.

▶**4**

"Princess, Princess. …Princess Raynesia?"

At her maid's voice, Raynesia turned.

"What is it…?" she asked, tilting her head.

The look was so adorable that if the palace knights had been there, they would have been smitten by it and pledged lifelong loyalty, but the person who was actually there was a maid who'd served her closely for long years.

"Were you thinking, milady? Lunchtime's still a ways off."

She returned a casually mean response.

Even so, for a remonstration, it was rather friendly. As far as Raynesia's actions went, "thinking" was unusual. She "brooded" much more than she "thought," and what she did most of all was "space out."

"Hm? ...Was that what it looked like, Elissa?"

Maybe because she was used to it, Raynesia didn't argue about any of it; instead, she responded to her question with a question.

Raynesia was seated at the vanity, and the maid she'd called Elissa circled around behind her and began combing her magnificent silver hair.

"Yes, it did look like that. It's an unusual thing for you, Princess."

At those words—truly unusually—Raynesia became lost in thought again.

The trick to telling them apart was in her gaze. When she lowered her eyes slightly and all emotion vanished from her face, she was "thinking."

But the expression where her gaze slid diagonally down, and she seemed to be enduring distress yet still trying to smile, was "brooding." When she was depressed over things—and they were usually the sort of things that made Elissa think, *Why that?*—this was the expression she wore.

This was the true identity of the smile university graduates and civil servants couldn't get enough of, the "Twilight mystic princess filled with melancholy" smile. ...Although what she was worried about were things like *I'm afraid I really did eat too much at dinner last night*...or *What if they throw away those old pajamas I've worn out?*

The expression that was highly popular with knights, military officers and other tough, physical types was the "spacing out" face. In that one, she tilted her head slightly with an entranced, dreaming expression and gave the faintest of smiles. If she spaced out even more, her eyes grew moist, making it even more charming.

In this case, since she was "spacing out," asking her about it would reveal that she really wasn't thinking anything at all. It would often be something like, "My, what lovely weather," or "I'd like to have a nap." Hearing that much made her sound dumb, but from what Elissa had seen, her mistress Raynesia *was* dumb, so there was no real mistake there.

...At least in ordinary, everyday life, at any rate.

Honestly! Beautiful people are so difficult to deal with. They really are.
There was nothing Elissa could do but sigh.

She was a lady-in-waiting who served the princess, after all, and compared to the average girl, she was considered quite a beauty herself. When she went to the castle town on her occasional day off, she was invariably accosted by men she didn't know.

However, although Elissa considered herself "a pretty woman," she didn't think she was beautiful or lovely. The ones who were beautiful in the truest sense of the word were people like Raynesia. Beauty on that level was an ability completely independent of the person it belonged to, and its effects operated in a separate dimension from Raynesia's own character and intentions.

I'm not particularly jealous, myself.

With a small sigh, Elissa kept combing the luxuriant silver waterfall of Raynesia's hair. Even a single skein of the hair that flowed coolly between her fingers was a treasure worth its weight in gold.

"...He hasn't come by today, has he?" Feeling as if she'd like to tease her a little, Elissa slipped the words into their current conversation.

"Pardon?"

"Master Krusty."

"—Why?"

"No reason. You often take lunch together these days, that's all. Considering the time, I thought it he was about due to invite you somewhere or pay a call."

"D-do you think so...?"

Raynesia's response was a bit flustered. This "slightly upset" Raynesia wasn't the "lovely princess" the knights adored.

She was a marvelously beautiful princess, of course, but rather than "lovely," she looked a terribly naïve and awkward girl...or, in common terms, a completely hopeless one. Elissa liked this version of her mistress.

"Yes, I do. Gentlemen are always so insensitive, aren't they? Here we are, doing our best with our traveling wardrobe and really struggling, and yet they don't even consider the convenience of our outfits. Good gracious me. …You wore the pearl dress, the lavender stole, and the amethyst necklace to yesterday's luncheon party, didn't you. The day before was the pale rose-violet satin… Yes, the double-tiered dress."

"Yes."

The Raynesia in the mirror looked back at Elissa with a blank expression. Apparently she didn't understand what Elissa was saying.

"Listen to me, Princess. This is not Maihama's Castle Cinderella. In consequence, there is a limit to your wardrobe. If you take lunch with one particular gentleman this many times in a row, there are only so many combinations we can use to make it look as though you have a variety of dresses. Since it is a luncheon party, you can't wear the sort of cocktail dress you'd wear to a supper party, and we must exercise restraint in how much skin we expose during the day. Of course, if dining in the courtyard, the shape of your cuffs must be appropriate, and if dining indoors, we must consider how the colors will look against the wallpaper…"

After mulling over Elissa's words for a short while, Raynesia spoke timidly.

"I could just wear what I wore yesterday…"

"No. Lunching in the same dress, two days in a row? Are you some backwater country girl?" Elissa promptly interrupted.

"Then… What about the silk dress-shirt with a highland kilt-skirt?"

"Those are to wear in your room. And really, that's what you wear *specifically* to laze around in, Princess!"

At her staff's ferocity, Raynesia fell silent, looking rather like a scolded puppy. Even then, she looked as if she were withstanding hardship while harboring melancholy: Beautiful people were a force to be reckoned with.

Still, inside her head, she's a failure of a human being. A highland kilt-skirt indeed! That isn't the sort of outfit one can show to gentlemen. She isn't a tavern wench.

"I really don't think Master Krusty would care about that sort of thing…"

"Not true. Gentlemen will *say*, 'I don't care, I don't care,' but inside, they're ruthlessly evaluating you. That is an absolute given. 'I love you just the way you are,' they'll say, but if you act fuzzy-headed around them, they'll be gone in a twinkling. That is what gentlemen are. What's required is 'to look natural,' not to actually *be* natural! Listen, Princess, in the first place, you are—"

However, just as Elissa was beginning to warm to her sermon, she was interrupted by a knock.

The man who came in, trailing his steward and seeming too impatient to wait for a response, was Raynesia's father, Phenel.

"Oh, Raynesia. Listen, and try to stay calm."

Exuding consternation, Phenel took a great gulp out of a glass of water that had been handed to him, then squeezed out the words:

"A huge horde of goblins is bearing down on the city of Maihama. There seem to be close to ten thousand of them. Even now, the enemy's numbers are increasing, and in a few days, they will probably be a massive army several times their current size. ...In the worst-case scenario, of course."

For a moment, Elissa was unable to grasp the meaning of the words.

Ten thousand. Ten times one hundred was one thousand, and this was ten times that.

The city of Maihama was the largest residential area in Eastal, but its population was only about thirty thousand, including farmers, merchants, and everyone else. Maihama's forces consisted of one thousand civic security officers who policed the city and the four hundred Maihama Knights who worked at the castle. Even including the patrolling chivalric orders brought it to a total of at most two thousand, give or take.

The moment she'd thought that far, Elissa felt all the blood in her body retreat with a roar.

A hostile army of ten thousand!!

If the enemy was demihumans, the citizen volunteers would hardly stand a chance. She'd heard the word *siege* before, but to a lady-in-waiting like Elissa who knew nothing of war, two thousand seemed to have no chance of victory against ten thousand.

"Of course it isn't certain that the ugly demons will attack our cherished treasure, the city of Maihama. The town of Tsukuba and several other nobles' territories are in the danger zone as well. However, the circumstances are unpredictable. I'm just about to hurry back to Maihama."

"Father! In that case, I'll go with—"

Raynesia was on the point of rising, her expression serious and sharp.

True, Raynesia was bad at associating with people; she was an idler, and spacey, and it was hard to believe she was the daughter of a great noble family.

However, while it was hard to believe that she was the daughter of a great family, it wasn't that she was *unsuited* to be one.

She wasn't unsuited. Not a bit. This half-hearted, irresponsible princess had inherited the blood of the Cowen family, one of only two remaining dukedoms in Yamato. The exalted lineage of the princess on whom Elissa waited and the latent abilities it held were the only things she had never doubted.

"No, there's no need for that. You stay here, at court."

"Why? If the domain is in crisis, the whole family should return—"

"No, Father is also staying at the court."

"Father" was the current head of the House of Cowen, Duke Sergiad. Raynesia's father had married Sergiad's daughter Saraliya, Raynesia's mother.

"This demihuman invasion is uncanny. From its size, it does not seem to be a cataclysm that has fallen on our city of Maihama alone. An attack made solely on Maihama isn't the worst that could happen. …Should worse come to worst, the goblins may lay waste to our entire land, all the territory of the Free Cities. As such, the Lord's Council must be in perfect unity. And as the leading lord, Father must not leave the Ancient Court, and you must support him. …You do understand, don't you?"

In all likelihood, he'd only come to tell her this.

Without waiting to hear his daughter's response, Phenel left the room at a brisk clip. Elissa could only bow her head deeply and watch him go.

Phenel was her employer. She saw him far less than Raynesia, whom she served directly, or Raynesia's mother Saraliya, but she had the impression that he was a sincere person.

The lord of the city of Maihama, on the other hand, was Duke Sergiad. He had ascended to the position of lord at a young age, he had a great reputation for being clear-sighted, and the people were deeply attached to him. His daughter Saraliya and granddaughter Raynesia were also extraordinarily beloved.

In contrast to them, it must be pointed out that Phenel, merely a son-in-law and an outsider, made—however rude it was to say it—a rather shallow impression.

Elissa's parents had told her that when it had been decided that a young man who was not the general of a chivalric order nor the relative of the lord of another country but an ex-civil servant—and one who'd been involved in practical business, at that—would be added to the royal family, the people of Maihama might not have been disappointed, exactly, but they'd felt mildly let down.

However, as Phenel showed not a scrap of hesitation in his haste to reach his territory, the sight of his back betrayed nothing of the softness and naïveté of an ex-civil servant. A man as weak as that could never have passed muster with Sergiad in the first place. Elissa felt deeply convinced.

"Father..."

"Princess?"

At the murmur, Elissa returned her attention to Raynesia.

She was brooding again.

Except...her expression was completely different from the one Elissa had noted as "the thinking Raynesia" just a moment before.

Her eyes seemed to gaze at something invisible, and they held a quiet, intense flame. She stood gracefully, but the noble determination that surged from her made it impossible for anyone to say she was "filled with melancholy" or any such nonsense.

"Prin...cess...?"

Raynesia kept biting her lip, as if she hadn't even heard Elissa's voice.

▶ **5**

The abandoned school was located on a gentle slope near the sea on the Zantleaf Peninsula. Its grounds were teeming with Adventurers.

They were exchanging murmured private conversations, but their expressions were filled with tension. They weren't a disciplined army, so there was no senior officer to badger them about rank and rules, but each huddled close to the people they knew or gathered in groups with people close to their level, and they all seemed to be waiting.

Although no one had specifically said to, all the Adventurers had finished inspecting their belongings and checking their equipment. Several large barrels had been placed near the big tent in the center, and staff members were distributing chilled Black Rose Tea to companions who brought over waterskins or canteens.

They were probably acting spontaneously. The Adventurers who'd been given tea returned to their companions and resumed talking in low voices.

A sun that seemed larger than it had at noon was sinking, dyeing the western sky crimson. It was already evening.

For a while now, several Adventurers had been constantly going into and out of the single large tent that remained standing in the center.

According to the plan someone had announced in a loud voice a short while earlier, the school would be used as their headquarters at least until the safety of all the training camp participants had been confirmed. However, conversely, the announcement had hinted that, once everyone's safety *had* been confirmed, there was the possibility of a mass exodus.

Marielle looked away from the scene outside the tent and sighed.

Inside the big tent, Nyanta, Naotsugu, Marielle, Shouryuu, Lezarik, and the other level-90 leaders were holding a meeting.

On paper, Marielle was the person responsible for the summer camp. Although the Crescent Moon League was a smaller guild, it was one of the eleven guilds that sponsored the Round Table Council. As guild master of the Crescent Moon League, there were only ten other players who were on equal footing with her. Those ten colleagues were currently scattered between the town of Akiba and the Ancient Court of Eternal Ice. Marielle was the one to whom the Round Table Council had entrusted the newbies' training.

They'd reported the sahuagin and goblin attacks to the Round Table Council, of course, and they were certain to be discussing remedial measures on that end as well.

"Miss Mari? I wouldn't stress about it too much. Leave that stuff to Shiro; he'll figure something. Henrietta's there, too, right? See, nothing to worry about. They'll cheat or do whatever it takes and come up with a good plan."

"Thanks, hon."

Marielle gave a great big, perfectly ordinary smile.

Even she thought that now wasn't really the time for smiling, but the brush with sincere human kindness had made her happy. This boy— or, no, that was weird; Naotsugu was only a couple of years younger than she was, so "this young man" was better—was capable of careful consideration for others to an extent you'd never imagine from the rough-and-ready way he generally spoke and acted. Ever since she'd noticed it, Naotsugu's solicitude had made Marielle incredibly happy.

"Right! That was glomp-worthy! Here comes a glomp!"

Partly to hide her embarrassment, she squeezed the flustered Naotsugu hard. The way he went bright red and panicked was cute, and she thought it was funny.

"Wai–! Wait. Miss Mari. Quit. Quit!! Cease-and-desist city, evacuate city, they're-touching-me city, bikini city?!"

He seemed *too* upset, really, but even as Marielle tilted her head in bewilderment, she kept hugging Naotsugu's head until Nyanta checked her, mildly:

"Mariellecchi? Listen. It might be best if mew changed into something else. It's already evening. ...Ahem. That is to say, mew see, a single parka over a bikini is a bit too stimulating for Naotsugucchi."

When he pointed this out to her, Marielle registered what he meant and hastily jumped back.

He was absolutely right. She'd been so tense up until now that she hadn't even noticed it. Why, she was practically half naked.

Nuh-nuh-not good! How could I be ditzy enough to go 'round dressed like this... Uu! I bet they think I'm a real dumb broad. Lucky Henrietta isn't here; she would've smacked me good for this...

The chest she'd pressed against Naotsugu was flushed and hot, and apparently it was from shame, because she felt the same heat in her cheeks. Marielle ran to the back of the tent and took a change of equipment out of her magic bag. Since she was on the other side of a standing screen and the others couldn't see her, she picked out a tunic shirt and light armor and began to simply pull them on over her swimsuit.

"Excuse me! Roll call completed for the over-level-thirty group! They're all here!"

Marielle was in the middle of changing and couldn't see, but she heard Nyanta take the team leader's report. That was probably the last of the roll calls. At the thought that they really hadn't lost any participants, Marielle felt as if a great weight had been lifted from her shoulders.

The battle they'd fought as they retreated from the coast had been a fierce one.

It wasn't that the enemy's level had been all that high. There had just been so many of them. The tactics required for long-term battles—in specific terms, those for MP distribution—were different from those for short-term ones.

As a Cleric, it went without saying that Marielle was a Recovery class. When a Recovery class ran out of MP, it meant the supply of recovery spells for the front line was cut off. Healers held the lives of everyone in the party in their hands, and it was necessary to pay very close attention to MP management. However, in *Elder Tales*, the only battles were those fought by normal parties during dungeon explorations and the like, and they lasted anywhere from thirty seconds to a few minutes. It was extremely hard to learn management techniques for use in battles that lasted more than ten minutes.

Fierce battles that went on that long belonged to a territory that only some of the major guilds experienced—raids.

However, the summer camp contingent had managed to get through that running battle somehow.

Some players had been injured, of course, but fortunately, none of the injuries had been so serious as to not be recovered by spells after the fact. Shouryuu had commented that making it through the first wave had given the newbies a sense of the attitude and courage needed for battle, and in that sense, it probably hadn't been a waste.

When Marielle had finished changing and was giving her hair a few swipes with a brush, she began to hear a hum of voices outside the tent.

"Miss Mari!"

Drawn by Naotsugu's call, Marielle went outside, where the sky was turning violet. What she saw, flickering in the forests on the distant mountain range, was the light of countless tiny flames, no bigger than grains of rice.

"...They're torches," Nyanta murmured.

It was a fantastical sight, and at the same time, there was something incredibly disturbing and ominous about it.

The forested hills of Zantleaf were sunk in shadow, backlit by the burning evening sun. Among them, innumerable tiny flames were flickering and moving, like lights carried by ants.

"Just at a glance, I'd say, what, a hundred, maybe a hundred and fifty?" Naotsugu muttered.

Of course, it didn't follow that there was just one goblin for every torch, but at the very least, there were that many goblins traveling through the mountains. Marielle understood that they'd abandoned even the idea of hiding themselves and moving in secret now.

Those myriad wavering flames were a wordless threat from the goblins: *We're about to attack you.*

"Bring a map!"

"Right, hang on. I'll summon a Magic Torch."

High-level Adventurers who'd come from Keel and the West Wind Brigade seemed to be calculating the goblin unit's position on a map. Serara looked nervous; she was hanging on to the tail of Nyanta's jacket. Nyanta was staring intently at the map and the written notes, but before long he raised his head and looked toward the southeast, straining his eyes.

While the sun was still up, Nyanta had ventured out on a griffin to do some aerial reconnaissance. At present, he was probably the one with the most complete knowledge of the goblins' movements.

Even faced with this eerie sight, the people in the square weren't all that agitated. Now that all the participants had been accounted for, in extreme terms, they could abandon the camp immediately and hold the closing ceremony in Akiba fifteen minutes later. Since Call of Home existed, it was probably only natural that no one felt as if they'd been chased into the jaws of death.

In this world, Adventurers were overwhelmingly the strong.

Well, either way, it depends on what we decide to do after talkin' it over with the Round Table Council. Still, now that we know we're all here, I should prob'ly report in...

Just as Marielle was thinking this, Nyanta came over with Serara and Minori. He was wearing a rather complicated expression. Naotsugu and Lezarik were near Marielle. Nyanta had probably come with some opinion or report to deliver to Marielle and the others, the senior management of the summer camp.

"What's the matter? Did somethin' happen?" Marielle asked.

"It seems we have a bit of a problem. No, I suppose there's really no need for us to trouble ourselves, but... Hm."

Unusually for him, Nyanta seemed to be having trouble choosing his words; he hesitated.

"What's up? Spit it out, Retiree." Naotsugu sensed that Marielle was bewildered, so he spoke to his guild mate, his tone direct.

"—Apparently, that mewnit plans to attack the village of Choushi. A midsized plunder mewnit, I mean; not the full army I found. The main force of the goblin army is far, far to the north... In other words, they intend to make Choushi their provisions storehouse."

"The village of Choushi doesn't have a town wall."

It was Minori who'd cut in.

Her clenched palms were trembling slightly, but even so, the middle schooler tensed her legs and stood firmly, speaking to Marielle.

"If we leave things as they are, Choushi won't last until morning."

▶ 6

"There are that many of 'em...?" Michitaka echoed, like a parrot.

There were five people in the small conference room:

"Berserker" Krusty, the leader of D.D.D.

Soujirou, the harem-prone guild master of the West Wind Brigade.

"Iron Arm" Michitaka, general manager of the Marine Organization.

Henrietta, proxy for the head of the Crescent Moon League guild.

...And "Machiavelli-with-Glasses" Shiroe, of Log Horizon.

The Round Table Council had swiftly convened a meeting to discuss the sudden crisis that assailed the Zantleaf Peninsula. Marielle, who was in Zantleaf to train newbies, and Krusty, Michitaka, and Shiroe, who were stationed at the Ancient Court of Eternal Ice for the negotiations with the People of the Earth, all participated by proxy, via telechat.

The conclusion reached by the telechat meeting was, in a word, *Wait*. At this point in time, they were unable to come to a conclusion. All they could do was stay in close contact, gather intel, and watch how the situation unfolded. That was the general outline of their conclusion.

However, that didn't make it all right for them not to prepare for an emergency.

One of the three measures Shiroe had proposed to the Round Table Council had been to reinforce the guard at the Ancient Court of Eternal Ice. Many nobles were gathered there, and they couldn't leave it defenseless. The aristocrats had brought bodyguards, of course, but from the Adventurers' perspective, that wasn't enough military power.

It was thus that after the Round Table Council, in response to Shiroe's request, the West Wind Brigade promptly rushed to the Ancient Court.

The Ancient Court of Eternal Ice was located roughly southwest of the ruined city of Eastal. It was hard to imagine that the goblins would attack it. This was a safe place, and there was no need for reinforcements. However, the movements of the Lords' Council were unpredictable, and in several of the developments Shiroe predicted, there was a possibility that either Shiroe or Krusty would be unable to continue their participation in the Council. To that end, the Ancient Court delegation requested reinforcements from the town of Akiba.

That said, under the circumstances, during this stare-down with the Lords' Council, calling in reinforcements on too large a scale might invite the lords' animosity. Because of that, Shiroe singled out the West Wind Brigade, a comparatively small guild that belonged to the Round Table Council and was composed of high-level players.

The West Wind Brigade was currently setting up camp at a point about ten minutes on horseback from the Ancient Court of Eternal Ice. Soujirou, the guild master, had gone ahead to the court, with only a few advisers.

In the League of Free Cities, the towns of Akiba and Shibuya were the two closest town zones to the Ancient Court of Eternal Ice. If they felt like it, they could reach it in under two hours, even traveling on horseback. That was how they'd managed to arrive that evening in response to a telechat conference held in the morning.

According to reports, the great horde of goblins had been sighted in a location that skimmed the edge of the Zantleaf Peninsula's root.

In the old world, the location Shiroe had roughly indicated on the map was in the vicinity of Abiko and Toride. There these towns had acted as bedroom communities for Tokyo, but in this world they were lush, green, undeveloped fields and mountains.

"They seem to be splitting into tribes and working with each other as they move, centered on this area. However, their coordination isn't perfect. They can sense the existence of the king, but the system of command is probably completely different between tribes. They're irregular, spread out over a large area. That's actually a problem," Shiroe commented.

When they looked on a map, yes, the location was already nearly touching the sphere of influence of the ruined city of Eastal. If the town of Tsukuba and the city of Maihama were connected by a rough straight line, Eastal was right in the center, where it would keep them from working together.

"In the first place, because their movements are so scattered, we can't get an accurate grasp of their numbers. We've had several reports, but… If we believe the latest aerial reconnaissance report, the goblin army is fifteen thousand strong."

"Fifteen thousand…"

It was Henrietta who'd spoken. She sounded as if she was at a loss for words. She wasn't a guild master affiliated with the Round Table Council; she was serving as Marielle's proxy while Marielle was in Zantleaf at the summer camp. As a result, she'd refrained from speaking much during this discussion and exchange of information, but the cry seemed to have slipped out involuntarily.

"The numbers aren't that much of a threat," Soujirou said nonchalantly. "A group of Adventurers can battle equal numbers of monsters again and again, you know. If the enemy is goblins, even a midlevel player can fight them ten times in a row, give or take. If there were fifteen hundred of us, we could annihilate them."

This was a sound argument, but on the other hand, it evoked blood-soaked carnage.

"Well, *we* might be fine, but I doubt it'll work that way for the Lords' Council," Michitaka countered Soujirou. At that, Soujirou gave an amiable laugh and scratched his head, saying, "Now that you mention it, you're right."

"Either way, as the telechat conference concluded, the Round Table Council has entrusted the response for this incident entirely to Krusty and the rest of the delegation. Since the goblins have attacked, it's all the nobles of Eastal are talking about as well, isn't it? In that case, it's more efficient to talk here, rather than in Akiba."

Although they'd decided to watch how things developed as a general rule, in a situation where they could expect to be contacted by the Lords' Council, they couldn't debate all responses in Akiba. As a result, this was the answer Akiba's Round Table Council had chosen.

During negotiations such as these, it wasn't advisable to restrict the authority of the people who were actually on location with the other party. They'd put their faith in the three of them as special envoys and given them full power.

"Well, mission accepted. We won't do anything to put Akiba at a disadvantage," Michitaka assured Soujirou, laughing brazenly.

After Shiroe had seen this, his eyes went to Krusty.

The big, handsome fellow wore a calm expression. He was gazing fixedly at the map, and he hadn't spoken at all; he seemed to be lost in thought.

"—Aren't the Knights of Izumo going to move?"

Shiroe was the one who accurately caught Krusty's quiet question. Accurately and deeply, meaning included.

"I think some trouble we're not aware of has come up. The Suzaku Gate Demon Festival, for example."

Like the Return of the Goblin King, the Suzaku Gate Demon Festival was a recurring game event that happened once every three months in real-world time. The event developed a story in which the gates of hell had been opened and demons had flooded out into the world.

The difference between it and the Return of the Goblin King was that the Return of the Goblin King took place mainly in the Tohoku region, while the Suzaku Gate Demon Festival occurred in the Heian City of Exorcism.

In other words, if a similar disturbance was occurring in the west, it was possible that the Knights of Izumo had turned their forces in that direction. He didn't really believe in the idea, but Shiroe mentioned it anyway.

"Hmm…"

It was hard to tell whether the answer had convinced Krusty or not. With his arms still folded, he retreated into silence again.

…There may never be another opportunity to confess.

Of course he'd run various calculations and predicted future developments. However, Shiroe had to call the reason for his final decision a premonition.

"I have one more thing to report."

"Hm? What is it, Shiroe?"

"Master Shiroe…?"

Waiting until all eyes in the room were on him, Shiroe began to speak.

"It's about 'death' in this other world. If we die, we revive in the Temple. We hadn't thought about it any other way. If we pay a penalty in experience points, we thought, our bodies come back to life. We believed it implicitly, and naïvely, because that was how it was in *Elder Tales*."

Krusty had been lost in thought, but at Shiroe's words, his head came up and he began to listen.

"According to the information I've obtained… It hasn't been confirmed yet, of course. This hasn't been completely substantiated, but death in this other world also carries commensurate risk. I don't mean losing some items or a few experience points. —At death, our yang energy is used to resurrect our yin energy and our bodies. Every time it happens, we seem to experience very slight memory loss."

The conference room was meant for a small group, and it wasn't very large. It was magnificent, though, and at a glance, it looked like a reception room. Currently, however, the air in that room was fraught with a tension that was practically palpable.

"It isn't clear how much of our memory we lose. We also don't know what sort of memories are lost… However, according to the hypothetical theory I discovered in a certain book, it does appear to happen."

No one seemed able to react to Shiroe's words.

After a long, long time, Krusty responded, briefly:

"Understood. …I assume that's why I'm missing memories from the old world, then. It makes sense now."

"……!!"

All eyes went to the massive warrior, who seemed completely composed. Even under those gazes, Krusty sat calmly, and his cool demeanor didn't flicker.

"D.D.D. is a combat guild. Before Akiba's renaissance, we conducted fierce combat training in order to adapt to battles in this world. I've experienced death a few times myself. I don't generally worry about it, but it's true that there are gaps. I can't confirm it, but…it seems as though memories of the old world selectively drop out."

"B-but that's…"

"What the hell?!"

"Specifically what areas, and how much?"

Henrietta and Michitaka had started out of their chairs, nearly shrieking. Shiroe checked them, looked steadily at Krusty, and asked his question in a firm voice.

"I've died twice since the Catastrophe. Pinpointing holes in one's memory is a fairly difficult task. If everything that relates to what you could pinpoint as missing is itself missing, it's very hard to notice it, you see. All I can say is that, at present, the memory loss is still partial. The name of the elementary school I attended, the faces and nicknames of my friends from middle school, the design on my computer's wallpaper, the lyrics of songs I liked— They're all still there. From what I can tell, subjectively, nothing has been lost. However, I know I kept a cat, but I can't think of its name or what it looked like. —The problem is that it's extremely hard to tell whether these gaps are losses stemming from the yin-yang energy issue, or whether they're ordinary forgetfulness. That said, my memory is comparatively good, so I presume it's due to special circumstances, in other words, to the influence of this matter. That's about all I can put my finger on. Right now, I don't see any losses concerning my own name or information on family members or people

I was close to. I don't know whether that's because important memories are protected, or whether it's just a coincidence. However, if my own case can be applied to others, dying a few times doesn't seem to result in memory loss that would inconvenience anyone. Even if one died several dozen times, it probably wouldn't be enough to affect day-to-day life."

Even dying several dozen times wouldn't be enough to affect day-to-day life.

True, simply forgetting a cat's name wouldn't cause some grave problem to occur immediately. It would have no effect on clothing, food, or shelter.

That said, even if it caused no inconvenience in their everyday lives, it was a shocking confession.

In a way, it was safe to say that Shiroe's guess had been correct. As he'd anticipated, the memory loss was partial, and they didn't lose everything by dying once. At the very least, his guess that memories disappeared in amounts the person in question wouldn't notice had been correct.

However, that didn't mean that the fact didn't shock him. After all, these were nothing less than *memories of the old world*. That was impact enough to plant an instinctive terror in the players; logic didn't even come into it.

The group was speechless. The corners of Krusty's lips curved into a smile.

"There's no need to be so pessimistic. Just don't die. If we avoid that, the memory loss won't occur. And besides..."

Out of the corner of his eye, he saw Soujirou comforting a pale Henrietta. Soujirou was a harem maker, and he always ended up improving others' opinions of him in situations like this.

Michitaka was dumbfounded. "Great Caesar's Ghost..."

However, to Shiroe, the last half of Krusty's sentence—the one the others probably hadn't heard—had been the important part.

Krusty had whispered it with determination, in a voice that might have been called gentle:

"And besides, isn't it true in either world that if there's no meaning to be found in it, life is more terrible than death?"

His words lodged themselves in Shiroe's heart.

CHAPTER.
2

A LAZY, COWARDLY PRINCESS

▶ LEVEL: **12**

▶ RACE: **HUMAN**

▶ CLASS: **NOBLE**

▶ HP: **909**

▶ MP: **455**

▶ ITEM 1:

[WHITE LUXE TREE RING]

A TOY RING MADE OF BRAIDED WHITE LUXE WOOD AND SET WITH PALE ROSE-COLORED STONES. RAYNESIA CAN'T WEAR IT IN ARISTOCRATIC SOCIETY, BUT SHE LIKES IT. IT'S SAID TO WARD OFF DANGER, AND IT HAS BEEN PASSED DOWN FROM MOTHER TO DAUGHTER FOR GENERATIONS.

▶ ITEM 2:

[CRYSTAL TONE MUSIC BOX]

A MUSIC BOX MADE WITH A MITHRIL DISC AND CRYSTAL FEATHERS. IT USED TO MOVE VIA ANCIENT ALV MAGIC, BUT WHEN THE ALVS WERE DESTROYED, IT STOPPED WORKING. SINCE GIVEN A CLOCKWORK MECHANISM BY HUMAN HANDS, IT PLAYS SONGS FROM BYGONE DAYS.

▶ ITEM 3:

[BLOSSOM ROSE DRESS]

A DRESS WITH A BEAUTIFUL TRAIN MADE OF LAYERS OF PALE PINK CLOTH, LIKE ROSE PETALS. THE COLOR OF EACH PIECE OF MATERIAL IS SUBTLY DIFFERENT, AND THE WAY IT CHANGES WHEN SEEN FROM VARIOUS ANGLES FASCINATES WATCHERS. NOT ONE THOUGHT WAS GIVEN TO HOW IT WOULD FEEL TO WEAR IT.

`<ROPE>`
BIND LUGGAGE
TOGETHER, CLIMB
CLIFFS, TIE UP
BAD GUYS...

▶ 1

Hurried preparations had been made.

Marielle of the Crescent Moon League was the only Round Table Council member on location at the abandoned school on the Zantleaf Peninsula, and her decision had been a pessimistic one:

All participants would move to the village of Choushi.

The band of Adventurers had no incentive to protect the People of the Earth's village. That said, abandoning the place in such a dangerous position would have left a bad aftertaste.

At the very least, they should warn Choushi. This was a provisional move based on that decision.

However, one group was moving in a way that had nothing to do with that intent: the five members of Touya's group.

The group had gotten their traveling equipment together promptly and had been the first of all the summer camp participants to set off for the town. At present, the roads seemed safe, but they couldn't be careless. Touya and the others were advancing through the dark countryside in a patrol file, spaced slightly farther apart than they had been in the dungeon.

The magic light Rundelhaus had summoned lit the area around them more brightly than a torch, but even so, in this primitive other world, the nights were black indeed.

"What about that one?"

Every time Touya spotted a hut beside the great river, he called out. As they went, they checked every single fisherman's hut. Depending on their location, the group sometimes shouted loudly, and if necessary, Isuzu conducted solo reconnaissance.

This was because, if People of the Earth were hiding in the huts for any reason, they'd lose their lives easily in a sahuagin or goblin attack. They needed to spend tonight in the village, Touya and the others had thought, and so they were performing this check voluntarily, without having been told.

"Hellooooo! Is anybody there?" Touya called toward a hut.

When he turned back to Isuzu, she silently shook her head. Apparently she didn't sense anyone. In that case, this one was probably okay. Touya and the others set off again, making for Choushi.

"It looks like everyone's evacuated."

"Uh-huh," Minori said, responding to Isuzu.

With their voices in his ears, Touya kept a vigilant eye on the area.

This farm road was fairly close to the coastline, and there were no goblins in sight. However, this close to the ocean, there was no telling when sahuagins might appear from its drenched darkness.

The group moved through the darkness, each keeping an eye on a different direction.

Having seen the countless torches on the mountainside, Touya had steeled himself, realizing that this had turned into something beyond belief. They might get pulled into combat. Awash in sunset light, Nyanta, Naotsugu, Marielle, and the others had been talking in low voices. He hadn't sensed much fear from their shapes, but he had picked up a strong tension.

As he had been gazing, arms folded, at the distant hills swarming with goblins, his sister Minori had come up to him.

Touya had been startled.

What's the matter with Minori?

He couldn't remember ever seeing her like this: face pale, lips drawn. Minori had glanced around hesitantly, but even so, when she spoke to Touya, her voice was not.

"Let's get ready to leave. I think we need to go to the village of

Choushi," she had said. "I...have to talk to Nyanta one more time, so you go persuade everyone, Touya."

After Minori had told him this, she'd turned her back on him.

As if awed by his sister's words, Touya had gone to invite their companions. They would leave for Choushi first, ahead of the summer camp group. ...Though that was a little risky, when he thought about it—as the vanguard, they were more likely to run into monsters.

Touya had thought that one or more of his friends might be reluctant, but unexpectedly, persuading them took almost no work. Only Serara seemed hesitant, and she had assented easily when Isuzu asked her to.

Yes, that had been unexpected, too: Isuzu had been terribly eager.

Touya focused, taking in the situation so calmly he had surprised even himself. Minori's earnest entreaty had mattered, but he also felt an instinctive aversion to the idea of leaving townspeople with no combat abilities on their own, even if they were just People of the Earth.

Without us there, the goblins will probably take that town out in no time flat...

Minori had told him in detail about the village chief, and how people lived. In Touya's mind, Choushi was a town of fishermen, a peaceful, expansive place. Choushi, which was located at the mouth of the Great Zantleaf River, wasn't a fortified city. It had no lord, and although it probably had a vigilance committee, it didn't have knights or other forces to defend it. It was a fishing and farming town that came under the influence of both the city of Maihama and the town of Tsukuba, and up until now, it had managed to stay relatively peaceful.

Unusually for the Peninsula, the surrounding area was flatland. What would normally be a hilly area had been carved away by the Great Zantleaf River, creating a fertile, smoothly sloping plain.

The areas closer to Choushi were cultivated and had been turned into fields that seemed to be marked off in squares, like a tile mosaic. It was a lush, beautiful sight: wheat and field mustard, and a handful of rice fields.

It was submerged in night's darkness now, but the land of Zantleaf, blown by summer sea winds, was a truly splendid place.

And now, a long procession of summer camp members stretched down the farm road that led from the abandoned school to Choushi. They were split into teams by level, or into guilds, or into groups of close friends.

Although they were traveling after sunset, even if they were newbies, they were Adventurers. Each had created a magic light, and they walked without any sign of fatigue. Some were on horseback, but since this was dangerous when you couldn't see your feet, let alone the path, most walked.

Minori's group was moving ahead of the very tip of that long line.

They'd walked for about thirty minutes when Minori abruptly began to speak:

"...Hey guys. I think we should protect that town."

Touya knew Minori's feelings.

He also wanted to protect the town, and he thought that they should.

However, there was no reason to do so.

That town was a People of the Earth settlement. It hadn't anything to do with Minori, Touya, or the others. They hadn't accepted a defense quest. Even if they saved the town, they wouldn't receive any items or cash rewards.

It wasn't even a player town. Were they close with people who lived there? No; it was only people they'd encountered for the first time once they'd arrived for the training camp.

It was strange to feel such an urgent sense of duty without a reason for reward. Still, the feeling was definitely there, as though a great rock were being rolled around in Touya's chest.

Since he couldn't think of a reason, he couldn't express it well. That was all.

It was possible that the other members felt the same way. Isuzu, Rundelhaus, and Serara were all silent, lost in thought as they walked.

There was a black, murky irritation inside them. There was no way for them to shake the impossible feeling of being trapped. They resented their own powerlessness, and no matter how they struggled to escape it, their arms and legs made no progress. It was like being in a nightmare. Touya and the others seemed engulfed by this feeling of helplessness.

"Well, you see...um. There isn't any reason we *have* to save them.

But, I mean..." Minori also seemed to be having trouble finding the right words.

When he looked up, beyond the foothills of the mountain, up in its forests, the torch flames that seemed to be lit on the tips of needles flickered and blazed, like malice in the darkness.

"I don't think...we can stop. It's scary, but even so." Isuzu's voice was forlorn, but it held determination.

Although their levels differed, two-thirds of the players in the summer camp expedition were beginners. Some were between level 20 and 30, like Touya's group, but others were even lower than that. In order to fight goblins, a player needed to be level 20 at least.

On top of that, they didn't know what the enemy's numbers were.

Nyanta had called it a midsized plunder unit, and Naotsugu had counted and said there were two hundred of them at most, but it was night, and it was hard to know how far those statements could be relied on.

There were lots of reasons to go on without saving them.

There was no reason *to* save them.

...But they *wanted* to.

As Touya and the others walked along in silence, the sound of the surf approached them, over and over. The sea might have been painted pitch-black; only the cresting waves that broke on the beach gleamed white, reflecting the moonlight.

As Touya drifted in the sound of the waves and the light of the moon, a thought abruptly occurred to him, a realization too modest to be called insight.

"Do we need a reason?"

"Huh?"

The blank question had come from Serara.

"Can't we just save them, without a reason?"

An odd, rather dumbfounded silence followed Touya's words.

"I think it's fine if we save them for no reason. I mean, we're Adventurers, right? Adventurers are called that 'cos they *adventure*. If we want to save them, I dunno why we can't do it without a reason."

As he spoke, the vague emotions inside Touya took shape. *That's right*, he thought. *What was I worrying about?*

Why had he been looking for a reason?

Had he been planning to justify his actions to someone?

No reason should be necessary to justify helping those who needed it in the first place.

"See what I mean? You, too, Minori. Guys. If we want to save them, let's just do it. Right? Because, I mean, we *want* to!"

Touya threw out his chest, practically shouting.

"Well said!" The first one to respond to Touya's words was Rundelhaus. He nodded firmly and set a hand on Touya's shoulder, expressing approval as though to shake off the silence of a moment ago. "Heh-heh-heh. To be honest, it seems that even I had lost my composure You're right. We are Adventurers. If we took to our heels now, we'd never know why we became Adventurers in the first place. That would have been getting our priorities backward. …Goblins! What can they do, anyway?!"

Rundelhaus shrugged off a concerned Isuzu's hand. "Even I am an Adventurer, in a minor way. I have no intention of shamelessly fleeing back to Akiba without saving the village!"

"W-wait just a minute! How?! How are we going to protect the village? It doesn't have a town wall, and the enemy is twice our size!"

As Touya and Rundelhaus hit it off, Serara broke in with a protesting shriek.

"Minori'll figure that part out."

"What?"

At Touya's abrupt through pass, Minori's eyes went round, as though he'd caught her by surprise. Touya felt a bit bad about throwing her a curve ball like that one, but if he didn't get Minori fired up as well, this enthusiasm would go to waste.

Getting Minori fired up was Touya's job.

As her twin, he knew that throwing her curve balls was the best way to do it.

"…Protect. Town wall… Can't. …The number of enemies… No."

Minori began muttering to herself. Touya saw her lips move: *What would Shiroe do…?* It made him feel very slightly bewildered, alongside a ticklish kind of joy. If his big sister was thinking like this, they had nothing to worry about.

Three steps, five steps.

As Touya and the others watched, Minori stopped in her tracks, then nodded once.

"I've got it… There is a way."

Yeah, that's how Minori's gotta be.

Touya's big sister was a very responsible type. Before, he'd felt as if she was fragile, as though the weight of that responsibility was liable to crush her. However, conversely, he thought it was Minori's strength as well. Since joining Log Horizon, it seemed to Touya that Minori had learned to convert that sense of responsibility into the power to move forward.

It was probably due to the way she idolized Shiroe. Touya idolized Naotsugu in the same way—as both a warrior and a man—so he understood her keenly.

"A way?" Serara asked Minori; she sounded nervous.

"Let's hear it, Mademoiselle Minori."

Rundelhaus and Isuzu, whose expressions were conflicted, gathered around Minori as well.

"There aren't enough of us to protect Choushi from the goblins. …Even if it was *just* the goblins, and it isn't: There are sahuagins, too. They've got more than twice our numbers. We don't even know if we'll all be able to fight. Besides—even if we managed to protect it, if the fields are ruined, it's sure to do great damage to the townspeople. And so… We can't protect it."

Minori's words were decisive, and their strength made even her brother Touya lose his voice.

Her hard-hearted words left every one of her friends speechless.

Minori looked around, as if confirming their expressions. Then, suddenly, she whirled around as though she'd been stung.

"Oh…"

"Hm. Mewr instincts have gotten better, Minoricchi."

"We young gents are patrolling to make sure none of you kids are trying to pull a fast one without permission!"

"I happen to be an old gent, thank mew."

"Nyanta!"

It was Nyanta and Naotsugu. Behind them, a short distance away, they saw Shouryuu and Lezarik as well. Serara had already latched on to Nyanta's thin, taut arm and was nearly hanging from it.

"Master Naotsugu!"

Touya also straightened up, on reflex. It wasn't that Naotsugu was the type of teacher who was strict about manners; the issue was Touya's mind-set. In front of this veteran Guardian, he naturally tended to stand up straight. Of course, ordinarily, even Touya and Naotsugu had careless locker-room conversations.

"Nyanta..."

Minori's expression was a little troubled, but she wasn't about to back down. Looking up at Nyanta with a force that nearly made it a glare, she bowed her head: "Please give us permission."

"Yeah. The manly thing is to keep quiet and let us go this time, Captain Nyanta and Master Naotsugu."

Touya came to stand beside Minori.

He was sure Minori had hit on something. Because she idolized Shiroe, because she'd tried to learn everything in order to follow in his footsteps, there was no doubt that she was harboring some way to break out of the situation. In that case, Touya couldn't let Minori stand in the line of fire alone.

"Permission? No, Adventurers are free. If mew've truly made up your minds, it doesn't matter whether your enemy's level is higher or mew're part of our guild. Adventurers have the freedom to carry through. Only... That in itself is quite difficult, Minoricchi."

Nyanta spoke as if he understood everything, and Minori nodded.

"All right. The nights are short—especially in summer. The pack is on the move, so mew'd best hurry. Understood, Minoricchi?"

Nyanta gave a skillful wink, with Serara still hanging from his left arm. Upon hearing him, Touya and Minori exchanged looks, then bumped their fists together.

▶2

"Approaching from the east ridge. One squad. One more unit forty behind them, and two units to the northeast, as expected."

In the nighttime forest, the shadows of the trees were jet-black in the moonlight.

Minori had called down from a treetop. She was peering intently through a pair of binoculars she'd borrowed from Naotsugu.

"Roger that."

"Understood. I'll begin chanting."

Minori's group was on a forested ridge not far from the Great Zantleaf River. The time was near midnight. Off the leaf-mold-covered track that wasn't quite a forest path nor farm road, in a grove about the size of a gymnasium on top of a rounded hill, Minori and the others lay in wait, holding their breath.

Minori had climbed a large tree that resembled a sturdy Japanese zelkova and was currently looking in all directions and reporting what she found to her friends, who waited on the ground. She used the binoculars to help her work as a long-range monitor.

Touya had had a Damage Interception barrier cast on him, and he was sprinting through the darkness, relying on the mirrorlike effect of the barrier spell.

He'd gone to draw in the goblin unit from the east ridge. Before long, the sharp twang of a bowstring echoed in the darkness, followed by the screams of the goblins and a sound as if someone was pushing through the undergrowth, coming closer.

Touya had received all-round combat training at Log Horizon that included projectile weapons, even though they weren't very practical in dungeons. It wasn't as if Samurai were ill suited to bows and arrows; in fact, they were able to equip both longbows and recurve bows, which were for use on horseback. This time, Touya had used a longbow to get the attention of the distant goblins, and he was now attempting to lure them back to Minori's group.

"...Approaching. As anticipated, two units have noticed."

At Minori's warning call, her companions readied their various weapons and took up fighting stances. In open spaces, the distance at which battles began naturally widened, which, understandably, necessitated a change from the combat methods they'd used in the cramped dungeon. When monsters and Adventurers caught sight of each other at a distance, it was only natural that projectile battles broke out as a preliminary to hand-to-hand fighting.

However, one problem with long-distance battles was that they drew attention from the surrounding area. The bow attack had put the goblins on their guard, attracting two squads—probably about ten goblins—to them. Minori had come to that conclusion from the flickering torches and the sounds of parting undergrowth; it wasn't possible to accurately grasp numbers in the darkness.

"Countdown, please."

Serara's voice was tense.

Through the binoculars, Minori strained her eyes in the darkness. The night was lit by moonlight, and a faint phosphorescence had begun to appear. Moon Fay Drops were midlevel eyedrops that could be made by an Apothecary. They cost quite a bit, but all you had to do was put them in your eyes and you'd be able to see as well as a cat, even in the dark, for twenty-four hours. They'd gotten them from Naotsugu before beginning this operation.

"Five…four…three…two…"

Minori focused her nerves and began the countdown.

Serara loaded the spell she'd had waiting into her staff, then—at Minori's "Zero"—activated it.

At a point about thirty meters away from Minori and the others, the trees suddenly rustled and the weeds writhed, beginning to grow thicker.

Druid was one of the three Recovery classes.

Each Recovery class had its own unique recovery spells, but they were distinguished from the others by more than just recovery properties.

As their name suggested, Druids used forest magic. The source of the magic they used lay in the mysteries of nature. This characteristic wasn't as obvious in dungeons, but when they were outdoors like this, the latent magic in nature held hidden power for them that couldn't be ignored. Since Druid wasn't a Magic Attack class, the power of their spells that dealt direct damage was weak, but in return, they were able to wield a variety of strong, unconventional magic.

Willow Spirits—the spell Serara had chanted—acted on the surrounding plants, making leaves and vines grow. They would wrap around the enemy and limit their movements.

"Here they come."

Flinging his catalpa bow under the trees, Touya drew his katana, gazing forward steadily. Minori had gauged the distance before activation so that the obstacle spell Serara had set earlier would only tangle around the second unit. That meant that beating down the first group of goblins was Touya and Rundelhaus's job.

"I can see clearly. The opening move is yours. Do it well, Touya."

During their recent team training, Rundelhaus seemed to have adopted a new mind-set.

He probably understood that his turn would come even if he let Touya go first. He no longer chose attack spells hastily, and he didn't show off. Even now, he was chanting the spell Icicle Blade to increase the attack power of Touya's katana.

When Rundelhaus's chant ended, freezing cold air gathered around Touya's katana, and it gleamed with a clear light in the darkness.

"That isn't like an Enchanter's spell. It will only add additional damage for a few attacks, so make sure you start with a large one."

In response to Rundelhaus's instructions, Touya nodded.

He's right. We'll have to finish them off quick.

The enemy was goblins, and they were stronger than Skeletons. On top of that, if they took time here, the second unit would probably slip free of their bindings and come after them. Serara's obstacle spell affected the land over a wide range, hampering monsters' movements, but it didn't last that long.

In addition, it wasn't just the one following squad; there were still lots of goblins lurking in the surrounding mountains and forests.

Two hundred at most, Nyanta had said, but even that was questionable. Many presences squirmed in the shadow-blackened forest tonight, and it was hard to imagine just how many enemies there were in this darkness.

"You save your big moves for later, Rudy, and keep them on the defensive with lots of smaller moves. I'll back you up for thirty seconds, but that's it… Maestro Echo!!"

Having steeled herself, Isuzu cast her support spell, and Touya and Rudy rushed the goblins.

Swords and spells danced wildly.

Understanding Isuzu's instructions, Rundelhaus abandoned powerful, stand-alone attacks in favor of a rapid series of lighter spells. In exchange for inflicting less damage, these lighter spells had short cast and recast times. They were spells that could be used back-to-back.

Once he'd discarded huge spells that took about five seconds to chant, Rundelhaus's serial magic attacks consisted of spells that were ready every second and a half, on average. Isuzu's perfect tremolo style turned each mad dance of flame and ice into a circular round.

Deep crimson notes for flame impacts. Marine blue notes for ice impacts.

Isuzu's own attack power was fairly low, however, given that she was a Bard.

That was the fate of all support classes, and there wasn't much to do about the characteristic.

On the other hand, there were things she could do precisely because this was so.

Based on the information her five senses gave her, Isuzu ad-libbed copies of Rundelhaus's spells and sang them with a slight delay.

This was a hidden Bard technique: the ability to copy other players' magical attacks and reproduce them on the spot.

Sorcerers had explosive attack power to begin with. What happened when all that power was doubled? The multilayer barrage, which even Isuzu's throat managed to sustain for only thirty seconds, annihilated the goblins in the blink of an eye.

When the second wave of goblins came, they attacked Touya and inflicted many injuries, but Minori's Damage Interception spell negated them, and the damage that did slip by was dealt with by the recovery spell she chanted immediately afterward. With the arrival of the two Recovery classes, who had switched roles, and Rundelhaus, who'd finished preparing for his big move, the group managed to wipe out ten goblins.

▶ 3

"Yeah. They're tough, but… 'S nothing we can't handle."

At Touya's words, Serara, who'd been treating him, suddenly said, "You mustn't get careless."

Isuzu took a swallow of tea from her canteen, then handed it to

Rundelhaus, who was retying his bootlaces. Accepting it, Rundelhaus admonished Serara: "Carelessness isn't good, Mademoiselle Serara, but if you caution against courage, victory will slip through your fingers."

While the four of them caught their breath, Minori was in the center of the group, desperately struggling with a folded map. Shiroe had given it to her when the summer camp began, saying, *I don't expect you to need it, but...* It was a highly accurate map centered on the Zantleaf Peninsula, and it showed the ruined city of Eastal and the town of Tsukuba.

Even though Minori could see in the dark, it was hard to make out the contents of the map, and so she'd used Bug Light to summon a lamp. She was now hiding in the bushes to keep the light from showing.

Over her shoulder, Serara's voice continued abruptly:

"Yes... Yes. We're fine. We're taking a short break now. You're heading north-northwest, aren't you? All right... About three kilometers, yes. I understand. You and the others take care too, Nyanta."

It seemed Serara was telechatting.

The maneuver Minori and the others had chosen was simplicity itself.

They planned to infiltrate the goblin plunder unit in the forested hills and strike from the inside.

If it was impossible to protect the town, they'd just have to attack ahead of time. They would use the forest in which the goblins were hiding to their own advantage and battle at night. There was no need to wipe out the entire unit.

Although goblins were vicious, too, unlike Skeletons they were demihumans. If the Adventurers struck hard enough, they'd probably damage the goblins' will to fight, and some might desert.

Even in terms of defending the town, if they cut down their numbers with a preemptive surprise attack, it would be much easier to protect it all the way to the end. It was a savage, almost desperate strategy, but at present, it was working far better than they'd expected.

That was the outline of the maneuver. If Nyanta and Naotsugu hadn't fine-tuned it and loaned them items, it probably wouldn't have gone this well. After all, Nyanta and the others were also deep in the forest, fighting separately from Minori's group.

Nyanta, Naotsugu, Shouryuu, and Lezarik were in an area where the fighting was much fiercer compared to where Minori's group was: They'd practically rushed into the center of the Goblin plunder tribe.

Nyanta's party of high-level players had, in fact, charged into the heart of the goblin unit. They had annihilated over and over, drawing attention to themselves. Minori's group was waiting farther south, attacking goblin units that had made it past Nyanta's group, along with any terrified, confused, or isolated squads. Two hours had already passed since the operation began.

In those two hours, Minori's group had defeated around twenty goblins. Lone goblin scouts were actually more trouble than organized squadrons of five or six, because it was often hard to tell what they were trying to do.

Come to think of it, their own maneuver had been an arbitrary act, too: They'd failed to discuss it with Marielle of the Crescent Moon League, who was in charge of the summer camp. Of course Minori felt terribly bad about that, but she'd tried not to think about it too much. When she'd reported in via telechat a little while ago, Marielle had read her the riot act, but she thought there was really no help for that.

This operation was built on the premise that most of their forces would be left in Choushi as a defensive unit. The fewer strike units there were, and the more confusion and damage they caused the goblin plunder unit, the more the gap between the power of the town security forces and the goblin attack units would shrink, and in turn, the higher the likelihood that the goblins would give up.

Minori's words probably hadn't convinced Marielle, but even so, at the end, she'd forgiven her: "Aw, for the love of—! You better be careful out there, or you're gonna live to regret it, you hear?!" (At any rate, she *thought* that had been forgiveness.)

"I think we've wiped out the enemy around here. Maybe we should move."

Isuzu had taken over Minori's binoculars and was looking through them.

"To the northwest… Oh! That's amazing—they're traveling really quietly," she continued to report, sounding impressed.

Nyanta's impromptu party had Naotsugu and Lezarik as its vertical axis, with Shouryuu and Nyanta as the attackers. In other words, it was built around two Swashbucklers.

Swashbucklers were the type that earned damage through attack speed. With two of them, it had been possible to conduct successive attacks across a wide range, without the magical attacks' glaring lights or explosions. In an extermination battle fought in the woods, they could display terrifying efficiency.

Okay, um... Move three kilometers north-northwest, then climb the ridge... They're heading for the ruined shrine from before... Yeah, that's it. In that case, we'll avoid the forest road...

That had meant going down into the valley, but the route would take them sideways, over the opposite ridge.

"What do we do? Minori?"

As everyone's eyes focused on her, Minori folded the map and stood up, nodding firmly.

"We'll go down into the valley for a bit, moving from west to north-west. Stay on the alert as we travel."

The party began to move, following the plan.

They received regular reports from Nyanta, which they then passed on to Marielle. Was Marielle speaking with Choushi's People of the Earth, in turn? Had the other summer camp members already used Call of Home and returned to Akiba instead? No, they thought, a few must have stayed behind for Choushi's sake...

As they walked along in the darkness, an indescribable unease and a sense that all their work was in vain threatened to surge into Minori's heart.

It sounded as though what they were fighting now was only a portion of the huge goblin army. Minori didn't know the details, but from what she'd overheard from Nyanta, the incident had begun with a huge outbreak of goblin tribes in the north, and they'd already closed in on the ruined city of Eastal.

In other words, the plunder unit they were fighting now was only a small part of the main goblin army. In fact, they could probably consider it an undisciplined group of irregulars.

When she began to think like that, futility welled up inside her.

Even if they beat back this plunder unit, it might be no more than a drop in the bucket. Wouldn't they just be buying time? The doubt billowed up like a black cloud, and she couldn't stop it.

"This's scary stuff. Fighting at night."

Touya, who was walking in front of her, spoke quietly.

"The silver streaks of light from my blade get in my eyes. Sure, I can see in the dark, but I'm still afraid I'm gonna trip on a root or in the mud and lose my balance. My heart pounds like a jackhammer, and the stink of blood is nasty—but."

Touya didn't turn around.

He was at the head of the line, and without breaking concentration, he pushed his way through gaps between the trees on a path that couldn't even be called a deer track, steadily descending into the valley.

"But it's okay if we do our best... It's okay if we save them."

Touya's voice was like a light in the darkness.

Minori raised her eyes.

She looked at her little brother's back. Somewhere in his heart, he really had been thinking, *We have to protect them. We have to save them.* In him, Minori could see a strength she didn't possess. Touya's will was simple and straightforward, and even if he wavered, he got there quickly enough to shake it off.

"Yes. That's enough, isn't it."

Isuzu was the first to agree.

I knew it...

If Isuzu, who usually took things at her own speed, was agreeing like that, then Minori's guess was right on the mark. Isuzu had been hesitant right up until they began fighting—she'd been worried about Rundelhaus. Which meant that they couldn't lose this battle.

Rundelhaus was Minori's friend, too, after all. In order to protect his pride and his secret, in order to save his friends, Minori and the others *had* to come here.

"What are you saying, Touya and Mademoiselle Isuzu? That's only natural. As if anyone could abandon someone who'd collapsed in front of him and still call himself an Adventurer! I'll do what I want to do, as I see fit. I became an Adventurer because I wanted to be someone spectacular."

Rundelhaus continued, indignantly.

Touya answered him, vigorously.

Minori watched over all of them.

Damage Interception spells weren't recovery spells.

On the contrary: The way Minori saw it, they weren't even magic.

They were a vow that one would protect one's companions to the end. The determination of a Kannagi. If Minori's friends were standing on a battlefield, she'd shoulder all the danger that came their way, protecting them so thoroughly they'd never even realize the aggression had occurred.

I don't have a lot of experience yet...and there isn't much I can do, but...

Still, she thought.

Even so, she thought.

She didn't plan to use woolly-headed words like *someday*. She would get that power. Tomorrow, even. Maybe today.

As a result, she didn't have time to be afraid of the darkness in front of her.

"Look sharp."

Isuzu's hushed voice pulled Minori's mind back to reality.

With narrowed eyes, Isuzu was looking at the end of the ridge. All that was there was vast, pitch-black forest without a single light in it, but the Bard's keen senses seemed to have found something in that darkness.

Giving a small hand signal, she left the front of the line and began scouting.

"They're magical beasts... I don't know what type, but I can see goblins riding creatures that look like big dogs," Isuzu reported in a small voice.

The wind that crossed the valley would probably keep their scent and voices from reaching the ridge. That was an advantage, but on the other hand, the enemy had the high ground, and that hurt.

"Three beasts and three goblins..." Minori murmured. "Dire Wolves. ...They're a powerful enemy."

She'd acquired basic knowledge from Shiroe's lessons. Dire Wolves were a larger, more dangerous variety of wolf. However, although they might be wolves, they weren't a wild species. They were full-fledged monsters, driven mad by mana and the moon, and their combat abilities were twice those of normal wolves.

"Weak points?"

"They don't have many. In this situation, we might be able to use… flashes and loud noises, I think, but that's about all. And those will probably only work once, too."

Minori answered Rundelhaus's question briefly.

Still, the group didn't hesitate. Even if they had, there was nowhere to run.

"Let's go. Rudy, you be the attack's main axis. We'll win by protecting him. Minori, you cast Damage Interception on him, too. Isuzu, you follow Rudy's lead."

After Touya summed up everyone else's views, the party made for the ridge, paying close attention to the direction of the wind.

The moon was high in the sky. The long night had only just begun.

▶ **4**

That night, at the Ancient Court of Eternal Ice.

The preliminary talk, which had begun in the middle of the night, dragged on, swallowed by a gloomy, oppressive atmosphere. It had been announced as being for "anyone who wished to attend," but nearly all the lords and counselors of the League of Free Cities were there, along with the three representatives—delegate and vice delegates—of the Round Table Council. That meant that it was a "discussion" among the same members as the great conference.

Ordinarily, with that many participants, even if they were quiet, their slight movements and coughs would have given the place a somewhat restless atmosphere. However, today, no one made a sound. It was as if they were afraid of pulling some sort of trigger.

The topic of discussion was "The Recent State of Security in the Northern Yamato Archipelago."

The conference had been convened by Baron Clendit, lord of the town of Utsurugi-Shinzen. That said, it was obvious to everyone that, rather than proposing the meeting himself, the baron had been swept away by the situation or caved under pressure and had had this important role thrust upon him.

As the one who had convened the meeting, the baron was presiding over it, but he was so flustered it was hard to look at him. As Shiroe watched, he kept incessantly fidgeting with his black whiskers and wiping away greasy sweat.

"You may well say that, but..."

"Hmm..."

"Haaah..."

The conference skated around and around the edge of the apparent topic, without making any progress.

"The army of goblins that sprang forth in the northeastern region of the Yamato Archipelago has departed from Seventh Fall...and... erm... Has, uh, laid waste to my territory... Yes."

Even so, having been forced to the top by the rest and speaking in a cracked, shaking voice, Baron Clendit had mentioned the topic several dozen minutes ago, and hadn't managed to develop it at all since.

It's probably an attempt by the lords to get us to bring up the subject ourselves so they can extract information or concessions from us somehow. Either that, or they may be trying to leverage our responsibility for not having captured Seventh Fall, or our sense of guilt...

As he observed the many lords that were present, Shiroe speculated. The lords' faces held all sorts of expressions: fear, resignation, anger, supplication...

They seemed far from relaxed. One whose attitude was fidgety and restless, and who sometimes turned resentful, hate-filled eyes on the Round Table Council members, was Marquis Kilivar, the lord of Tsukuba.

Tsukuba... That's one of the places closest to the goblin army, along with Maihama. It's practically on the front line. On top of that, compared to Maihama, the largest city in the east, its military strength is poor, and its wall can't be that sturdy. ...I hear it's a town of magic-users, too, built around a school for philosophers. I'd imagine he has a few thoughts about us.

"Ah... Ahem, harrumph! And so, for these reasons... At present, this invasion of demihumans, this unparalleled disaster, iiiis, as an urgent situation, occurring *here*, in our Eastal, the League of Free Cities. With regard to this state of affairs..."

Baron Clendit's verbose presentation began again, but this time, the murmur of whispered conversations didn't stop. Both the lords and the civil servants who waited behind them were talking to nearby companions in hushed voices. Each individual voice was low enough to keep the words from being heard, but together, they made for an undeniably agitated atmosphere.

When he glanced to the side, Michitaka gave an exaggerated shrug.

If this kept up, the conference wouldn't take shape.

However, even so, when they considered the future of the Round Table Council, giving in on their end would be conceding too much.

"Could someone who's familiar with the movements of the Knights of Izumo be kind enough to inform me of them?"

With no way around it, Shiroe spoke. The conference room had been on the verge of growing noisy, but his words seemed to abruptly dash cold water on it. Some of the lords' eyes went perfectly round, and they stared at Shiroe with their mouths half open.

What a reaction... What is this? Do the People of the Earth think we're brainless monkeys? ...Ahh, good grief. I suppose there's no help for that. Up until a little while ago, we were underestimating them as NPCs, too. I guess this makes us even. That said... Apparently the Knights of Izumo really aren't in a situation where they're able to move. Not only that, but... Would simply not being able to move warrant a reaction like this? Is there a deeper reason?

"The— The Knights of Izumo are the guardian deities of Yamato. They mustn't be summoned for a battle like this one. Never mind that, let me pose a question to the gentlemen of Akiba's Round Table Council: Why have you not risen up in Yamato's time of crisis? I am told that the knights under Sir Krusty's command are incomparably powerful. Does the Round Table Council not intend to dispatch troops for this incident?"

"We thought the conference was being held in order to hear each of the lord's opinions on that. Did you hold it to get Akiba's opinion? The Round Table Council's decision was to gather more information."

Michitaka answered brusquely, scratching his head.

His attitude seemed to say that they were attending the meeting, after all, and they didn't mind being asked for comments, but it was irritating to be used as a device to divert the discussion.

"I hear the knights of Akiba are invincible in both the east and the west," added a skinny noble whose name they didn't know, in what was nearly a yell.

"I'm not sure what sort of rumors you've heard, but neither the Round Table Council nor the town of Akiba has the sort of standing army or chivalric order you seem to be thinking of."

Shiroe shrugged his shoulders in something approaching disgust.

He finally understood that, particularly for the People of the Earth, "chivalric orders" were the standard unit of military force for war in this world. Their knights weren't elite soldiers who rode on horseback; they were professional soldiers. It didn't seem to be too much of a stretch to consider that "chivalric order" meant "a specific military force that was always standing by for combat."

In this world, where the Adventurers existed, you almost never heard the word *mercenaries*. In addition, militias made up of ordinary citizens who'd armed themselves were only seen defending farming villages. This was apparently due to the fact that the lords weren't comfortable with the idea of armed farmers.

In other words, chivalric orders were the only type of military force the nobles could understand.

However, Shiroe didn't feel that that meant the town of Akiba had to match their style.

"Then what the devil are the Adventurers for?!" Marquis Kilivar railed with bloodshot eyes, and Michitaka reacted:

"'What are the Adventurers for?' …What's that supposed to mean?"

"That should be obvious. The Adventurers' abilities are a divine favor, granted by the gods. You have a duty to save the land!"

"I don't recall hearing anything about it."

"Don't be daft! Immortal, indestructible! With abilities like that, you still intend to neglect your duty to the world?! *Shame*, gentlemen! You're blessed with such a wealth of abilities— How can you be so arrogant?!"

"—Don't give me that crap!"

Michitaka's bellow resounded, making the air shiver.

Before beginning this conference, as they talked with each other and discussed the intelligence that had been gathered since noon, they had examined the memory loss in detail. …That, along with the possibility of going to war.

Certainly, the idea of missing memories was terrifying. Losing memories of the old world would be as lonely as losing their birthplace and getting lost in this other world. Still, that said, it was clear that they couldn't avoid living here.

To Shiroe and the other Adventurers, even death no longer meant "the end." There was no telling how long it would last, but… For now, the only way open to them was to live a life without end.

Since that was the case, even if they managed to avoid sending soldiers to meet the Goblin army, they'd inevitably be pulled into a war they couldn't avoid someday, somewhere. The Round Table Council had been unanimous on that point. If they had to fight somewhere, it would be fine to rise up in this clash with the Goblin King, although of course they'd need to figure their odds of victory. They had decided that they were prepared for it, and had placed that authority in the hands of the three who were in charge of on-site negotiations.

However, letting themselves be unilaterally used would set a bad precedent. Shiroe had stressed that easily providing soldiers would scar not only the Round Table Council and Akiba, but, in the future, the League of Free Cities. There was nothing wrong with joining forces, but it would have to be done through the proper channels.

Then they'd gone over their roles for that night's conference.

Shiroe would approve of sending soldiers from the Round Table Council, drawing out information as he did so.

Michitaka would oppose sending soldiers from the Round Table Council, extracting concessions.

Krusty would make the final decision.

In other words, when Michitaka had taken exception to Marquis Kilivar's demand for troops, it had technically been in line with the scenario. However, Michitaka's bellow had exuded more anger than the acting had planned on.

…I guess that's only to be expected after hearing, "You're immortal, so there's no risk. Since there's no risk, get to work…"

Now that the Adventurers were aware of the memory loss, language like that was enough to incur their wrath. It was no wonder Michitaka was angry.

Is it the arrogance of the weak regarding the strong...? No, that's not funny at all. We may have gotten arrogant, too, while we weren't paying attention...

"First off, we're not lords in your League of Free Cities. We haven't gone through that ceremony deal we need in order to participate yet. That's why we weren't called to the full conference yesterday. Am I right?"

Michitaka kept talking, fixing them with a hard glare from his intense eyes.

They knew from Akatsuki's investigations that the lords had convened in secret the previous night.

The lords' spies had kept her from learning what was being discussed, but from the way this meeting was progressing, it was self-evident.

"That's fine. We haven't actually been decorated or whatever yet, and that's a fact. However, gentlemen, is it right for you nobles to conduct a full conference by yourselves, then demand one-sided cooperation from the Round Table Council and Akiba? Are you telling us we have a duty to submit to demands from a conference we didn't participate in? What do you think, Baron Clendit?"

"That's not... It was never intended that you... I mean, you do not. You have it all wrong, Sir Michitaka."

"I'm not a 'sir.' Like I keep telling you, we haven't been decorated."

"P-please don't say such things. ...You believe we, the lords of the League of Free Cities, are...colluding? With each other... That we are relying on numbers and demanding that the town of Akiba send soldiers? That is most decidedly not the case, and..."

Michitaka's ferocity left poor Baron Clendit discombobulated and at a loss for words.

"Hm. Then demanding soldiers from Akiba was an arbitrary decision by Marquis Kilivar and had nothing to do with the general consensus of the League of Free Cities. Is that what you're saying?"

Shiroe responded to Baron Clendit's words.

At that, it was Marquis Kilivar's turn to lose his composure.

"Wha—?! Do you mean to say that I, blinded by personal interest, would arbitrarily advance matters regarding an incident like this?! Gentlemen! Count Kashiwazaki! Marquis Taihaku! Elder Suwa Lakeside!! Why will you not say anything to the Adventurers?!"

"Well..."

"Certainly, it is not the general consensus. It isn't... But. At the very least, it is true that we have heard such voices in our midst, and that there are a significant number of them. Or do you intend to tell us that Akiba's proud, ultimate forces care nothing for Yamato's calamity?"

A greasy, middle-aged lord pressed Michitaka in a voice that seemed to cling stickily.

"We're not dogs or cats. 'You don't die, so go clear out the goblins'? Is that what you're telling us? As if anyone who went along with hogwash like that and drove his comrades out onto the battlefield could gain the trust of the people of Akiba!"

Michitaka was on the verge of completely blowing his top. Shiroe pulled his arm, drawing him back into his chair.

As far as their roles were concerned, it wasn't a problem if Michitaka objected. Still, if he let his emotions get the better of him and kept yelling like this, and the information about the memory loss got leaked to the People of the Earth, things could get troublesome.

Hm... This isn't good...

Shiroe thought he'd made a bit of a blunder.

Marquis Kilivar and Michitaka's confrontation had completely deadlocked the conference. Personally, Shiroe didn't mind sending troops or cooperating with this expedition. In fact, ultimately, he thought they'd need to cooperate.

Given the option, he'd intended to take a bit more time to search for common ground, but a fissure had developed in the conference before he'd had the chance. As things stood, it would be hard for him to add his opinion.

Come to think of it, it was a mistake to say we'd draw out compromises without setting specific goals... Capital, for example, or economic cooperation, or possibly the conclusion of a treaty. Either way, going in without setting targets was a bad move.

An oppressive mood hung over the frozen conference.

Even Old Duke Sergiad was unable to speak in an atmosphere like this one. Just as Shiroe, racking his brains, was about to attempt to raise a question somehow... Without warning, the big double doors opened.

A lovely girl entered, bringing with her a cool wind that must have been blowing through the corridor.

The girl, who wore a dress the color of a pale dawn and had put up her silver hair, was Raynesia.

▶ **5**

Raynesia was mentally kicking herself.

As a matter of fact, she'd been kicking herself absolutely nonstop for a while now.

Raynesia was kicking herself so assiduously that if those who knew her as she usually was could have seen her, they would have wept sentimental tears. Setting aside the fact that, since kicking oneself is usually an unproductive act, the adjective *assiduously* is not generally used to describe it...

Raynesia didn't have the wherewithal to pay attention to little things like that today.

For instance, the great hall was even bigger than she'd imagined.

To be perfectly honest, Raynesia had been listening to what was going on from an adjoining room.

Of course, as the daughter of a duke, Raynesia would never do something as ill-mannered as eavesdropping (and did not have the skills for it). Elissa was the one who had done the listening.

Although she'd burst in as though compelled to do so by the way the conference was going, her knees were quaking, and her heart was hammering. As a young lady of the aristocracy, Raynesia excelled at smiling elegantly and dancing in public, but this was the first time she'd ever made an appearance at a political affair like this one. What was more, there hadn't been any plans for her to do so in the future.

Aristocratic culture held sway over the League of Free Cities, and the nobles did not consider women, particularly unmarried women, to be full-fledged adults. She had never been allowed to speak on an occasion like this one, and no doubt she never would be. Raynesia had been raised to be "an ideal, modest, ladylike young woman," and so she knew this very well. It was one of the reasons the incident she was in the middle of perpetrating frightened her.

However, something in Raynesia's heart had pushed her into motion, and it wouldn't allow her to hide in the shadows of her parents or the knights.

So even while, internally, Raynesia perspired great drops of cold sweat, outwardly she crossed to the center of the conference room on graceful feet.

"That's..."

"As beautiful as ever..."

"That's Duke Cowen's granddaughter, Princess Raynesia, isn't it?"

"She's like a lake naiad on a moonlit night."

The conference room held not only the lords, but many young knights and advisers as well. They'd become Raynesia's admirers at first sight on the night of the ball, and these were the sort of things they were whispering to each other.

Of course, some of the gazes went past curiosity: contemptible gazes, sullied with lust.

The soft, oval outline of her cheeks. Her large eyes, filled with melancholy. The neat bridge of her nose. Her spun-silver hair was swept up today, and it harmonized beautifully with a dress that generously disclosed the beautiful line from the nape of her neck to her collarbones. Her limbs seemed slender, but their curves were quite feminine enough. The combination of all these things meant there was no one who would argue that she was not the most beautiful princess in the Free Cities.

On top of that, marrying her meant inheriting the Cowen dukedom, which boasted what was no doubt the greatest or second-greatest power in all Yamato. It was only natural that she should receive not only looks of pure longing and yearning, but proposals stained with greed.

Inside the conference room, tables had been set up in a U-shape. At the end of the room, in the center of the table that formed the short side of the U, was Baron Clendit. He was probably conducting the conference proceedings. Next to him was her grandfather, Sergiad.

Even to his granddaughter, Sergiad always seemed to be a strict, frightening grandfather. As she prayed that he'd let her get away with this, just for today, she advanced to the center of the room, then gracefully bent her knee in the traditional greeting. First to the center, then to the east. Finally to the west.

Her thoughts had been frozen for a while now.

It was as if her head had been stuffed with cotton. She couldn't think. The elegance with which she performed the courtesies was like that of an automated doll, something she'd acquired after long training. "The real Raynesia," who was watching it, was hiding in the depths of her heart, quaking and shivering, panicking and holding an (imaginary) cushion over her head.

However, the instant she straightened up and raised her eyes, they met those of her target.

The paragon of rudeness whom she'd met nearly every day over this past week or so. The hypocritically courteous giant. The mind-reading menace. The devilish tormentor in the guise of a battle-tried knight.

Krusty, the representative of the Round Table Council.

To Raynesia, Krusty's frame was so large it seemed practically colossal. He was wearing jet-black clothes with very little ornamentation, and even in the midst of this hopeless conference, his usual expression was firmly in place.

In other words: the mean-spirited expression where he hid his eyes behind thin, rectangular glasses and wore a smile so faint it was barely there at all.

Raynesia watched Krusty steadily.

Krusty also looked back at Raynesia, but before long, he whispered, hardly seeming to move his lips:

"Your chronic 'idleness' is better today, then?"

Was there any need to ask something so obvious?

It wasn't better at all.

She wanted to head straight back to her comfortable room. She wanted to change into her flannel pajamas—the well-worn set, the ones that were getting stretched out of shape, which was exactly what made them so supremely comfy as far as Raynesia was concerned—and laze around in bed.

She wanted to nap to her heart's content, without talking to anybody.

After that, she wanted to crawl out of bed, eat lunch without really bothering to wash her face, then go right back to sleep.

…And so she gazed steadily at Krusty.

She didn't have the presence of mind to smile her usual elegant-noblewoman's smile.

She only watched Krusty, disgracefully, gritting her teeth, her lips drawn. On some level, Raynesia could feel Elissa behind her, worrying, but she didn't even have the leeway to pay attention to that. She kept staring into Krusty's eyes.

The conference room began to buzz.

What was this sudden turn of events?

The lords thought it might have been instigated by the leading lord, Duke Sergiad. Unable to stand the silence, dubious murmurs began to escape them.

"Raynesi…"

"Master Krusty."

Interrupting her grandfather's words without even looking at him, Raynesia spoke to the young foreigner.

She was hoping that her voice wouldn't tremble.

Even as she felt a vague premonition that once she'd said it, things might never be the same again, Raynesia spoke to Krusty, prepared to abandon everything.

This man isn't human. He's a menace. He's a monster, so…

Even as she shivered internally, she remembered the peaceful atmosphere Krusty wore. The tranquil air of the man who'd spent so long with her and hadn't once tried to connect with her as an individual. The nearly supernatural insight of the man who'd never said a single kind word to her.

Right. His sociability and his hypocrisy.

When it came to keeping up superficial appearances and pretending all was as it should be, she and Krusty were accomplices.

Over this past week, the two of them had teamed up and completely fooled all of Eastal, the League of Free Cities. Using calm smiles and mild manners, they'd kept the modest secret of their respective true selves, of their idle prank, a secret to the end.

That's right… I probably…believe in this man's insincerity. I trust the lies of a liar. I trust him to see through me, to play along with this absurd joke…

"Yes, Lady Raynesia."

As Krusty deferentially returned her greeting, Raynesia took a step forward. She faced him across the conference table; there was less than a meter between them.

"I am about to depart for the town of Akiba. Accompany me, please." Raynesia spoke clearly.

The inside of her head went perfectly silent, and even the hum of the conference seemed to come to her from a distance.

Her own pulse, the heat of her burning earlobes. She saw the change in Krusty's expression as it narrowed, ever so slightly, with much more clarity than usual.

"Master Krusty, you swore on your knight's sword that you would wait upon me for the duration of the conference. Hence my request. I must go to the town of Akiba."

"To Akiba. To do what?"

"To recruit military volunteers."

As Raynesia spoke, she felt the lords gasp. Akiba was governed by the Round Table Council. The Adventurers of Akiba were forces belonging to the Round Table Council. In this world, *forces* meant "knights."

In other words, she intended to go to a town that was not her territory, and, without permission, directly urge its knights to participate in battle. To the common sense of aristocratic society, this was an act that would damage the authority of the Round Table Council, something she had no right to do.

However, if Krusty, the representative of the Round Table Council, were to accompany her on this journey to recruit volunteers, there was a possibility that the tide might turn slightly.

Of course, Raynesia had only asked Krusty to guard her, as an individual knight. Logically, even if Krusty agreed to act as her guard, it didn't follow that the Round Table Council would have to lay down their arms. In the worst-case scenario, Raynesia might be declared an agitator and sentenced to beheading.

That said, it was also certainly possible that she might influence the Round Table Council's decision for the better. Surely they would hesitate to behead a princess who had been guarded by their own representative.

Even so, Duke Sergiad couldn't possibly allow his one remaining

granddaughter to do something so willful, could he? A com
groan, something between disappointment and understanding
delight, rose from the nobles.

There was probably no chance that Krusty would accept Raynesia's
extraordinary proposal. After all, it was no more than the whim of a
girl.

However, Raynesia continued to look straight at Krusty.

"I imagine that's going to be terribly, terribly troublesome..."

"—Yes," Raynesia agreed, with a meek, ladylike expression.

However, although her profile struck the conference participants as
graceful and melancholy, internally, she wasn't nearly as calm as she
appeared. She'd been driven so far into a corner that, if it had been
possible, she would have liked to cling to Krusty in tears.

"Why are you doing this?"

"...You yourself said that the Adventurers are free, Master Krusty. I
am only a foolish woman, you see... I know nothing of politics. I can't
even understand why my grandfather and the rest are hiding the fact
that the Knights of Izumo have disappeared."

This time, the conference was enveloped in roars of anger.

Voices criticizing Raynesia's imprudence created such a clamor that
the walls practically vibrated. To protect her mistress, Elissa drew
a dagger she'd had concealed. At the sight of it, the lords, who were
already on their feet, howled even more loudly.

"This is quite the beautiful mess you've created."

"When I take responsibility for it, apologize along with me, if you
would."

As Raynesia answered Krusty, her face was heartily disgusted.

It was an unsuitable expression for "the single winter rose that
blooms in Eastal," but almost none of the participants in this vast conference room were up to noticing slight changes in Raynesia's face at
this point. The voices denouncing Duke Sergiad's granddaughter for
betraying the Lords' Council and leaking secrets to the Round Table
Council knew no end.

"What are you thinking?"

"So there are things even you don't know, Master Krusty. ...Noth-
ing. I'm thinking nothing whatsoever. As a member of the House of
Cowen, I merely wished not to be discourteous."

Just then, the young man next to Krusty, the one who looked like a magic user, clapped his hands together. The sharp report shivered the air, and for the briefest of moments, all the lords and knights in the conference room seemed paralyzed.

It was probably some sort of psychological magic.

In the momentary silence that fell, Raynesia turned around, standing as if to shield Krusty behind her, and raised her voice.

As she'd told Krusty, Raynesia wasn't thinking at all.

She only put words together, as though impelled to by the mass that overflowed in her heart.

"The Adventurers are free! They're human, and freer than we are. ...We may be weaker than the Adventurers, but that doesn't give us license to become aggressive about it. We have no right to relax into our weakness and use their people as our tools. I intend to go to the town of Akiba and entreat the Adventurers directly. It was Master Krusty who said the Adventurers were free, so if any Adventurers respond to my request, doubtless he will not attempt to stop them. I go to find people who will lend us their strength, even if there are only ten or fifteen of them. If they are free and we are asking a favor of them, it is only natural that we should accord them every courtesy, is it not? My grandfather taught me that treating someone with courtesy doesn't mean using high-flown language. I plan to go to them directly, stand in the street, and plead with each Adventurer individually."

She'd said it.

She'd finally gone and said it.

Her blood retreated. Just as Raynesia seemed about to fall, in the midst of a dizzying dimness, a hand supported her shoulder.

"Can I leave the rest to you, Shiroe?"

"Absolutely not. What a waste."

"...To Michitaka, then."

She felt light and detached, and the words they exchanged seemed to come to her from far away.

The sharp sound of a whistle rang out. The conference room buzzed.

The sound of hasty footsteps. Loud voices raised in some sort of argument.

Led by the hand as though she were being escorted at a ball, before she knew it, Raynesia found herself out on the terrace, in the midst of the night wind. When she looked back, she saw the conference room in chaos, and several knights who'd slipped out of it and were in hot pursuit. In the lead, she found her stern yet beloved grandfather's face.

"Are you coming?"

Even though her mind was too confused to think, those words came to her like letters of light written in the clear night sky, and Raynesia nodded plainly. She thought she saw her grandfather break into a broad smile, but it was probably her imagination.

She was only able to think these things for a moment.

Terrifying winged monsters—griffins—glided right over the balcony, riding a strong updraft, and before she even had time to scream, she was picked up bodily, like cargo.

"Pardon me."

The cool voice belonged to Krusty, the sable warrior.

Cradling her in his powerful arms, Krusty leapt up onto the back of the griffin, using only the muscles in his legs.

"Feel free to cling to me."

She might have fainted if it hadn't been for that calm voice speaking to her as the griffin leapt up into the starry night, the two riders on its back.

Beside them was another griffin, which carried the young man who looked like a magician, and a black-haired girl.

She'd left her grandfather and the nobles behind.

Raynesia clung desperately to Krusty's chest, to keep the wind that roared in her ears from snatching her dress.

And so it was that Raynesia's "whim" began tumbling down an infinite slope.

▶ 6

"Why are you laughing, my liege?"

Akatsuki twisted around in Shiroe's arms and looked up at him.

For a little while now, Shiroe had been chuckling to himself, making small noises deep in his throat.

The griffins were slicing through the wind between the stars, heading due northeast. If they went on this way, they'd be able to see Akiba in just a few minutes. A journey that would have taken several hours on the ground grew very short—only around twenty minutes— on the back of a magical beast that was beating its powerful wings.

"Nothing. I just thought that was brilliant."

"Hm?"

Shiroe laughed as if he found it really funny.

"I've never seen Krusty make a face like that before. He managed to hide it, but still. …He was really on the ropes back there. Ahh, that felt good."

"Were you still holding a grudge about that, my liege? …About the ball?"

"No, not at all. …Well, maybe," Shiroe answered Akatsuki, who fit snugly into his arms.

"That princess is really something, too. Doing what she did at a time like that… 'Courtesy,' hm? I hadn't thought of that. Still, the League of Free Cities had reached an impasse over this, and she saved them. No matter what anyone says, she took action to save them, and she succeeded."

The League of Free Cities needed the Round Table Council's fighting power. Shiroe didn't know what sort of particulars lay behind it yet, but if the Knights of Izumo weren't able to move, the Adventurers would need to be sent out. If they failed to do so, they'd plunge into a messy war of attrition.

The circumstances were such that it was conceivable that several of the chairs belonging to the League of Free Cities' twenty-four lords might end up empty.

Since that was the case, the League of Free Cities had needed to pull the Round Table Council's Adventurers out onto the battlefield, no matter what conditions they were required to swallow.

However, they'd gotten one thing very wrong.

The Round Table Council was in charge of Akiba's self-government, and it bore a certain amount of responsibility for its management. However, it did not *control* Akiba.

Adventurers were completely free. The idea that the movements of separate guilds and individuals should not be restricted was so established that there had been no need to codify it in Akiba's founding principles. To Shiroe and the others, who'd played *Elder Tales* as a game, this was self-evident to the point that there hadn't been any need to confirm it.

The town of Akiba governed itself through an unstable council system, and restricting the freedom of the Adventurers who lived there was bound to generate a huge amount of stress among them.

Naturally, Krusty and the other special envoys from the Round Table Council could commit to cooperating in the defensive war against the Goblins. However, it wouldn't be unconditional. The condition would lie in whether they could get sufficient support when they announced their decision to the Adventurers of Akiba.

If they did it any other way, the people of Akiba would abandon Shiroe and the other special envoys in the blink of an eye.

At present, in terms of defense, Akiba's fighting capabilities were more than sufficient. In economic terms, although they had difficulty supplying their own food, since they'd begun to develop items using their knowledge from the old world, it was almost certain that advances would be made in the future.

In other words, the situation was such that finding a way to reward the town of Akiba was fairly difficult. Even if they tried to lure them in with bait of some sort, Akiba was quite wealthy.

If paying with money wouldn't work, and providing technology was difficult, the League of Free Cities would naturally reach a deadlock. Of course, there were several things even Akiba wanted, with food supplies at the top of the list. After all, Shiroe and the others knew the old world, and their craving for further comfort in everyday life was strong. It was much too late for them to return to the soggy rice crackers of yore.

However, the lords didn't know them very well, and they hadn't been able to pick up on that.

If the conference had gone peaceably, Shiroe had privately intended to bring the negotiations to a close by casually presenting these requests on behalf of the Round Table Council.

However, Marquis Kilivar and a few of the other nobles had gone off half-cocked and stalled the conference, and the circumstances had no longer been the sort in which he could play any cards.

She probably isn't aware of it, but she saved the lords, and she's also saved the Round Table Council.

As a matter of fact, Shiroe himself was in favor of dispatching troops.

Life in this world seemed to be an inevitable fate, and since it was something they couldn't avoid, they should fight under conditions in which they had the advantage.

The lords had viewed the Adventurers as invincible soldiers and had wanted to send them into battle, but their understanding had been flawed. In fact, the Adventurers were also saddled with risk: the loss of their memories. From Krusty's statement, they'd learned that they weren't likely to lose all their memories by dying once or twice, but even if that was the case, the pressure was still terrible.

This information hadn't yet gone beyond the Round Table Council, but someday, they would probably have to announce it to all the citizens of Akiba.

When that time came, what would it take for the Round Table Council to maintain the current public order? Shiroe had spent many sleepless nights worrying about that. At this point, he thought the answer might be "understanding." It might also be called "resolution appropriate to the risk."

When life lost its absolute end—when death was made meaningless—chaos would come of its own accord. No longer a one-way corridor that led from beginning to end, a life that had lost its other shore—its original destination—would be compelled to wander.

Shiroe and the other Round Table Council special envoys couldn't simply let themselves be used by the League of Free Cities, even if they did decide to cooperate with them. Doing so would damage the "understanding" the Adventurers of Akiba had of the world.

And directly opposite that, was her...

In the face of all that, Princess Raynesia had said, *I will persuade them.*

She would plead with the Adventurers, who were free by nature, on an individual basis.

She'd declared it outright.

"World Fraction"...

The menace of that phrase pressed at Shiroe's heart.

Where were he and the other players?

To Shiroe, the demihumans were monsters, his enemies in the game.

However, Li Gan had said they were the nightmares of warped souls, born from the curse of the first World Fraction.

Shiroe had been an ordinary university student living on Earth. *Elder Tales* had been just an online game. However, Li Gan said that Shiroe and the other Adventurers were beings that had been summoned to this world by the second World Fraction.

Shiroe's immortality was only natural: This had been a game. However, Li Gan considered the restoration and repair of yin and yang energy through the Spirit Theory to be part of a great system that was tied to the secrets of the world's beginning.

Where did he stand?

The question made Shiroe terribly uneasy.

Which was the dream? Was it the body that was racing through the sky on the back of a griffin, or was it the self that had sat at a computer desk, clicking away? The boundary was growing vague.

If his memories were taken while he harbored this unease, he was sure he'd be plunged into the darkness of delusion. No doubt most Adventurers would be. And who would save them if that happened? No such convenient outsider existed.

All there was, Shiroe thought, was "understanding."

Even he didn't know how to go about obtaining that understanding. Not only that, but this world wasn't likely to give him time for that doubt, or to find an answer. Each day came at ferocious speed and was swept away into the past.

The Adventurers might—no, probably would—travel that precarious, painful road, and they were the ones the ladylike Princess Raynesia had meant when she said, "It's only natural that we afford them every courtesy."

I suppose I should have expected no less from Krusty...

In his arms, Akatsuki pressed her cheek against Shiroe as if she were cold. Shiroe's expression softened as he sheltered her under his arms.

Marquis Kilivar's emotional outburst had cut off the Round Table Council's path of retreat as well. Because he'd spoken as though he saw the Adventurers as mere tools, Shiroe and the others had lost their chance to contribute to the war, even if they'd wanted to.

If they'd let that attitude coerce them into promising to cooperate, it would have hurt the pride of Akiba's Adventurers, and the

Round Table Council would have lost their trust as an organization of self-government.

"My liege, there lies Akiba."

"Indeed."

"Does battle come next?"

"Most likely."

In this other world, *night* meant "darkness."

A pitch-black world spread out below them. Due to the stars scattered across it, the sky was actually brighter. He had no watch, but he thought it was probably about midnight. Even so, the town of Akiba wasn't asleep.

Thanks to the telechat he'd sent through right after the griffins took flight, the Round Table Council should be ready and waiting. Roderick of the Roderick Trading Company would probably also respond to the measures he'd taken.

In the midst of the dark world, the lights of the town of Akiba shone like a watchfire.

As they drew nearer, the single blaze seemed to break apart into countless bonfires, and before long, they could even make out the circle of fire that enclosed the plaza, like a tiny ring. It was an impromptu landing site that D.D.D., Akiba's largest combat guild, had quickly set up to receive their leader.

In the midst of enough light even for mounts whose eyesight failed in the dark, the two magical beasts descended to the town of Akiba. The long night was still less than halfway over.

CHAPTER.
3

EXPEDITIONARY FORCE

► LEVEL: **14**

► RACE: **ELF**

► CLASS: **ELDER MAID**

► HP: **629**

► MP: **589**

► ITEM 1:
[LACE PARASOL]

A GORGEOUS PARASOL MADE OF FINE THREADS, METICULOUSLY WORKED TOGETHER. ITEMS MADE WITH LACE WERE DEVELOPED AFTER THE MAY INCIDENT AND ARE CURRENTLY IN VOGUE. A MUST-HAVE ITEM FOR ATTENDANTS SEEKING TO PROTECT NOBLE PERSONAGES FROM THE SUN'S FIERCE RAYS.

► ITEM 2:
[BROWNIES' DUSTER]

A MAGIC CLEANING IMPLEMENT AWARDED BY BROWNIES, THE HOUSE FAIRIES, AS THANKS FOR A QUEST. WHEN USED BY CERTAIN SUBCLASSES, IT HELPS THEM, AND IF YOU GIVE IT TO NPCS AS A PRESENT, THEY'LL LIKE YOU MORE. IT ISN'T CLEAR WHO GAVE THIS ONE TO ELISSA.

► ITEM 3:
[MAID OUTFIT]

A FULL UNIFORM FOR A MAID. THERE ARE SOME USED BY PEOPLE OF THE EARTH, TOO, BUT THE ONE ELISSA HAS BEEN WEARING LATELY IS SPECIAL DEFENSIVE GEAR FOR THE MAID SUBCLASS. APPARENTLY SHE LIKES IT BECAUSE IT'S COMFORTABLE AND STURDY.

<Chopsticks>
Traditional Yamato dining
utensils. It's said that a
professional can snatch flies
out of the air with these.

▶ 1

After the griffin descended, Raynesia couldn't move a muscle while she was being carried down from its back. She'd been held around the waist during dances, but for as far back as she could remember, she'd never been handled so carelessly, like luggage.

She hadn't thought being treated this way by the opposite sex would be so disconcerting. She tried to smile with her face tense, but even she knew it looked drawn and stiff.

Partly because she'd been highly determined during the conference, it hadn't felt real to her. She'd felt as if she were delirious with fever as she carried out her plan.

Now that she thought about it, Raynesia had spent too much time with Krusty over this past week. She'd been able to give herself courage by thinking that, compared to this alabaster, practically supernatural young man who guessed her most private thoughts, speaking defiantly in front of the lords was nothing at all.

However, she really wasn't comfortable around Krusty himself.

She knew that while they were flying on the griffin, he'd been casually solicitous toward her, keeping her from being blown away by the wind or getting cold. However, the more solicitous he was, the more it felt as though every one of her innermost thoughts was an open book to him, and she was beyond flustered.

She wasn't all that concerned anymore that he'd find out she was a fake, that she was really a lazybones who hated people, that she was a terribly hopeless person who thought of nothing except loafing around in her room.

However, if possible—no, at all costs—she wanted to keep Krusty from finding out that she was flustered over him.

"Milady."

For just a moment, she took the hand Krusty held out to her and descended to the ground.

She was in the town of Akiba.

Even though it was the middle of the night, lights were lit all through the town. When she'd looked down on them from the sky, she'd thought they were a type of watchfire, but now that she'd descended, they proved to be lights of all different sorts. The seven big bonfires in the plaza were orange, the lamps that were resistant to wind and rain were yellow, and magic lights were a phosphorescent white.

"I… Thank you very much."

She'd lowered her eyes as she spoke, but Krusty's interest was already elsewhere. A group who wore overcoats with white, undyed crests like the one on Krusty's mantle was approaching from that direction, stepping briskly.

Krusty exchanged greetings with the group, then turned to speak to the young man who looked like a magic user, the one who had just lifted the black-haired girl down.

"Shiroe. Can I ask you to take care of her outfit and management?"

"Yes, of course. Only… Are you sure?"

"There's no help for it. I'll brace myself."

After Krusty had spoken to the young man he'd called Shiroe, he left with the group that was dressed like him. At the same time, the griffins also took off, whipping up a gust of wind.

Raynesia was standing there, at a loss, when the young man named Shiroe addressed her:

"I believe this is the first time we've spoken directly, Princess Raynesia. I'm Shiroe of Log Horizon. This girl is Akatsuki."

At Shiroe's introduction, the petite girl he'd called Akatsuki nodded briefly. Apparently she was the quiet type.

"All right, then. Follow me, please."

Shiroe turned his back to her and began to walk away. Most of the people on the street seemed to be Adventurers, and apparently they were moving with some sort of purpose. A flurried atmosphere hung in the air.

Raynesia had rushed out, declaring sharply that she would persuade the Adventurers of Akiba, but she'd given no thought to the specifics of how she was going to do it. She'd had the vague idea that she'd make an entreaty at the Round Table Council—which she assumed was a place like the Lords' Council—and, after obtaining permission, would meet with the major Adventurers one after another.

The town of Akiba was nothing like Maihama.

Unlike the beautiful, brilliant Maihama, where fruit trees hung with crystal lined the streets, this town seemed to make use of the ruins from the old days. Maze-like streets ran through the gaps between buildings that were five or ten stories tall, and Raynesia was wary, knowing she'd get lost in moments if she were to become separated from the young man who was guiding her.

A woman who was coming up the street, carrying a large load, nimbly yielded the right of way to Shiroe; she whispered something to him very quickly, then bowed her head. Raynesia thought that Shiroe must have significant status on the Round Table Council. He'd been chosen as a vice envoy, after all.

He is walking a little too quickly, though.

The girl he'd called Akatsuki was keeping up with him without difficulty. Raynesia had heard tales of the extent of the Adventurers' physical abilities, but she'd never imagined she'd feel the difference in something so basic.

Shiroe had one hand to his ear, covering it, and was talking to no one as he walked. He'd probably contacted someone with some sort of magic.

But before long, they arrived at a big, blackish building.

"Shiroe!"

"Thanks for coming, Calasin."

The man who was waiting for the three of them just inside the building, in what seemed to be a reception hall or lobby, was dressed like a young merchant.

"This is Princess Raynesia."

"Oho! I've heard a lot about you. You're the young lady of the Cowen dukedom, aren't you? I'm Calasin, a merchant trader. I'm the head of Shopping District 8."

Apparently, the man who'd called himself Calasin really was a merchant. He greeted Raynesia with an affable smile. However, to Raynesia, a noble, his brand of courtesy felt extremely pragmatic and simple.

The Adventurers all seem to be very candid, and to dislike empty formalities...

With a ladylike smile, Raynesia returned a greeting that was elegant, but quite abbreviated by her standards. "Shopping District 8" was an odd name, but considering the way he'd used it to introduce himself, it was probably the name of one of Akiba's influential houses.

"I am Raynesia of the House of Cowen. I'm very pleased to make your acquaintance."

Calasin turned red and averted his eyes. This was a reaction Raynesia was used to.

"So, Calasin," Shiroe said.

"Mn?"

"Hm... What to do... What should we go with...? We need to make an impact. The first impression has to be hard-hitting. ...Valkyrie Mail. Do you have a full set?"

"Wha? Ah...huh. Of course I do, but... With that one, the legs are... Are you sure?"

However, Raynesia's relief was fleeting. She didn't really understand what was being said, but Shiroe and the merchant Calasin had begun to talk about something she couldn't just let slide.

"Yes. It's not a problem. Something like that is just what we need, in several ways. One set, if you would. I've got the cape somewhere, so we won't need that. Would you also pick out a likely-looking weapon? A one-handed long sword with a good design; if the equip level is four or under, it should be fine. ...Akatsuki, go get us a room. A small one will do. We'll pay by the hour. —No, attack power doesn't matter at all. It just has to look good."

What followed was a whirl of shame and confusion.

Having been shown to a simple room, Raynesia was stripped of her clothes and changed into the battle costume she'd been handed. The girl called Akatsuki dressed her.

There were many nobles who regularly left the task of changing their clothes to their maids. Raynesia was one of them, of course, and she wasn't reluctant to show her skin in public.

The source of the embarrassment and confusion lay in the battle costume, the first she'd ever worn.

First, it was as light as down.

A robe woven from thin, dazzling silver chains, and a cuirass.

The gauntlets and what seemed to be metal leg protectors were graceful things, embossed with arabesque patterns, and they reminded her of elven craftsmanship.

The problem was…

The chain robe, and the waist armor. They only hid the bases of her thighs by the barest margin, leaving most of her legs exposed. Some dresses were designed to leave the upper arms naked this way, but she'd never in her life (probably) worn any garment shameless enough to show her legs.

"Skirt…next." The scrap of cloth that was put on her after that minimalist sentence was made of green silk. In terms of area, it was more like a sort of loincloth or scarf than a skirt.

I-I knew it. My legs will be entirely exposed… And this cuirass— The chest is sculpted to be a bit too realistic, and…it's making them look bigger than they are…

Akatsuki hung a sword belt around the discombobulated Raynesia's waist, then cinched up various belts here and there. As they tightened, all the armor pressed closely against her skin, and she felt the weight of it even less.

Raynesia marveled at its lightness and comfort, thinking that it must be a terribly famous magic item… However, it accentuated the lines of her figure as well, meaning the wretched spectacle was too horrid even to look at.

She didn't think her figure was all that bad, but weren't these clothes far too, too—scanty? Raynesia groaned.

"Erm… Miss Akatsuki? I really do think this shows my figure too—"

"You're tall, so live with it."

Finding herself the target of a cold glare, Raynesia fell silent.

Akatsuki took a comb out of an inner pocket and began to run it through Raynesia's hair until it lay smooth. Her movements were flowing, and Raynesia thought she was more careful than any of her maids, but her tension only grew.

For a while now, she'd felt an excessive pressure from the tiny girl, possibly because she didn't say much.

Catching Raynesia's hand as she sniffled and complained, Akatsuki opened the door and pulled her outside. Shiroe and Calasin were waiting for them. They seemed to have been having a meeting right where they stood in the corridor. When Calasin looked at Raynesia—who was trying to hide behind Akatsuki, even though their heights were different—he broke into a smile.

The expression of genuine admiration on his face was the same as the ones worn by the knights and civil servants. On the other hand, Shiroe's was appraising, and Raynesia added him to her mental list of people to watch out for.

"That's not bad at all. …Is it, Calasin."

"Yes, I think she's terribly beautiful."

"…Th-thank you very much."

Raynesia very nearly lifted the skirt a bit to curtsy, but she checked herself hastily. The scrap of cloth she was wearing right now (she really didn't want to call it a skirt) wasn't long enough to lift.

"All right, let's get down to business. It's fine. Yes, don't worry. I rate you quite highly, Princess."

For some reason, Shiroe's words and smile gave Raynesia a chill, but for now, all she did was nod in agreement.

▶ **2**

And then…

"Thank you for gathering before dawn like this; that's good to see. I'm Shiroe of Log Horizon. It is early, after all, and the military situation is urgent, so I'll explain the present circumstances right away."

It was dawn.

Akiba's plaza was filled with a crowd of Adventurers. There was no telling how many there were, but the square was packed. She thought there must be far more than a thousand of them.

Akiba's central plaza.

They'd cleared away the rubble over the past few months, which meant there was about 20 percent more space than there had been right after the Catastrophe. When *Elder Tales* was a game, the rubble had been background objects and they hadn't been able to shift it, but now they could both move and break it.

In combination with the neatly repainted, enterprising shops that were already opening, even at this hour, this made the town of Akiba look even livelier.

Raynesia didn't know about any of these things, of course, and to her, Akiba seemed to be an almost frighteningly energetic town. Dawn hadn't yet broken, and blue had only just begun to steal into the eastern sky. She'd never experienced a full-fledged war, and, to her, the fact that such a large crowd had assembled so early on a summer morning seemed to be an extraordinary situation.

Not only that, but not all the people who'd gathered looked like knights.

There were elves and dwarves, and even artisans and merchants. Unlike at military or noble meetings, food and drink was being sold to the people in the plaza, and the sight made her think that this sort of assembly might be an everyday occurrence in this town.

Although Raynesia wasn't aware of it, the Round Table Council members who'd been answering Shiroe's telechats in shifts around the clock had made all the preparations at his request. This was also true of the able Adventurers who'd gathered in the square, of the stage that had been set up, and of the "secret weapon" moored on the river that ran behind the town of Akiba. However, these were things Raynesia didn't yet know.

What Raynesia saw from the tent that formed the backstage area was a platform brightly illuminated by Lumieres—light spirits conjured by a Summoner. It looked as though they'd used a precious magician—and a Summoner at that—as a mere stagehand, and the idea was nearly enough to bring Raynesia's common sense crashing down, but what completely stunned her was the continuation of the talk.

"—Due to the factors I've just mentioned, a tribe of goblins a little less than twenty thousand strong at the maximum has appeared in the forested hills of the northeastern region, centered on the base of the Zantleaf Peninsula. The pressure of this force is exerting influence in all directions. Reports from multiple Adventurers staying in Zantleaf have also been confirmed. Eastal, the League of Free Cities, an organization that governs eastern Yamato, is currently being exposed to this threat. That said, according to predictions from the Round Table Council, the threat will remain a mere threat. Even if we do nothing, the League of Free Cities will not be annihilated. However, it is conceivable that they will lose about thirty percent of their total fighting strength. …While it's true that these figures are close to annihilation, it isn't as though the People of the Earth will be completely wiped out down to the last man."

The information Shiroe was delivering was more detailed than what the League of Free Cities' Lords' Council had obtained. His words were merciless, and if her ears weren't deceiving her, she sensed sharp thorns in them.

However, what truly astonished Raynesia wasn't Shiroe's attitude. It was the fact that there was a clear light of understanding in the eyes of every Adventurer who heard what he said.

From what she could see from where she peeked out of the tent, not a single one of them looked bored or as if they couldn't understand. A few of them even had bundles of paper—probably maps—open and were jotting down the main points of the address.

To Raynesia, a Person of the Earth, it was an astounding sight. Weren't the people gathered here Akiba's equivalent of ordinary townsfolk? How could they comprehend so much?

The Adventurers in the plaza, the ones Raynesia had assumed were soldiers, had understanding that was on par not only with military officers, but with royal civil servants. All these people had knowledge of topography and military affairs. Not only that, they seemed to be well informed even about the political situation of Eastal, the League of Free Cities, and the fact was enough of a shock to crumble the very ground under Raynesia's feet.

What were nobles? What were commoners? What were farmers?

Inside Raynesia, the worldview she'd placed her trust in up until now shivered and broke apart.

"On the other hand, as far as we're concerned, I don't think it will be very difficult to defend Akiba from this army. This town is quite self-sufficient in everything except food, particularly with regard to technology, and we have a certain amount of defensive strength. Nothing says we have to save the League of Free Cities. In terms of profit and loss, there's no need to save them. Let me repeat that: There is absolutely no need to save them. Now having said that, there's something I'd like you to hear."

Everyone in the plaza seemed to be holding their breath.

In the midst of the intense silence unique to large gatherings, Shiroe looked toward the tent and beckoned to someone with his fingers.

Huh?

As Raynesia stared blankly, a hand suddenly caught her arm.

When she turned… Krusty stood there, wearing armor the color of a dull dawn. Was it for ceremonial or practical use? But with his usual calm smile, the one that didn't betray what he was thinking, Krusty said, "Well, shall we?"

"What? Pardon?"

"Come."

Just like that, she was dragged from the tent. Abruptly, a light strong enough to make her vision go white filled the area.

It was the first rays of dawn. The morning's first light had begun to stream down into the plaza from the eastern sky.

Raynesia was suddenly thrust out into the wind of an early summer morning, which held no heat as yet.

She was in the center of the stage. On the front line, with no place to run.

Raynesia flushed from head to toe. She felt giddy. She had no idea what to say or do. There were several thousand Adventurers in front of her. Beings who were not like the People of the Earth. They might look the same and speak the same words, but the slight contact she'd had with them over the past short while had convinced her that they were fundamentally different creatures.

Her lips trembled, and her knees were on the verge of quaking.

Just then, a sharp sound rang out from behind her, to her right.

When she turned, there was Krusty, looking as imposing as a heroic deity charged with protection. His hands were folded over each other on the pommel of a giant, two-handed ax that was braced on the floor. The sharp sound had been the ax hitting the stage.

The dull, loud thud she heard next came from behind her on the left. Shiroe had retreated to that point, holding a ceremonial priest's staff he hadn't had earlier. It was about as long as he was tall, and he was resting it on the stage as if it were a spear.

With Krusty and Shiroe to either side of her, Raynesia took a step forward on the great stage. The heat she'd felt was rising, and her vision warped dizzily, but her mind was oddly clear. The sound of her own breathing was loud in her ears, but strangely, she could hear the voice of an Adventurer whispering in a corner of the plaza quite clearly.

"—It's a pleasure to make your acquaintance. I am a Person of the Earth. My name is Raynesia Elarte Cowen. I belong to the House of Cowen, which governs the city of Maihama and is involved with Eastal, the League of Free Cities. I've come here today to ask a favor of you."

Even she was startled at the clarity of the voice she managed to produce. In the morning air, her words reached all the way to the edges of the plaza.

"As Master Shiroe has just explained, the land of Yamato is heading toward crisis. Let me speak plainly, concealing nothing: The whereabouts of the Knights of Izumo, whom you know as Yamato's guardian deities, are a mystery, and the League of Free Cities is being compelled to handle this matter with nothing to rely on but its own power. The numbers of this goblin army are greater than any invasion we've seen before, and their movements are as fast as lightning. Regrettably, we have already let them advance deep into the heart of the Free Cities. Of course, the People of the Earth have town walls and defensive barrier magic, and we do have soldiers. But, should war break out, it isn't clear how reliable these things will prove to be. Even now, I believe my fellow People of the Earth are polishing their swords, patching up the town walls, and preparing for battle to protect the land of our ancestors. However, if that is all we have, we will be unable to avoid great bloodshed."

Raynesia's gaze went distant.

What she saw was not the throng in front of her, but the scene from a few hours before.

"Although I am ashamed to admit it, even now, at the eleventh hour, we of the League of Free Cities have been unable to come to an agreement. At the conference that was in progress until immediately before I came here, everyone was so concerned with the safety of their own territory that they could not cooperate. Moreover..."

She faltered.

However, it was too late for her to stop. "Moreover, they ended by devising a strategy to force our own sacred duty, that of protecting the land of our ancestors, onto the emergent town of Akiba's Round Table Council. Immortal Adventurers... They were counting on your power, and they tried to use your military force to protect themselves and their territories. I do not have the right, but...I felt badly about it. What makes me feel even worse is that I have also come to make this selfish request of you."

She didn't realize it, but the set of Valkyrie Mail and the bright violet cloak that Shiroe had chosen emphasized Raynesia's feminine form better than anything. In the dawn light, she was a goddess of war that anyone would idolize.

Raynesia didn't know.

She didn't know that as she faced the Adventurers and spoke to them, behind her, Shiroe had glanced slightly to the side and winked. Or that Krusty, who looked completely disgruntled, had given a wry smile in response.

"Neither I nor the League of Free Cities can offer much by way of payment. ...I don't even know if there's anything we *can* give the people of a town as prosperous as yours, nor do I think it's possible to compensate you fairly for your freedom. Even so, as a daughter of the House of Cowen, I love the city of Maihama, and I have a duty to protect it. And so—I will go there."

It was far too pitiful, and far too selfish, and so...

Spontaneously, Raynesia knelt. She bowed her head very low.

If the Adventurers here had been knights, or civil servants, or, in other words, "nobles," she could have gotten by without bowing her head. In aristocratic culture, ladies were treated as articles of value. The safety of a woman of high rank was protected first and foremost.

However, after meeting Krusty, she'd learned: The Adventurers were different.

Even in the town of Akiba, a title like hers would have won her respect as a daughter of the nobility. However, there was no doubt that it would not win her hangers-on who would be swayed by the slightest change in her expression, as it did in aristocratic culture. At the most, the respect would be the sort due to a neighbor.

This town was alien.

In it, she would not receive the warm welcome she'd received as a princess up until now. However, on the other hand, she would also not be subjected to aristocratic society's unique discrimination against ladies.

In aristocratic society, women had no rights as human beings.

They were pampered, of course, and they received gifts. They were given compliments, empty love poems, and enough sweet words to bathe in. If she merely looked anxious, the young knights would attempt to find any medicine for her, no matter how costly. However, none of this was because she was loved for herself, as an individual.

She was only being treated courteously because, as a lady, she was a prize in the diplomatic competition among the nobles.

In aristocratic society, ladies were treated as jewels. Even among those ladies, she had been beautiful with a certified pedigree: the ultimate trophy. No more than that.

Raynesia, who had closed herself up in her room and wallowed in melancholy thoughts, understood this better than anyone. She also knew she didn't have the strength to deny it.

"I am lazy and a coward, an empty-headed ornament, but even so… I am going…to the battlefield. And so, if you please, if there are some of you who don't mind, would you come with me? Would you help me, in the name of your goodwill and freedom? I would like to protect the 'Adventurers'' freedom to the best of my abilities…"

But even if I say that… Even if I tell them I'll protect their freedom…

While she was a daughter of the House of Cowen, she'd been born a woman, and she didn't have that much authority. She could coax her father and grandfather into buying her dresses and jewels. She could probably choose one or two Adventurers and ensure that they received rewards. She could also hold a party.

However, in fact, that was the full extent of her political authority.

Even Raynesia felt as if she'd just made an empty promise.

That said, it was a wish more than a lie.

Krusty, who'd been the first person to acknowledge that she had the freedom to go to battle. The Adventurers, who probably didn't even doubt her. She herself had gone a very long time without being given freedom, and the desire to protect their freedom was the first wish that had visited her heart.

"Please. I beg you."

She almost murmured the words. The moment she finished, she heard the heavy sound of steel. In the center of the plaza, a group in navy blue overcoats marked with undyed comma-shaped *tomoe* crests were rattling their various weapons and clicking their heels together.

A group wearing black armor dropped matching long swords into their scabbards, declaring their intent to go to war. From the crumbling terrace of an abandoned building, a group of elves with longbows slung across their backs blew hunting horns, and dwarves with axes raised war cries.

Even minority races such as felinoids, wolf-fangs, and foxtails didn't seem to be particularly discriminated against in this town.

Oh...

Krusty came up and stood beside the astonished Raynesia. A step behind him, Shiroe advanced to stand on her other side.

"Starting now, this town...will embark on its first military expedition. Those who wish to go to the front must be level forty or over. This is a quest from the Round Table Council. There is only one reward for this quest: The respect of the Person of the Earth standing here. Those who think, 'That's for me!' mount your steeds and go straight to Maihama! In light of the urgency of the situation, this will be a blitzkrieg. Since that's the case, directions regarding organization will be issued while we're on the march. I ask for self-restraint and cooperation from every one of you. I, Krusty, will act as supreme commander for the expedition."

"And I, Shiroe, will act as counselor. First, we'll organize an advance strike battalion. I will make contact via telechat within fifteen minutes from now. If I contact you, please leave the town of Akiba and hurry down the Akiba River to the experimental dock. The *Ocypete* will pick you up there. Those of you who have not been contacted after fifteen minutes will be the main force. Please go to the registry office set up

at the city's east gate, pick up your quest documents and register for telechats, then depart according to the instructions you receive. We'll conduct party matching on the way, and I'll issue orders for squad organization. You have fifteen minutes to prepare for the expedition. Thank you for your cooperation."

"Uh, uhm..."

In front of the speechless Raynesia, an army more than a thousand strong sent up war cries.

"Why are you dithering?"

"Wha— What are you talking about? Saying something like that... For a nobleman... For a nobleman, that's..."

Raynesia faltered; her voice was shaking.

Still, the plaza was filled with clamor and the sounds of armor, and it didn't reach any ears that shouldn't have heard it—except for Krusty's.

With aristocratic elegance, Krusty held out an arm. He and Raynesia exchanged stubborn glances that were filled with suspicion, but also with mutual understanding. To onlookers, though, they only looked like a beautiful couple, smiling beautiful smiles.

In any event, it had been decided that they would march.

The enemy was the army of goblin tribes, estimated at more than ten thousand strong, facing the ruined city from the Zantleaf Peninsula. And so it was that Akiba's first expedition turned the tip of its sword toward Zantleaf.

▶ 3

It was near noon, and Minori's party was making its way toward the village of Choushi.

They were tired, but their faces had lost none of their vitality.

Although it had only been one night, the intensity of the hours they'd spent in the darkness had honed the group's latent abilities. Of course, it was also true that the battles they'd been fighting since Forest Ragranda had raised their levels slightly.

Every battle they fought gradually refined their teamwork, and there were moments when they felt they could hear what their companions were thinking without speaking to them.

As Minori and the others walked down the country road, although they were more relaxed than they had been in the forest, they kept their guard up. Even as each kept an eye on the surrounding area, covering each other's blind spots, they were able to walk along in an amiable atmosphere.

Fighting is still scary, but…

It was scary, Minori thought, but there was no longer anything to fear.

What was really frightening was the feeling of terror that was running through her veins and making her limbs cringe: the feeling of being about to let go of her own life. That was very similar to "giving up."

In this deathless world, "giving up" meant the same thing as "death." Conversely, as long as you didn't give up, you had a chance. Even if it was shameful, even if you were shaking, as long as you stayed standing, there was a possibility that something might happen.

The hour was already too late to call morning.

It was probably a bit before noon.

"Helloooooo! Heeeeey!"

As they'd confirmed via telechat a short while ago, Naotsugu's party was resting where they'd detoured around the bushes. Nyanta, Shouryuu, and Lezarik were there as well.

In this other world, resilience meant that equipment that was only dirty cleaned itself automatically. Equipment had set durability values, and, in numeric terms, normal wear during use was very slight. Since the figure was so small, little realities like dirt were lumped in with that number…and that was why the dirt came off, or so the reasoning went.

However, on the other hand, since there *were* set values regarding wear, rough treatment would steadily grind down the number. In specific terms, long-term battles gradually destroyed weapons and armor. This was why it was necessary to periodically take them to weapon and gear shops to be repaired.

The four people in front of Minori were all skilled level-90 Adventurers, and their power was many times greater than that of Minori's group. However, relying on that power, they'd probably leapt into the center of the goblin plunder unit, caused thorough confusion, and attacked again and again.

Even though they'd fought in a mobile formation centered on the two Swashbucklers, the ferocity of their battles must have been far beyond what Minori's group had experienced.

"You guys okay? Yo, Touya. Did you protect everybody?"

"Yes, Master Naotsugu!"

Touya responded with a deep, respectful bow, and Naotsugu patted his head.

Serara had already made a dive for Nyanta.

Minori gave Shouryuu and Lezarik a brief report of how the previous evening's battles had gone. They both seemed relieved, and they took a look at their equipment and wounds for them. Shouryuu aside, Lezarik was a Cleric from a major guild. Minori had thought they might be rebuked for their selfish actions, and their consideration made her feel both abashed and apologetic.

They had no wounds, but the wear on both had been great.

It had been so bad that Minori's group had been afraid they'd run out of potions partway through.

When the sun had risen that morning, the attacks from the goblin plunder unit had decreased like a wave rolling back. They probably also understood their own characteristics and numbers, and the effectiveness of attacking at night.

As the enemy retreated, Minori and the others had withdrawn to a spot near Choushi.

"All right, let's wrap up our break and return to the village. I'll be uneasy until I see it with my own eyes."

It was Lezarik, the Knights of the Black Sword's Cleric, who'd spoken, and his expression had been very serious. The group agreed and began walking, making straight for Choushi.

It was a summer morning after a very bloody night, but the sky was blue.

Zantleaf's distinctive sea wind came to them from the coast, across the fields, and buffeted their cheeks.

Under the bright sunlight, the colors of the distant scenery looked pale and overexposed, and the shadows of the beeches and zelkovas fell darkly across the farm road, creating a beautiful contrast.

But after they'd walked for a little while, they began to see goblin corpses. They hadn't simply been left on the road; they had been gathered here and there in piles. The sight made them realize that Adventurers must have been fighting goblins in the area the night before.

"Looks like they handled it. That's a big-boobed, big-sister type for ya," Naotsugu murmured, sounding happy.

It was just as he said: Even Minori's group hadn't thought they'd be able to protect Choushi with the infiltration strike idea alone. Minori's friends and Nyanta and Naotsugu's group had fought their goblin enemies in the mountains as mobile units. It was a strong-arm-guerilla tactic that used the advantages of surprise attacks and their night vision to decrease the number of goblin squads.

If they managed to reduce the goblin unit's numbers this way, the attacks on Choushi would grow less intense, making it possible to defend it… This was the tactic Minori had come up with.

Although Minori didn't know the technical term, the strategy the goblin tribes had taken was a saturation attack. This was a tactic that used an overwhelming difference in numbers to break down the enemy's position.

If they fought one-on-one, for example, or squad versus squad, the goblins would lose to the Adventurers. Any slight different in fighting power would be repelled by the Adventurers' combat abilities.

For that reason, the Goblins unleashed small-scale units in numbers the Adventurers couldn't handle, all at once. Of course many of the goblin squads would be blocked by the Adventurers, but the difference in numbers would inevitably create holes. The Goblins simply had to throw their abundant resources at these holes.

Once they'd invaded through the holes and sunk their teeth into the fruit that was the village of Choushi, they could probably set fire to it and create a panic. The Adventurers' discipline would be disrupted, and they wouldn't know whether they should return to the town and deal with the plundering goblins or keep battling the goblins that were there in front of them. They would then dispatch the confused Adventurers one by one. This was a conventional goblin invasion tactic.

However, Minori's group had begun attacking before the goblins had, and they'd done so at a distance from the town.

When Minori had proposed this operation, her idea had been a simple one.

The goblins had no base to protect, while Minori and the others did.

Not only that, but their base—Choushi—didn't have a protective wall and would be easy to invade. This was a weakness. Therefore, in battle, they'd be at a disadvantage.

In that case, we just need to fight in a place where we won't have to worry about our weakness.

It was a simple, easy conclusion. Of course they'd needed skill and courage as well, but Minori and the others had put that conclusion into action by brute force.

Their maneuver had reduced the goblins' numbers, but even so, the goblins had attempted to launch a night raid, in accordance with their earlier plan. Choushi had been attacked.

However, decreasing the goblins' numbers hadn't been the maneuver's only goal. Several times the number of goblin squads that Minori and the others had actually destroyed had been wary of Minori's group in the mountains, or had tried to detour around them, and had ended up taking more time than was necessary. That meant the goblins hadn't been able to act together and attack all at once.

The main point of a saturation battle was to create a situation the enemy couldn't cope with by concentrating all your power on one point. The goblins hadn't been able to assemble, and their timing had been staggered; they'd followed their unit commanders' orders and attacked Choushi anyway, but they'd done so as individual units, little by little, charging as they arrived. From the Adventurers' perspective, this attack method had made them ideal prey.

Even Adventurers who didn't have much power and whose numbers were insufficient could handle sporadic attacks like those.

As such, Naotsugu had talked Marielle around to the idea. In turn, Marielle had persuaded the summer camp members, and they'd managed to defend Choushi until dawn.

"Welcome home!"

"Hey, welcome back!"

"I bet you're tired!"

When they entered the village of Choushi, familiar Adventurers called to Serara and Shouryuu. The two of them looked after the newbies at the Crescent Moon League, and so they knew a lot of people. Nyanta, Naotsugu, and Lezarik also seemed to be discussing intel with the veteran Adventurers.

The roads of the village, tramped firm by many feet, showed no sign of having been disturbed.

The goblins seemed to have been unable to invade the village.

"Heh! Check that out. We did it!" her little brother's voice declared triumphantly.

When Minori looked his way, there was Touya, in the sunlight, with a huge little-kid smile on his face.

At the sight of that smile, Minori's heart grew warm.

Minori's brother had hung on to his unclouded cheerfulness all through the night. Spontaneously, Minori smiled, too. She was also glad they'd managed to keep Rundelhaus safe. Touya held his fist out to her, and Minori bumped it with her own.

"Minoriii! The People of the Earth set up a place for us to nap in the tavern! Let's take turns and go rest! We can't get careless yet."

"Mademoiselle Minori. Ah, and Touya. It sounds as if they're going to let us wash our faces, at least. Many thanks to the kind staff at the inn!"

Isuzu and Rundelhaus were yelling to them across the street, and Touya and Minori began to walk, their steps light in the summer sunshine.

▶ **4**

The *Ocypete* was an experimental, steam-driven transport ship.

It had been created as a test ship to inspect the possibility of large-volume transport, combining a steam engine with large, external paddlewheels. The steam engine had been made to be more compact than the ones that had actually been used in paddlewheelers on Earth, and because it used a heat source (a Salamander) conjured by a Summoner, one couldn't overlook the fact that there was no need for fuel stores. As a result, the *Ocypete* had a carrying capacity that was more than ample.

Paddlewheelers were a type of steamboat that had structures like enormous waterwheels attached to either side. These two wheels were turned by the steam engine, and their revolution moved the ship forward through the water.

In terms of performance, paddlewheelers weren't as efficient as propeller ships. The energy was the same, but there was a greater loss when converting it to driving force.

However, due to the difficulty of manufacturing and installing the components, it had been determined that paddlewheel construction was appropriate for Akiba at this point in time, and they'd run experiment after experiment.

Although paddlewheelers did fall behind propeller ships in terms of propulsion efficiency, on the other hand, they didn't need to draw deep water, and they were perfect for traveling down the Sumida river, as they were doing now.

Steam engine experiments with small boats and barges had succeeded less than a week after the uproar surrounding the establishment of the Round Table Council, but it had taken the intervening two months to arrive at the *Ocypete*, their experimental steamship.

At present, the *Ocypete* was carrying about 130 Adventurers. Although it was crowded, it was a large ship, and it didn't seem filled to bursting.

Raynesia stood idly on the deck, all alone, near the bow. It wasn't as though she'd never been on a boat before, but the way this ship was traveling was different from sailing ships. She couldn't rid herself of the feeling that their power-driven, wave-cleaving progress was unnatural, but they were certainly moving fast.

The Adventurers around her were relaxing in various attitudes or walking around making preparations. Although there were all different kinds of people, nearly half of them wore overcoats with the same crest as Krusty, and she assumed they were from the same clan.

Still, Raynesia was in a dull mood.

It wasn't that she was seasick. As the daughter of the lord of Maihama, she'd been familiar with boats of all sizes from the time she was small.

This sunken mood was due to her disastrously reckless temperament.

I went and said it again...

Why was it that someone like her—a shy, idle person who thought everything was too much trouble—grandstanded when push came to shove? She thought it might be a reaction to the "perfect lady training" she'd been subjected to ever since she was small, but never mind the reason: She wanted to bury her face in her hands.

Since just last night, I intruded on the Lords' Council meeting and caused a scene, even though I'm a woman; I made my grandfather and the lords lose face; I picked a fight with a mind-reading menace... and then ran away with him. ...On top of that, he embraced me on the back of a griffin...

Remembering the warmth of Krusty's arms, even in her depression, Raynesia squirmed in agony.

No, I didn't mean... And then, when we reached the town of Akiba, I was forced into embarrassing clothing. Which I am still wearing. ...And I gave a speech like that one...

She buried her face in her hands.

Even she couldn't believe herself.

Still, personally, she wanted to be particular about courtesy and her promise.

As a Person of the Earth, she wasn't like the Adventurers. She'd heard that assumption from her grandfather and had understood it intellectually, but until she'd stood there, she hadn't been able to truly understand what it meant.

That enormous crowd of high-level knights, who'd simultaneously had the intelligence of civil servants... She'd never heard of such a thing.

If they'd been the people known as heroes, it would have made sense.

The Ancients, beings with both the sword skills of knights and the magic of philosophers, did exist, after all. There was no inherent problem with a certain individual being superhuman. She couldn't put it into words well, but the strangest part of all of it was the way there had been several thousand such people, as if it was nothing out of the ordinary. That uncanny group had been Adventurers.

She thought that the Lords' Council, which had believed they could negotiate with the Adventurers by threatening them, soothing them, and dangling noble titles in front of them as a reward, had misread them on a fundamental level. What sort of negotiations had they planned to conduct by rewarding people who had that much understanding and wealth with a prize they'd thought up themselves?

The nobles were wrong.

Through her irritating yet easygoing relationship with Krusty, and through that speech, Raynesia had come to understand this very well.

It was just the same as the way jewels and invitations to dances were no incentive to Raynesia. All she wanted to do was laze around in cotton pajamas, doing nothing but eating and sleeping. The Adventurers, these alien beings, were like that, too. There was no way that jewels or gold or rank or territory would serve as a reward for them. When you looked at it that way, there was really nothing to do except beg and make promises.

In any case, I am a woman, and I haven't received any training in politics... There's really no help for it.

To make a firm promise, no matter how small, and earn trust by following through on it...

To bear the same amount of risk as the Adventurers, when they were exposed to danger...

Continuing to accumulate these things was all Raynesia could think of.

Even so...

Declaring that she would go to the battlefield as well had been incredibly bold. Had she been out of her mind? Could it have been the fault of this odd...excessively leg-exposing costume?

She wanted to crouch down and curl up right where she was, but— possibly because of those long years of training—the common sense that one had to stand up straight and behave in a ladylike manner in public was too ingrained to allow that. She wasn't even able to act listlessly.

She'd been taken in by that smirking Shiroe's glib words, and just look what had happened. The villainy of it all nearly brought tears to her eyes.

"You look as if you'd gotten carried away and said something insane on impulse and now regret it, but have no way to take it back and are writhing in agony."

"Yeek!"

He must have come up behind her while she wasn't paying attention. Krusty stood there, blocking the sea wind, and his words made her jump as if an electric current had run through her.

"Ha-ha-ha. Master Krusty. That isn't true at all."

"You're twitching."

Raynesia, whose chance of continuing the conversation had been summarily cut down, turned an expression "filled with melancholy" on the waves.

"You look worn out."

"...Rrgh. Well, that's true—but don't get me wrong! I don't regret it. I'm asking you to risk your lives, so it's only natural that I'd go myself and stand on the battlefield with you. And no, I don't think a life such as mine is equal to the swords of even ten Adventurers. That is, in other words, um..."

"It doesn't matter. It's enough..."

"Pardon?"

For just a moment, something about the tone of Krusty's words seemed strange to Raynesia. However, the sense of oddness was broken by the voices of the sailors announcing their arrival, and she came back to herself.

—Fast.

True, they'd only cut across the bay, but they were carrying more than a hundred knights, and they'd arrived after noon... What incredible speed. Why, it had only been about fifteen minutes since they'd put out to sea.

By the time she noticed it, Maihama's familiar Castle Cinderella was practically right in front of her nose.

They seemed to be planning to bring this huge ship along the bay-side pier.

She could see that the residents of Maihama working at the port were in an uproar. They'd probably been startled by the strange, enormous black ship. That was only to be expected. The news probably hadn't made it to the townspeople yet.

This was normal.

This was the reality of People of the Earth society, the one Raynesia had lived in up until now.

An army that had methods of individual long-range communication, in which all the soldiers could not only read and write, but perfectly understood military operations and goals— That was abnormal. If the people who worked at the port had been Adventurers, no doubt they'd already know why this warship was coming toward them, its objectives, and its later plans.

Just as when Raynesia had stepped down from the griffin in Akiba, all preparations had already been made.

However, the Maihama where Raynesia lived wasn't like that. Since she was the only Person of the Earth on this ship, it was probably her job to reassure them.

Prompted by Krusty, as she waved from the bow of the ship, there was no trace of the idle, people-shunning princess about her.

▶ 5

Meanwhile, Shiroe and the General Staff Office were leading the main body of the Akiba Expeditionary Force.

The strategy Shiroe and Krusty had adopted this time emphasized "fast and loose" over "slow and careful," since there was no telling how the goblin army in the center of the archipelago would move from here on out. However, if they consumed all the available provisions in the mountains, it was clear that they would invade one or the other of the towns nearby. Because there was no telling where that attack would be aimed at this point, the group from Akiba had lost its initiative: The fact that the choice of battlefield lay with the enemy was a big disadvantage.

To compensate for that, speed was the most important thing at this stage.

Fortunately, even in this devastated other world, the land between Akiba and Maihama was comparatively safe and open. The biggest issue with regard to travel—after they had left Akiba—was where to cross the great river.

Precisely because the line of march was expected to be relatively safe, Shiroe had abandoned the idea of assembling a large army in one place and having it march in an orderly fashion. Instead, he'd organized the Adventurers who were ready into squads, and sent them off one after another.

Shiroe's General Staff Office was made up of a telechat communications team composed of Shiroe, Calasin, and about a dozen other members. A communications network had been set up between participating guilds, and solo Adventurers who were participating on their own were also registered with the communications team.

Through these preparations, Shiroe and the others had created a high-speed communications and report network that covered the entire army. However, of course, they hadn't been able to take time building the relay network—it would be issuing simple instructions, requesting mutual communication between guilds, and having players register a communications officer to their friend list and vice versa when they confirmed their participation.

The advance units who'd already left, the core units, and the rear guard units that were being kept in reserve were all linked by the current communications network. It was a monstrous expeditionary force with completely unprecedented communications abilities, and the issue Shiroe and the rest of the General Staff Office were facing at the moment was how to organize it.

First we'll need to draft a register categorized by level, but... That's going to be almost impossible to do on the move. Should we divide up the work roughly at our destination?

For now, their destination was approximately where Matsudo would have been in the old world. It was north of the city of Maihama, at about the midpoint between it and Abiko, where the hill country began. According to Shiroe's knowledge of *Elder Tales*, that area had many ruined buildings, and as a battlefield, the topography would give them a disadvantage.

However, there were no other suitable candidate areas, so there was no help for it.

According to the telechat transmissions, after the *Ocypete* had called at Maihama's port, they had taken a few People of the Earth onboard as guides and sailed to the abandoned port of Narashino.

Krusty, meanwhile, was commanding an advance strike battalion with ninety-six members.

Parties were composed of six Adventurers. Full raids, being made up of four parties, consisted of twenty-four members. Legion raids brought together four full raids. This last group, with a total force of ninety-six members, had been the largest battle unit in *Elder Tales*.

Krusty looked like a young nobleman with glasses, but on the inside, he was the charismatic warlord who led D.D.D., the largest combat guild in Akiba and, therefore, on the Japanese server.

He'd understand the crux of this strategy, the speed of the advance. It was a sure thing that, after reaching Narashino, he'd lost no time in beginning their march.

Shiroe, on horseback, dexterously rummaged through his bag and took out a portable map.

The distance from the abandoned port of Narashino to the central forests where the main goblin forces were believed to be was about twenty-five kilometers north-northeast, as the crow flew. For normal knights in this world, the march would take from two to three days, but Krusty might even manage to open hostilities by the next morning.

Meanwhile, the main army was traveling, not by sea, but overland by horse. Although there was really no help for it, their ranks were strung out, and they weren't under control.

Let's have the lower levels set up a military post about five kilometers north of Maihama...

Shiroe's finger skimmed over the map.

He selected candidate areas, analyzing the geography of the area centered on Maihama and remembering the features of the zones as he did so. This military post would be built around lower-level players, and in addition to conducting defensive formations and peacekeeping activities, it would be used as a place to accumulate resources. It would probably need to be relatively spacious.

Midrount Equestrian Gardens.

Before long, his fingertip stopped on a small, green oval. According to Shiroe's memory, it was an equestrian garden with an exterior that looked like an enormous coliseum. Wild animals appeared in the surrounding area, but there were no dangerous monsters. It was an ideal location.

"Communications team! Transmit this, please. Midrount Equestrian Gardens is the temporary destination for the northbound army! Select units will continue on to the coast. Once the advance units arrive, have them guard the surrounding area and set up camp immediately. Please clear away the rubble and create a large open space."

Various possibilities flickered in Shiroe's mind.

He shifted his glasses up; he seemed to be holding his breath. His profile showed fierce concentration, exuding an atmosphere like glass.

Either way, this war is a blitzkrieg. We don't need to pay too much attention to supply lines… Our total numbers are…

The main expeditionary force that Shiroe was currently commanding was about 1,200 strong. In other words, roughly 10 percent of Akiba's Adventurers were participating in this war. If he excluded artisans and looked only at the percentage taken up by combat-type players, the number jumped to more than 20 percent.

None of them, Shiroe included, had any experience in large-scale battles fought by more than a thousand people. However, Raynesia's speech had definitely set fire to the souls of a great many Adventurers, more even than Raynesia herself had suspected. The high morale was visible in the eyes of the small units heading past him, to the north.

Shiroe's role was to avoid trouble and guide this war to success without breaking that morale.

People said there were things to be learned from mistakes. However, as far as this expedition was concerned, Shiroe didn't think there was anything they could learn from failure.

The Adventurers' self-confidence and pride. Their future influence, and their survival, in this world. And, most important, "understanding," and the self-government of Akiba. All sorts of conditions demanded victory from Shiroe and the others.

They must not suffer defeat.

Besides, a force of 1,200 was more than enough to actually win a victory. He wasn't Soujirou, but, *All we have to do is have each player take out ten Goblins.*

It was Shiroe's job to eliminate unforeseen trouble and turn the fighting spirits of those 1,200 Adventurers in a set direction on the front line.

Ten kilometers to Midrount Equestrian Gardens, hm? Even if we don't hurry, we'll reach it after noon. We'll camp there tonight. We'll also structure and organize these 1,200 players. Half will deal with the goblins by guarding the area and scouting over a wide range. I'll lead the other half; we'll follow Krusty and attack the main goblin army. Or should we leave the defense of the town to the People of the Earth and lead the whole army into the mountains…?

As Shiroe rode his horse at a walk, he ran all sorts of simulations regarding the coming war in his mind.

► 6

Meanwhile, the speed of Krusty's advance had been even more rapid than the fastest speed Shiroe had imagined.

He'd judged aptitude through interviews onboard the ship, and had already finished organizing his legion raid.

"Organize" was easy to say, but it was a pretty difficult task.

For example, every spell had a restriction known as "range." The range of the average recovery spell was twenty meters, and the maximum range of Bard support spells was also twenty meters.

In other words, it was possible to recover or support allies only within that range, and so there was a general concept of the party as a battle unit that could act within that range.

Taken the other way around, it meant that the battle unit known as a party assumed teamwork within a range of twenty meters.

In that case, all parties needed to have at least one Warrior for protection and two Recovery specialists.

Even when four parties were assembled into a full raid, their formations had to be balanced according to this principle.

It was the same with a legion raid composed of sixteen parties: Even if twenty four of the ninety-six members were Recovery classes, it wouldn't do to create four six-member parties made up entirely of healers.

However, on the other hand, simply organizing all units so that their classes were balanced wasn't enough. When one considered a variety of cases, it was necessary to give them special characteristics for tactical purposes.

For example, if only one Recovery class was assigned to each party, they would be dogged by the possibility that the Warrior wouldn't be able to completely absorb attacks from a large magical beast enemy. It was preferable to assign two Recovery specialists—or even three, if possible—to units that could be expected to battle large magical beasts.

That said, conversely, if no attack units were heavy on Attack classes, when it came right down to it, there wouldn't be any melee units that could wipe out the enemy, and the battle lines would be plunged into a war of attrition.

Thus, if all units were organized equally, their ability to respond would be lowered.

In addition, a party couldn't display its true strengths without regular team training.

Taking that variable into consideration, it was preferable to put members belonging to the same guild in the same party, or in parties that would mutually support one another. On the other hand, veteran Adventurers who were well-known on the server could work with any party they happened to be placed in as if they'd trained alongside them for ages.

In addition to the compatibility between the classes of individual Adventurers, how accustomed players were to combat and how they adjusted to the system of command also needed to be taken into account.

It was common sense among veteran players that, even in a perfectly ordinary six-person party, it was vital to communicate during team plays in combat.

In a full raid, in which a total of twenty-four players participated, the level of confusion on the battlefield inevitably grew. Who was supposed to do what? Should they emphasize recovery or offense, and what about their position? Decisions on these matters were required frequently. To that end, each party had to choose a leader and secure a line to receive orders from the raid leader.

In a legion raid, the raid leader would also take orders from the legion leader. Maintaining this chain of command in the midst of ferocious combat required quite a lot of concentration and experience.

When *Elder Tales* was a game, very few game quests or events had called for a legion. This was because it was terribly difficult to assemble nearly one hundred members whose skills were at a certain level, within a certain time. In addition, the training needed to facilitate organic teamwork among those nearly one hundred members boggled the imagination.

Legion raid wars were content whose threshold was too high for ordinary players to challenge. If most players weren't able to attempt them, the company that administered the game couldn't make them a development focus, either.

The bottom line was that legion raids were "too hard." They became content that was limited to a certain demographic of top-level players, and as a result, although the winners were promised vast wealth and fame, there had never been many challengers.

One group that had challenged that type of high-level content was D.D.D. Krusty, D.D.D.'s guild master, was one of fewer than twenty players on the Japanese server who had experience commanding a group the size of an army.

He put that experience to work, organizing the formations with a speed that left everyone dumbfounded. At first glance, his member allocations seemed careless, but an examination of the details showed that they were quite reasonable.

On disembarking from the *Ocypete*, Krusty's group organized itself into the ninety-six-member legion raid to use in the advance strike, and a twelve-member detail that did double duty as both Raynesia's guard and the observation team. Having received a brief description of the surrounding topography from the People of the Earth guides, Krusty added that information to his military map, and then, with no hesitation, began the march.

Each of the full raids that formed the legion raid was given a number, one through four, and they disembarked on the Zantleaf Peninsula in the late afternoon. They were heading for the western area of Kasumi Lake, a point about twenty-four kilometers away.

The Akiba expeditionary force mounted their horses as a body and rode straight north, toward the Goblin plunder army. Rotating the leading unit in order to avoid exhaustion, the group raced over the old, decaying national road like a gale.

They looked like a bolt of black lightning that was blazing through Zantleaf.

Onward! Onward!!

Like an arrow shot from a bow, the expeditionary army's advance unit, led by Krusty, rushed headlong toward the main enemy force.

CHAPTER.

4

CHASE THAT BACK

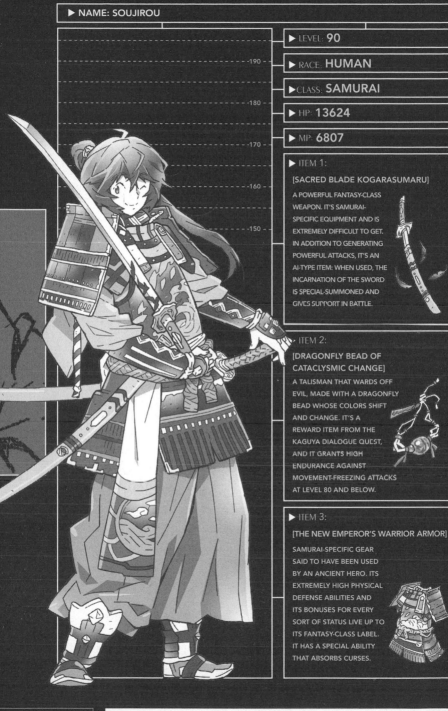

▶ NAME: SOUJIROU

▶ LEVEL: **90**

▶ RACE: **HUMAN**

▶ CLASS: **SAMURAI**

▶ HP: **13624**

▶ MP: **6807**

▶ ITEM 1:

[SACRED BLADE KOGARASUMARU]

A POWERFUL FANTASY-CLASS WEAPON. IT'S SAMURAI-SPECIFIC EQUIPMENT AND IS EXTREMELY DIFFICULT TO GET. IN ADDITION TO GENERATING POWERFUL ATTACKS, IT'S AN AI-TYPE ITEM: WHEN USED, THE INCARNATION OF THE SWORD IS SPECIAL-SUMMONED AND GIVES SUPPORT IN BATTLE.

▶ ITEM 2:

[DRAGONFLY BEAD OF CATACLYSMIC CHANGE]

A TALISMAN THAT WARDS OFF EVIL, MADE WITH A DRAGONFLY BEAD WHOSE COLORS SHIFT AND CHANGE. IT'S A REWARD ITEM FROM THE KAGUYA DIALOGUE QUEST, AND IT GRANTS HIGH ENDURANCE AGAINST MOVEMENT-FREEZING ATTACKS AT LEVEL 80 AND BELOW.

▶ ITEM 3:

[THE NEW EMPEROR'S WARRIOR ARMOR]

SAMURAI-SPECIFIC GEAR SAID TO HAVE BEEN USED BY AN ANCIENT HERO. ITS EXTREMELY HIGH PHYSICAL DEFENSE ABILITIES AND ITS BONUSES FOR EVERY SORT OF STATUS LIVE UP TO ITS FANTASY-CLASS LABEL. IT HAS A SPECIAL ABILITY THAT ABSORBS CURSES.

<Carpet>
A type of rug.
Apparently there are flying
ones out there somewhere.

▶ 1

After Raynesia's departure, a chaotic despondency ruled the conference room. Krusty, the Round Table Council representative, had gone with Raynesia. Shiroe, who had struck the Lords' Council as a counselor and a moderate, had gone as well.

The only remaining Round Table Council envoy was Michitaka, who seemed like a resolute hard-liner.

The Lords' Council was also unsure where to bring down the fist they had raised. Rather, in the first place, although they'd raised their fist, it was questionable whether they actually managed to bring it down at all. Those with the ability and the will to handle the situation at the conference had gone, and their purpose was confused.

During the discussion that followed, poor Baron Clendit completely lost his ability to preside as the chair. He turned pale and red by turns, the desperate care of his retainers proved useless, and at last, gasping feebly, he requested permission to retire.

Although theirs wasn't as severe as Baron Clendit's, all the lords were harboring the same sort of confusion to a greater or lesser degree.

As a result, at around midnight, the conference was temporarily adjourned.

In the corridor, Michitaka exhaled deeply.

This couldn't be more of a pain in the butt.

In the first place, although Michitaka was in charge of a merchant guild, he wasn't particularly skilled at fine negotiations. He was the sort of guy who thought that a merchant's job was to make good things, sell them at fair prices, and open up new markets, and nothing else.

And anyway, I'm a blacksmith...

He still considered himself an active artisan. Even now that he was on the Round Table Council, he plied his hammer every day. Now that the number of players heading to high-level dungeons had fallen off, the magical materials needed to create magic items were running thin and things were a bit dreary, but it wasn't impossible to work around.

Michitaka's opinion of himself was that he'd just happened to like hanging out with other people and hadn't had any aversion to talking, so his friends had kicked him upstairs.

He'd probably sounded like a hardliner to the Lords' Council, but as far as Michitaka was concerned, he'd only been giving a bunch of rude idiots an earful, and he didn't feel any ill will toward the League of Free Cities as a whole. He'd been against sending soldiers mostly because that was the role he'd been given, out of the three Round Table Council members. Personally, he wasn't actually against contributing troops.

In any event, he was a production player. Compared to the Adventurers who would leave the town to fight with the expedition, he was in very little danger of dying. Even when the war began, it was likely that he and his guild would simply provide logistical support from Akiba. He couldn't deny that, privately, he felt guilty about someone in a position like his easily approving of war.

Grousing now that things are in motion, huh...?

He shoved thick fingers into his black hair, scratching at his head. He was in a rotten mood, and he really couldn't stand it.

Michitaka walked down the long, deserted corridor, trailing a man from his guild behind him. At the corner of the corridor, he casually glanced out at the terrace. There wasn't any real significance to it. It was only that, as he'd turned the corner, the moonlight had been shining in, so he'd looked that way.

"Master Soujirouuu. These egg sweets are delicious, too."

"Master Soujirou, listen to my story, too!"

"You're tired, Master Soujirou. I'll sing you a gentle lullaby, so please nap for a little while…"

There was a magnificent sofa on the moonlit terrace, set up as a place to be used for tea parties. On it sat Michitaka's comrade Soujirou, guild master of the West Wind Brigade, surrounded by People of the Earth princesses and ladies-in-waiting. For some reason, Michitaka was assailed by a feeling of desolation.

The dark clouds that hung over Akiba's future and had weighed on his mind, his own guilt, and that indescribable unease… None of it seemed to matter anymore.

Compared to the aura that hung around Soujirou and that view, worrying about the Round Table Council and the League of Free Cities seemed truly pointless.

Aah, I bet my face looks like something somebody scribbled with their left hand…

Without approaching Soujirou, Michitaka turned his steps toward the area that held his own room.

So, that was it for tonight. What should he do about tomorrow?

Michitaka began to think these things, but in a moment, it was clear that such a laid-back development wouldn't be happening.

Waiting in front of the division the Round Table Council was borrowing was Rayncsia's grandfather, Duke Sergiad Cowen. The old duke—whose retinue consisted of a single knight who was holding a lamp—bowed to Michitaka silently. It had been a very long conference. There was no way he wasn't tired, but the old duke's aura betrayed no fatigue. Michitaka respected him for that.

The duke spoke briefly to Michitaka: "Shall we?"

Guessing what he was after, Michitaka began to walk, leading the way.

He invited him into the small conversation room where the Round Table Council—Krusty, Shiroe, and Michitaka—routinely held their meetings. The "small" was only in relation to the standards of the palace: To the Japanese Michitaka, the conference room, which was really two rooms and could be partitioned off at the center, looked big enough to live in.

When he motioned for him to sit, took tea out of his bag and poured him some, the old duke seemed very slightly startled. There was no way someone like the duke didn't know about magic bags, and Michitaka didn't know what the reaction meant, but he decided to ignore it for now.

"My apologies for visiting so late."

"No, don't worry about that. If we don't get that conference squared away, neither of us is going to be sleeping well."

"Ha-ha-ha, I suppose not."

The old aristocrat who was seated across from Michitaka put a hand to his splendid whiskers and laughed confidently.

"I mustn't let my granddaughter's thoughtless actions bring about the fall of the House of Cowen."

Come to think of it, his position was extremely precarious at present.

Of course, as the leading lord of Eastal, the League of Free Cities, Duke Sergiad had great influence. However, in this case, the very strength of that influence could prove to be a handicap.

"As you've guessed, the girl's actions may cause a rift in the league of lords."

He was pointing out the possibility of the story that the House of Cowen had stolen a march on the Lords' Council. Maihama, which Sergiad governed, was powerful. If Maihama and Akiba joined forces and took in a few of the other lords, their forces would be large enough to drive out the remainder of the League.

Of course Princess Raynesia probably had no such ambition. Michitaka and the other Round Table Council members thought the event had been a sort of freak accident, and that it hadn't had any deeper meaning.

However, in this situation, what was important was the way other people interpreted it.

Even if there had been no deeper meaning, meaning could be assigned after the fact.

The fact that we're talking like this now might give somebody somewhere the wrong idea, too...

"Because it's possible that Maihama could take in Akiba and establish a new power, right?" Michitaka asked directly. He wasn't good at scheming and beating around the bush.

"That is one idea, yes, but… Hmm… What do you think, Master Michitaka?"

Michitaka had expressed a dislike for being called *sir* in the conference, and he felt favorably disposed to the duke for using *master* instead. *Sir* was just a word to Michitaka, and it didn't particularly please or repulse him. However, this old man had avoided the word because Michitaka had expressed anger about it. It felt as if he was trying to deal with the other man as an individual, a human being.

Well, let's see, now. I'm not a brain like Shiroe…

Michitaka thought hard, tilting his head on its thick neck.

Just then, there was a subdued knock.

When Michitaka gave permission, Henrietta entered with a cart that held a late-night snack. The group of delegates from Akiba, which had grown due to Shiroe's proposal, included Chefs. The area the Round Table Council was borrowing had been set up (although they'd probably had a terrible time doing so) with the various things needed in order to create the banquets that accompanied small conferences and tea parties.

Henrietta had probably brought the midnight snack and drinks out of consideration for them.

"Hey, that's perfect. Come join us, would you, Henrietta?"

"No, I was simply—"

"C'mon, it's fine."

Henrietta knit her brow at Michitaka's invitation, but when he pressed her, after she set out the light meal, she sat down beside Michitaka.

"You're the young lady who danced with Master Shiroe at the ball, aren't you."

"Yes, I'm Henrietta of the Crescent Moon League."

"The Crescent Moon League is one of the eleven guilds on the Round Table Council. This young woman is one of their advisers."

After he finished the introduction, Michitaka took a breather.

He didn't plan to shove all the responsibility off onto Henrietta, of course, but the matter was much too serious. Henrietta would probably notice pitfalls Michitaka's brain had missed and come up with a set direction for the conversation.

For the moment, the three of them began on the meal in front of them.

Cold chicken sandwiches and a salad of cooked vegetables. In addition, there was fruit and thinly diluted liquor.

They commented on each of the dishes and made small talk for a while, letting the conversation wander where it would.

When Michitaka and Henrietta briefly explained their positions, and Duke Sergiad described the city of Maihama for them, the conversation came full circle, returning to the topic of the evening's conference.

"I understand the matter now, in general. Let me see…"

As she spoke, Henrietta set down her teacup elegantly.

Sergiad looked like a genial old man, and so she continued easily, pressing him with questions:

"The important point of departure here is your vision of the goal you wish to achieve, Duke Sergiad. I think the crux of this discussion is whether you'll be able to share that with the Round Table Council."

Michitaka grunted.

In a word, that was all it was, but there was something pitiful about summing up the pain and confusion of that five-hour conference in just one line. However, that was probably due to Henrietta's intelligence. They said that two heads—or three— were better than one, but from his experience on Earth, even Michitaka knew they probably couldn't expect that sort of thing from a conference like that one.

"I expect that's it exactly. Hm…"

Duke Sergiad closed his eyes.

"It's weird for me to say this, but I doubt we'll make any headway if we keep trying to sound each other out. We'd like to hear what you have to say, candidly; whatever you, personally, are hoping for," Michitaka added.

He was fed up with being treated like a dog or cat, but he didn't think this elderly man would speak to them that rudely. If he did, then he did, and if the man who was leading lord of the Lords' Council held opinions like that, he wasn't worth dealing with.

"First, there's the immediate issue of the goblin plunder army. I would like to cooperate with you on this, to have you defend us against them and eradicate them. We are locked in a long, long struggle with the demihumans. Our ultimate issue is protecting the land of our ancestors."

Michitaka could agree with that.

Any noble who didn't have the will to protect their territory and their people wasn't a noble at all.

To them, that hope was less a condition or requirement than it was the premise of the discussion and its point of flight.

"In addition, I no longer wish to invite you to join Eastal, the League of Free Cities, as its twenty-fifth noble member."

Michitaka was startled into silence.

"I now feel that our initial mistake, the basis of our error, lay in treating the Round Table Council as if it was the same as our lords, who hold fortified cities and territories. I don't intend to boycott the Round Table Council or to put distance between us. This isn't that sort of conversation. It's more accurate to say that at this point, I am aware that the power of the Round Table Council is equal to that of Eastal, the League of Free Cities. The structure and the actual strength of the Round Table Council, and of the town of Akiba, equal those of our League of Free Cities in all respects. In the League, the lords discuss matters and cooperate with one another. This is extraordinarily similar to the Round Table Council, which was born as a federation of your houses—or your guilds, I should say; that was the word, wasn't it? Since your territory is a single town, and it isn't a large one, we took you lightly, and that prejudice led us to make a very rude, selfish proposal to you. I would like to apologize for that discourtesy."

Michitaka thought about Duke Sergiad's words.

"The area of the town of Akiba's territory is not in proportion to its power. This isn't a nice way to put it, but if we forced it into the League's framework, sooner or later it would cause friction, and I believe it would destroy us. We may be able to bell a wolf, but I doubt we can chain it up. Even less so if we are dealing with a griffin that soars through the skies. I feel that the proper relationship between Eastal and the Round Table Council would place both parties on equal terms. I think we should conclude nonaggression pacts and treaties of commerce, and build our relationship on them."

"Agreed."

At Michitaka's response, Duke Sergiad's eyes went wide.

"In the first place, the Round Table Council has no territorial ambitions or plans to invade. We just want to protect our home in this world, and... If we manage to get our wish, to find a way back to our old world; that's enough for us. Of course, in order to do that, we'll have to live in this world for the time being. We'll need to travel to ruins that are located all over, and we'll need to trade for food and the like. That said, that doesn't mean that we can't cooperate with our neighbors in order to get these things done. Nothing would make us happier than being able to cooperate."

After Michitaka had responded that far without pausing, he glanced at Henrietta. Henrietta frowned; she seemed to be thinking. Then she added, speaking quickly:

"This is, of course, an extremely general, basic policy, you understand. Even if the relationship is an equal one, until we see the wording of the treaty and learn just how the principle has been incorporated, we can make no promises in the truest sense of the word."

She sounded slightly flustered. Michitaka nodded in agreement.

He'd been hoping she would cover for him when it came to details like that.

Duke Sergiad seemed to have been a bit surprised by how ready and frank their response had been. For a short while, he was at a loss for words.

"However, regarding mutual nonaggression pacts and treaties of commerce made from the standpoint of equals... Those would mean that we will not attack each other, and that we will conduct trade. I'm very sorry, but the defense against the current goblin invasion will be outside the scope of such treaties. Of course, I don't intend to declare what is and is not within the scope of the treaty at this point, when we have yet to conclude a treaty of any kind. However, I believe the question of how to handle this irregular situation is very significant, both for the League of Free Cities and for the territory of Maihama, is it not?"

Both Michitaka and Duke Sergiad nodded at what Henrietta had pointed out.

In the end, the conversation had come right back to it.

The inequality of the burdens on the People of the Earth and the Adventurers.

The mutual distance that stemmed from the difference between their separate positions and the things they looked at.

"Let's set that aside for now."

Michitaka shrugged his shoulders as if poking fun at the atmosphere, which had been on the point of growing heavy.

That image of Soujirou was in the back of his mind, and just remembering it made stressing about anything seem dumb.

The Adventurers had unlimited power; would the People of the Earth grow jealous of it and plot against them? That sort of aristocratic political corruption had weighed on him, but the moment he'd seen Soujirou's harem-forming nature in action, he'd stopped caring. That experience had drained the strength out of his knees. Jealousy and anger and suspicion were all pretty easy to understand compared to that.

In any case, there was no need for Michitaka to shoulder all that by himself.

"Since Krusty and Princess Raynesia, the two people in question, aren't here, there's no way to wrap things up neatly. Besides, they might have some specific idea in mind. It isn't fair for us to have to worry about it on our own. We should pull in Shiroe and have those three think about it; that would make for a better division of labor."

Michitaka's opinion was a little reckless, but the other two felt the same way.

At any rate, whether they came to a conclusion here or failed to reach an agreement, the die had already been cast. At dawn, an army would probably depart from Akiba. It was no longer possible for either Michitaka or Duke Sergiad to stop that army.

Now that Krusty and Shiroe had made their moves, there could be no such thing as an impasse.

It wasn't possible for those two to rise up and not carry through to the goal.

To Michitaka, that future was already assured.

In that case, the only thing to do was watch events unfold.

"Well, no doubt Master Shiroe will do something about it."

Henrietta agreed, pouting; she seemed to be sulking a little. Her words seemed to disparage Shiroe, but no matter how you looked at them, her eyes were brimming with trust. Privately, Michitaka felt convinced.

"All right. In that case, let's have my granddaughter take responsibility for the whole affair."

With Duke Sergiad's statement, which sounded somehow entertained, they parted ways.

▶ **2**

Wait… Did something rustle…? There, in those bushes under the trees… It couldn't be… It can't be… Goblins?

Beside Raynesia was a female knight from D.D.D. in an austere military uniform. She wasn't carrying a weapon at the ready; instead, she kept up a running telechat as she looked at the map of the battlefield and a sheaf of reports she held in one hand.

"Large-scale group at two o'clock. Enemy attack unit at nine o'clock, total number over eighteen. Two large magical beasts."

As she delivered terse reports, her voice's demeanor was unlike that of any knight Raynesia knew, and it also didn't sound as if it belonged on the sort of battlefield she'd heard about in rumors.

When Raynesia's eyes hadn't yet adjusted to the darkness and she was afraid, the woman had gently applied a salve to Raynesia's eyelids.

After she'd blinked a few times, a rose-colored light had enveloped her surroundings, and it had grown easier to see.

Even so, the sounds in the darkness were frightening.

This area wasn't all that deep in the mountains, but Raynesia had grown up in a castle, and her tolerance for such things was low. Every time the bushes swayed in the darkness, no matter how she tried to keep them under control, her knees began to quake.

C-calm down. Walk tall… That's right, relax…

Her spirit was still strong.

She hadn't yet lost the courage to move forward.

However, her body was more honest, and possibly because it felt that her life was in peril, it would instinctively tense up or begin to shake. Drawing upon all the ladylike training she'd accumulated and polished over long years, she tried to advance boldly and confidently, but she felt her mask was on the point of slipping.

"Princess Raynesia, they say the view opens up if we go a little farther up the ridge. Let's go that way and rest for a while," the female knight told her.

The warriors around her seemed to have been expecting that order: They changed formation as smoothly as flowing water. The only ones who stood dazedly in the center were Raynesia and two People of the Earth. Those two were telling the female knight about the local topography in detail, when she asked them. There was a creek small enough to step over, and once they'd crossed it and gone up for a while, the ground would turn rough and rocky, and they'd find a hill from which they could look down into the valley.

And just so, Raynesia and the others advanced, parting the underbrush.

Of course the warriors at the front of the group moved the bigger branches out of the way, but the sharp grasses of this animal track tried to tangle around her mercilessly. However, the Valkyrie Mail Raynesia wore must have been terribly high-performance: It seemed to cast a wall of air around her, and it wouldn't let them near.

I have no complaints about the performance. …But. Honestly.

The only thing about it that concerned her was the tremendous amount of leg it made her show.

If it had been winter, she could have said something about catching a chill and asked for a mantle, but that wasn't possible in summer. What Raynesia was actually wearing was a thin cape that barely fell to her waist, an article far too pathetic to call a mantle.

Oh...

She must have covered more distance than she'd thought while her mind had been elsewhere. Once they'd detoured around a spinney of what seemed to be huge beech trees and climbed a slope that was about as tall as she was, the view abruptly opened up. It was a clear, rocky area about six meters square, a ridge that looked down into the valley. From the rocks, she could see the trees below the cliff and the flowing river, stretching away.

Were the hundreds of gleaming lights the torches of the goblin army? They seethed restlessly, reminding her of a march of malicious insects.

"This way."

The female knight had directed her to a simple folding chair. It had no back or armrests, but she was grateful to be able to sit down and close her legs properly.

Raynesia thanked her politely, accepted the chair, and sat down.

That speech had brought it home to her: Adventurers were fundamentally different from Raynesia and the other People of the Earth. It was probably best to assume that all of them—not only Krusty and the other Round Table Council representatives—had the education and manners of nobles.

That meant it wouldn't do to be careless about gratitude and politeness.

However, on the other hand, Adventurers also seemed to dislike empty formality. Had her thanks been appropriate? She watched the lady knight, trying to see, but the woman was in the middle of a telechat, and was briskly reading from a map. It had probably been all right.

Around her, the Adventurers were bringing out folding pieces of furniture one after another: a little collapsible three-legged table and several tubes that were probably telescopes.

"It's starting."

"Pardon?"

The moment the lady knight's words made Raynesia turn, a flash of light dropped into the valley. The roar followed a split second later. Eerie tremors shivered through the area. Raynesia was flustered, but the female knight pointed a white finger into the depths of the darkness, at a corner of the valley.

When Raynesia focused her attention on it, she felt her faintly shining vision pull the distant scene toward her. The trees and even the outlines of their leaves leapt into view, as real and vivid as life.

"It's Fairy Balm for snipers. Even your long-range vision is good, isn't it? Don't expand your visual field too far... They'll be there soon. Watch closely."

The white light lasted a mere instant.

The thunderbolt seemed to have pierced right through the center of the goblin squad. Unlike an actual thunderbolt, though, the crushing blow that had fallen down from the heavens had enough force behind it to gouge up the earth, exploding the land and scattering the goblins.

In the midst of that flash, quite clearly, Raynesia saw Krusty's form. A tall shadow, sprinting through the forest, holding a long-handled, double-bladed ax. It had to have been as long as Raynesia was tall, but he carried it as if it weighed nothing.

Krusty ran along the stream that flowed through the forest, with the nearly one hundred members of the strike unit following behind him. It was as if the mantle that streamed down his back had stretched and spread, eroding the forest.

Whenever the unit encountered goblins, they sliced or gouged, inflicting lethal damage, devouring them. The glinting flares of light were probably magic. At this distance, there was no way to make out the details, but she could tell they were overwhelmingly destructive.

However, what struck Raynesia even more than the force of the unit's overpowering attack was Krusty himself.

Krusty, who ran at the head of the unit he commanded, leading the knights with his back, was exuding a strange aura. The oddness she'd sensed on the deck of the ship had become tangible and was creating mountains of corpses, rivers of blood.

Lips curved up like a crescent moon.

Eyes narrowed with joy.

Glasses that reflected the silver light.

Krusty was sprinting across the battlefield, filled with exultation, as if he were a child running to the plaza on a festival day.

Krusty's hands swung.

The ends of the ax became invisible, as if it were a whirlwind.

Then clear space opened up around him for three meters in every direction.

Or again, when magical beasts leapt at him. An enormous wolf the size of an ox charged toward him, but Krusty thrust out his left hand, stopping it easily, and called to those around him. The wolf's gigantic body was riddled with dozens of arrows and slashed with magically strengthened swords.

Krusty flung away the wolf's body, now just a ragged clump of dead meat, as easily as if it had been a sack of wheat. His attention turned to the next goblin unit.

It was ominous.

It was unearthly.

It was so dreadful it provoked revulsion.

However, to Raynesia, more than anything, the sight was somehow terribly sad.

It was probably her own ego that made it look ominous and unearthly. She felt it was rude of her to feel these things about a hero who was protecting her homeland.

Still, the sadness… What was that?

What was making her feel so lonely?

"Fifty ahead, two hill giants. Recovery teams in position to the right and left. Annihilate them, starting with the surrounding squads."

Faintly, she could hear the lady knight's telechat.

She'd squeezed her eyes shut involuntarily, and when she opened them, she saw Krusty heading toward two huge giants the size of siege towers.

Raynesia gasped.

A loglike club bore down on him, but Krusty leapt away like a swallow, fielding the blow with his two-handed ax, and stood between the giants. To the princess, the size difference seemed overwhelming, and it looked as if the giants were unleashing attacks that would blot out Krusty's life. However, Krusty's smile only widened, and she couldn't sense a trace of fear from him.

On the contrary, Krusty's weapon shone red, and every time it struck, the giants began to focus on Krusty obsessively, as if they'd forgotten themselves.

In the faint light of dawn, as the giants were whipped into a frenzy, Krusty continued to field their attacks.

The two giants had probably been that goblin attack unit's secret weapons, and they were surrounded by a host of goblins with crossbows and spears. However, Krusty's legion raid began to work freely, as if they'd just been released from all restrictions.

The unit had been roughly split into four, and each of these split into four again, attacking the goblins as scattered squads. These small attack units began to spread an encircling net over the surface of the forest where the goblins were.

Even as Akiba's forces shifted dizzyingly, they showed no openings, and the goblins' system of command had been unreliable to begin with. They had no hope of matching them. In the darkness, one after another, they fell to spells and swords.

In Raynesia's eyes, strengthened by Fairy Balm, they dashed through the forest like flitting shadows.

Krusty was at the center of that dance.

He brought his arms down, like a conductor.

A barrage of fireballs swallowed up the horde of goblins like a fiery avalanche.

Krusty looked as if he was enjoying himself.

He seemed far more free than he had during his time at the Ancient Court.

That, more than anything, made Raynesia sad.

Without knowing why she felt sad, or lonely, Raynesia kept gazing at the chivalric knight.

He swung his ax with all his might, hacking through enemies, blocking attacks; and even though blood streamed from both his arms, his steps were firm, and his commands spurred on his unit. He looked like a god of war.

To Raynesia, Krusty seemed to become more and more transparent, so free that sometimes she thought he might simply dissolve into the moonlight.

That's...

For some reason, the sorrow bore down on her heart until it was nearly painful.

How could Krusty, who seemed so powerful and invincible both at the Ancient Court and on the battlefield, look ephemeral? Raynesia was sure there must be something wrong with her mind.

Krusty seemed to be having fun, but, abruptly, the suspicion welled up that beyond that fun lay absolutely nothing. There might be no one there at all.

Krusty and the Akiba expeditionary force continued their advance through the forest.

As Raynesia watched them, she sat very tall and straight, continuing to seek out the back of the tall Adventurer with single-minded intent.

▶ 3

Marielle and the others had commandeered a fishing gear storehouse located near the mouth of the Great Zantleaf River as a temporary headquarters. They were relaying telechats from patrol units they had sent to the area directly around the town and were putting together a plan for defense.

No goblin sightings had been reported for more than half a day now.

At the very least, the goblins seemed to have completely retreated into the forest-covered mountains. The Adventurers in the area were napping in shifts, at the inn and in their storehouse.

A full day and night had passed since that first night. During that time, Marielle's group had successfully defended the village of Choushi.

Marielle had been startled by the fact that the most adaptable and enthusiastic players were the ones she'd discounted as newbies.

Maybe that was only to be expected, though, she thought.

Come to think of it, these kids are the type who decided to try playin' Elder Tales *because of the rumors about the expansion pack. They don't have much gamin' experience. ...Meanin' they don't have many biases, either...*

Having very little experience in *Elder Tales* meant that their character levels were inevitably low, and that they weren't skilled in combat. Because of those disadvantages, the veteran players had seen the new players as weak, and nothing more.

However, not having any preconceptions about the game system or the world could also be considered an advantage.

To Marielle and the other veteran players, Shiroe's declaration—that the People of the Earth were humans who had the same senses, spirits, desires, and intellects as they did—had come as a great shock.

However, the shock probably hadn't been all that big for the newbies.

In the first place, since they hadn't been playing the game for very long, the conditioning that *Elder Tales was* a game hadn't sunk in all that deeply. In that sense, to them, the situation was the same as if they'd been abducted to some other world, one that had nothing to do with *Elder Tales*.

Marielle had been happy when these players had actively called for the protection of the People of the Earth and had sprung into action. The newbies in the summer camp group had taken up the defense of the village of Choushi without Marielle having to persuade them with impassioned speeches.

When they saw the newbies roused to action like this, there was no way the veteran players could go without taking a stand.

The summer camp had begun on what was very nearly a volunteer basis. The veteran players who had signed on for it were people who were good at looking after newbies. They couldn't possibly disgrace themselves in front of those newbies while they watched them blaze with hope.

Once the support of Marielle's smile, which Marielle didn't really notice, was added to the mix, morale would rise no matter what.

When Minori and Nyanta had conspired with each other and headed into the mountains, it had really hurt her, but in the end, the maneuver had proved to be a great success. From what Marielle knew, during that first night, there had been twenty-six defensive encounters in the area around the village. That was an average of four battles per party, which meant they'd had a far easier time than they would have had capturing a dungeon.

Yet when dawn broke, the newbie Adventurers' expressions had changed.

Battles in this other world had a special difficulty that hadn't been there in *Elder Tales*: one that was less the intensity of combat itself than it was the hideous atmosphere of the battlefield.

Their bodies seemed to be based on those of their game characters: They were high-performance, and although their stamina, strength, endurance, and agility did depend on their game class, none of those posed a problem. Recovery spells healed wounds quickly, and even without a spell, if you toughed it out, minor cuts and scrapes would heal naturally in half a day or so.

The terror of battle lay more in its psychological aspects.

Taking a life with your own hands, even if that life belonged to a monster, was a terrible feeling, and some Adventurers were truly traumatized by it. It was a feeling Marielle could understand.

If they wanted to continue fighting in this world, there was no choice but to get used to it, and until they did get used to it, newbie players needed motivation and veteran players who'd stick close to them.

In terms of motivation and opportunity, the defense of Choushi was not only a big challenge, but a chance for the newbies.

It was newbie Adventurers with high morale who first noticed the change from the sea. High morale made itself known in endurance and fighting spirit as well, but the most striking effect was probably increased concentration, like now.

A team of three newbies who had gone on guard duty spotted white waves heading for the coastline and immediately contacted Marielle.

Their memories of being attacked on the white sandy beaches of Zantleaf were probably still with them. This time, that terror had worked in their favor.

When the veteran players ran to the scene, the sahuagins were still far beyond the distant, shallow coastal waters. They'd spotted them very early.

The Great Zantleaf River grew extremely broad in this area. Because the mouth of the river met the ocean, the flow of the tide mingled salt water with freshwater, and several piers jutted out into the river.

When the veterans had rushed over and looked at the sea, they had let out groans of despair. There were numerous white waves. Far more than one or two hundred.

This is...

Marielle felt it, too.

Choushi was a peaceful town that was designed around fishing and farming. This meant that the town was built along the Great Zantleaf River, and its shape was long and drawn out. Consideration had been given to flooding and the ebb and flow of the tide, of course, and even at the narrowest places, there were at least a hundred meters between the residential areas and the beach. ...But that was still close.

To make matters worse, that hundred meters wasn't a hundred meters of forest or mountain.

It was simply open beach a hundred meters wide, sandy or rocky, which fishing tackle and boats were normally dragged over.

It would be next to impossible to defend the town—which exposed its long, broad side to an open space like that one—from that many sahuagins.

Maybe not even "next to" impossible... Sure, we can survive pretty easy. All we have to do is run home. I bet we can prob'ly even beat all those sahuagins, although it's gonna take time. But completely protectin' the town and keepin' all the People of the Earth in one piece... We might not be able to do that...

Still, as Marielle stared wordlessly at the foaming surface of the ocean, she heard the creak of bowstrings being drawn back on either side of her.

On her right was Naotsugu. Touya stood next to him.

On her left, newbie Assassins and lots of Warriors were nocking arrows. Shouryuu wasn't good with bows, but even so, he was holding a throwing knife that looked like a thick metal skewer at the ready.

"Hand down an order, Miss Mari. Give us a shot in the arm."

Naotsugu was grinning widely.

At that smile, Marielle's feelings grew lighter.

There was nothing to stress about.

Marielle always had encouraging companions with her, friends who had supported her. Their smiles alone made her feel as if her heart had grown wings.

"Sure thing, hon. Um, let's see. …Uh, okay, folks!"

Marielle raised her voice.

The foaming water in front of her seethed more restlessly, surging toward the mouth of the river.

"Thanks a bunch for helpin' out up till now! Thanks to you, there wasn't one single death from Choushi, and we made it through the goblin attack without lettin' too many fields get ruined. That's somethin' we should be real happy about. It's gonna be just a bit longer, though. The show isn't over until we beat this enemy, too… We won't have protected the village all the way through. Help me out for one more battle. I know you can do it. Okay, let's go! Move out!!"

Bowstrings sang one after another.

When this had happened three times, Naotsugu took the lead, running for the coast. Shouryuu and Lezarik followed. Nyanta, who brought up the rear, gave Marielle a jaunty little wave.

Here and there, parties of Adventurers were charging toward the coast.

However, a closer look revealed several groups that weren't charging. When she sent a questioning look at Minori, who had withdrawn to a bend in the farm road and sat down where she had an open view of the coast, the answer that returned to her was "They'll need alternates soon."

The opinion was so level-headed that Marielle was a bit taken aback; it made her wonder if Minori was really a middle schooler. Still, she was perfectly right: If they were going to hold back numbers like this at the very last minute, right before they came up on land, the fatigue would make alternates a must.

A fierce battle was beginning at the coastline. As such, it would probably be a good idea for Marielle to rest up, too.

Long-term battles took a ferocious mental toll on the Recovery classes. Marielle was a high-level Cleric, and her abilities would be sorely needed in the fight ahead.

Midrount Equestrian Gardens.

At present, simplified defenses were being set up here, and units were being organized at fever pitch. Since the military units that had been organized and issued posts had already departed in rapid succession, the camp held only about a third of the entire army now.

The situation was extremely fluid, too.

Apparently Krusty and his infiltration strike unit had already begun to engage the enemy before dawn that morning. Reports from the observation team estimated about one thousand casualties on the enemy's side. In the near future, they'd probably learn just how much significance that number had as a part of the whole.

Although he'd been given the nickname Counselor, Shiroe wasn't well versed in real-world military affairs or tactics. As a result, he didn't know whether that number was large or small, or whether the damage would be enough to cause the goblins to retreat.

In general, he'd heard that if 30 percent of an army's total forces were rendered unable to fight, the army was said to be nearly annihilated. To Shiroe, this wasn't much more than trivia, but something about it perplexed him.

During battles with the goblins, had any enemies ever fled? When he thought about it, although he couldn't say there hadn't been any, he thought that, in most situations, it had been to the last goblin standing. *Elder Tales* had been a game, after all. Game monsters wouldn't take to their heels, let alone surrender, until that stage.

That meant his faintly remembered knowledge might be wrong, or maybe that sort of real-world tactical knowledge didn't apply in this world. It was also possible that goblins or demihumans in general were exceptionally bellicose and had no concept of "retreat."

On the other hand, though, there had been good news as well.

During that morning's battle, Krusty's group hadn't sustained significant damage, and they'd wiped out the goblin army's magical beasts and two giants. Provided the main forces of the goblin army didn't have anything really extraordinary, it was probably all right to leave them to Krusty's legion raid.

In any case, if an enemy Krusty and his group can't handle shows up, our chances of victory won't rise no matter who in Akiba goes up against it.

Of course, compatibility varied among enemies. If they got intel on the enemy, they could take steps to counter it by reorganizing.

In other words, even if Krusty and the others lost, it wouldn't mean the enemy was one they couldn't beat. In the days of *Elder Tales*, during large-scale battles, they'd learned how to win by being annihilated over and over again. Information always saved the ones who came after. In a contest of practical strength, it was only natural that the contestant with the most information on their target had better odds of winning.

However, in a confrontation where they had no intel, the legion raid Krusty was currently leading was without a doubt the strongest weapon Akiba had.

We can leave the nerve center of the goblin plunder army to Krusty.

With a small *tunk*, Shiroe placed a black pebble in the center of the map. That was Krusty's position. Next he set a whitish, misshapen pebble at Midrount Equestrian Gardens, and a smooth, green pebble at the village of Choushi.

At the moment, the place that needed the most watching was Choushi.

Of course he'd received reports that they'd been attacked by sahuagins, and that pained him, but what was more important was the fact that if the sahuagins managed to take that cape, they might even go ashore in Maihama.

One thing both towns had in common was that neither was expecting an invasion from the sea.

Why had the sahuagins even appeared?

He wasn't clear on the reason, but Shiroe thought the cause lay with the army the Goblin King had unleashed. After all, they'd appeared simultaneously. It could also be a maneuver by the Sahuagins meant to capitalize on a war that had already begun, but either way, it meant their army would be split in half.

I'd already made allowances for that...or I'll just have to bluff that I had, I suppose.

Shiroe had been fiddling with a slightly larger pebble, and he set it on the map with a *thunk*. The pebble was streamlined, and oddly cute: It looked a bit like a waterfowl with folded wings. He'd placed it on the ocean.

The experimental steam-driven transport ship *Ocypete*.

They were using it at maximum rotation.

After Krusty's group had disembarked, the *Ocypete* had waited for reinforcements at the abandoned port of Narashino, but they would have reached the ship by now. It would be out on the ocean, leading the four full raids Shiroe had organized, bound for Choushi.

The *Ocypete* was a transport vessel, and it wasn't armed. In that sense, it was a plain, unaffected ship.

However, since the ship was a prototype, they'd reinforced its hull so that they could run various strength tests, and with all the armor plating it had, its defense was probably high. In addition, as far as shipboard weapons were concerned, all they had to do was put the Adventurers on it.

The units Shiroe had specially organized were heavy on Summoners and Bards. Summoners were weaker at direct long-range magic attacks than Sorcerers were, but when you took into account the fact that they could use long-range attack spells based in the spirits they summoned, their range expanded to twice that of Sorcerers. Bards could provide backup for their magic attack power, avoiding the risk of exhausted MP.

Then it was just a race against time.

Shiroe consulted with the telechat operators who were constantly coming into the tent, determining organization and placement for unit after unit.

In this war, simply winning wouldn't be all that difficult. However, the trouble was that, if they destroyed the goblins' main army, it was just as likely that many goblins would form rogue tribes and go around wreaking havoc on the territories of Eastal.

Shiroe remembered the People of the Earth village they'd stopped at on their way back from Susukino. That good-natured old man, and the village laborers with their sheep. Of course, in a dangerous world like this one, they would be expected to defend themselves, and, although it wasn't likely to happen, even if they did die, he thought there would probably be no help for it. However, if there was still a chance to save them, it was only natural that he'd want to do it, and fortunately, Shiroe was in a position that would allow him to try.

No doubt it would be fine to leave the subjugation of the main goblin army to Krusty. The problem was how to deal with that goblin plunder army of just under twenty thousand when it disintegrated and dispersed.

By organizing smaller, mobile units that were separate from Krusty's strike unit—the one that was attacking the central forces—and using them to surround the perimeter, they'd keep any damage the goblins did contained in the mountains somehow. He needed to draw up a strategy for that maneuver and give concrete shape to its tactical aspects. That was the issue Shiroe was currently facing.

The key to the general strategy was to drive the Goblins into the hilly region at the center of Zantleaf.

In order to make that happen, Krusty's group was fighting at the edges of the main goblin unit and working clockwise from the west, as though they were "peeling" the army. Fortunately, the goblins were taking advantage of any chances they got, and they'd already sallied quite far in the direction of Zantleaf. If they continued to lure them in, it should be possible to lead them to an ideal position.

If he distributed Akiba's forces in such a way that they'd support Krusty, and they managed to seal the goblins into Zantleaf—the tip of Chiba on the Bousou Peninsula in the real world—it would make the surrounding areas significantly safer. The ultimate weak spot in that strategy was the defense of the village of Choushi, and the soldiers that were being sent over on the *Ocypete*.

"Aren't you going to the battlefield, my liege?" Akatsuki asked.

She'd followed him all the way here—in order to guard him, she'd said—and she was sitting on a cushion that had been set out inside the tent.

"I'd like to. I can't leave this place just yet, though. I haven't finished all the organizing... Well, the end of that should be in sight within a day or two. When that time comes, I'll move."

"I see."

Akatsuki nodded.

Shiroe was a griffin rider, one of fewer than two hundred on the server. In terms of speed in the air, only wyverns were able to match them.

If they had to mobilize a unit and march through the mountains, it would take time, but if Shiroe was traveling alone, he'd be able to race to either Krusty or the village of Choushi in about thirty minutes.

That was one of two reasons Shiroe was currently based here: One reason was that being close to a large number of telechat operators meant he could quickly issue orders to the entire army. The other was that, in a fluid military situation like this one, he wanted to stay halfway between Choushi and Krusty's unit so that he could run to either one.

Shiroe was in the middle of building an army-wide communications network.

If they managed to get that in place, the expedition was already an assembly of experienced Adventurers, so they'd probably be able to carry out the operation semiautonomously. The plan was to set up leaders for each party, establishing lines for reports and orders. Shiroe's group would organize a horizontal network between units, and position telechat operators as a vertical network. They would sort out the information that came up through the telechat operators and note it down on the map, making developments visible.

The strategy Shiroe came up with wasn't terribly advanced, nor were his tactics.

It was a familiar situation:

Order the situation and make it visible. Once you discover discontinuity, investigate it thoroughly, find points worth noting, then "produce" them in order to show them off to good effect. Shiroe's "scheme" was really only a collaboration between investigation and production.

…And most of it was the sort of work he was doing now: Dull tasks that would never be seen publically. *Good grief,* Shiroe muttered to himself. *I'm just a paper-pusher.*

However, as if to drown out Shiroe's thoughts, a telechat operator's voice echoed through the tent.

"Mister Shiroe! The summer camp group just encountered sahuagins at the village of Choushi. It's sixty Adventurers against at least a thousand sahuagins. They're drastically outnumbered!"

"Tell the *Ocypete* to hurry! Then call Calasin. The final organization materials are already drawn up. We'll get the communications network up and running in a day—no, half a day!"

Shiroe spread documents with a vast number of notes out on his desk. About a dozen telecommunications officers stood around him, looking down at them. As Shiroe began to fill them in on his predictions for the future with clipped words, his voice held no hesitation.

For now, they had to complete the command transmission network as quickly as possible.

And then— Shiroe bit his lip, his mind racing.

▶ **5**

"Haa…! Haa…!"

Calming his ragged breathing, Naotsugu gulped down the water he'd taken out of his bag.

As he ran his eyes over the area—covering for Shouryuu, who was so tired he'd sunk down to the ground—he gave a strained smile: *This is a pretty nasty situation.*

Naotsugu, Nyanta, Shouryuu, and Lezarik were currently taking a short break at the foot of a pine tree a little ways from the coast. You couldn't really have called it a rest, though.

The battle that had begun that morning had gone on for four hours already, a merciless, continuous struggle under the blazing summer sun.

This was Naotsugu's group's third break, and the previous two hadn't lasted more than ten minutes each. The sahuagins were trying to come up on land at many points, and there weren't many Adventurers. In a situation like this, when they had to make defensive cover function effectively with small numbers, teamwork between parties was vital. If the Adventurers gathered in one place, the sahuagins would invade through the holes that would inevitably open up.

And if that happened, the village of Choushi was right behind them.

Of course they'd asked the village chief to have the People of the Earth take refuge in buildings whose defenses seemed solid, and the young men had probably taken up arms and were preparing to fight.

However, even so, they were nothing more than the ordinary residents of an unwalled town. How much of a fight could they give the sahuagins? The answer was: Only enough to buy some time before they were overrun.

At the waterline in front of him, three groups of newbies were fighting again and again. True, from Naotsugu's perspective at level 90, they were clumsy about a lot of things, but their fight was worthy of being called a brave one.

Still, even so, the heartbreak of being midlevel remained: Sometimes their defensive formation loosened or came close to cracking apart.

There was no help for that. The power and range of their techniques was far too different from what Naotsugu's group had. The fact that they didn't have the high-level magic items that Naotsugu and the others practically took for granted also made a big difference.

Elder Tales had an Item Lock system. Nearly all high-level magic items needed to be "locked" in order to be equipped, and afterward they could be used only by the Adventurer who'd locked them.

It was probably easiest to picture if you imagined having an item that was calibrated to you, for your exclusive use. Since locked items couldn't be equipped to strangers, it was harder to steal and resell them, and even if you died, you wouldn't lose them. They sometimes unlocked hidden abilities as well.

Once they'd reached level 90, like Naotsugu's group, even players who belonged to regular guilds had a few high-level magic items. Veteran players like Shiroe who went on tough adventures ordinarily had several dozen high-level items, and even some legendary items.

These magic items weren't simply high-performance weapons or defensive gear. Sometimes they came with unique special abilities, and some of them could even rewrite their bearers' special skill performance.

In Naotsugu's case, this was true of the magic sword he used, Chaos Shrieker. This weapon rewrote the range of Taunting Shout—a special skill that had the effect of enraging monsters—from ten meters to fifteen. That changed even the usability of the skill.

Midlevel Adventurers didn't have the support of these powerful, high-level magic items, and so it was only natural that their battles would look different from those of the high-level Adventurers who owned them. In addition, because of the Item Lock system, they couldn't lend them their powerful items.

Anxious, Naotsugu started to get up, but Nyanta checked him from behind.

"Right now, our job is to rest."

Unusually, Nyanta's tone brooked no argument.

Naotsugu, Nyanta, Shouryuu and Lezarik had all exhausted their MP. Unless they were being influenced by some sort of special effect, MP recovery during battle was practically nonexistent. Even if they went back into the fray now, since they had no MP, the front line would break down in a heartbeat.

When they fought goblins in the mountains, they'd been able to lie low in the darkness and rest at regular intervals. In this battle, they weren't able to set the pace themselves, and responding to the sahuagins' charges had them in heavy rotation.

Of course, even so, Naotsugu's group was able to hold the front line for much longer stretches than the newbie Adventurers. Even then, though, there were limits. Even the MP of level-90 tough guys like Naotsugu and the others wouldn't last through a battle that took over an hour.

Not only that, but this time Naotsugu's party had four members, not six. Each of them had to work one and a half times as much as they normally did to make combination plays happen.

"Naotsugu. Here."

"Thanks, man."

He drank the potion Lezarik had handed to him. The blue elixir was medicine that recovered MP, but its effect was very slight. *Elder Tales* had lots of ways to recover HP, but far fewer methods of recovering MP, and the amounts recovered were small. This potion certainly wasn't a cheap item, but its effects were still limited.

Even as Naotsugu fretted, he watched Touya fighting in front of him.

The boy kicked up white sand, swinging his blade to draw the sahuagins' hostility, charging again and again.

Touya had certainly gotten stronger.

His techniques and his fighting methods were still rough, and you couldn't say he had gotten *skillful*, but he was stronger. And actually, subtle "skillfulness" wouldn't be necessary for a while.

One of a warrior's essential attributes was spirit. This was the same spirit as the one that showed up in the phrases "full of spirit" and "in high spirits." It meant being prepared, and having a proactive attitude when trying to make something happen.

Touya's fight had spirit. This was an irreplaceable attribute for a warrior who supported the front line. In order to protect comrades, Naotsugu thought that sometimes you needed the sort of savage courage that was involved in smashing a glass door with your bare hands. The sort that wasn't afraid of shedding its own blood.

Touya's gonna keep right on growing...

When he shifted his gaze, his eyes found the girl called Isuzu and the Sorcerer named Rundelhaus. Isuzu had been a Bard, if he remembered right.

Unlike Touya, she *was* skilled. The positions she took, the attacks she paid out: They all showed an exquisite sense of distance and rhythm. An amateur wouldn't have been able to see her skill. Even a player who was well versed in battles might have seen her as an unremarkable Adventurer and overlooked her. However, her unerring support raised each element of her friends' combat—offense, defense, movement, and recovery—to the next dimension.

The combinations she executed with the Sorcerer were particularly noteworthy. The prescient timing and positioning of her support made it seem as if she knew exactly what the young man wanted. The Sorcerer's defensive power was low, and she watched the battle from his perspective as she moved, keeping him from being exposed directly to enemy attacks, but giving him room to target all the sahuagins with one attack.

The young Sorcerer who was on the receiving end of this support was practically energy incarnate. Sorcerers had high attack power in the first place. If compared at the same level, they shared the distinction of being strongest of the twelve classes with Assassins.

However, the young man's attacks held a desperate determination, more as if he was packing all the thoughts and emotions he had into each and every spell than as if he was relying on his class's performance. As if possessed by his tenacity, lava shells leapt and bounded, and spears of ice pierced the sahuagins.

The girl named Serara, the one who'd gotten attached to Nyanta...

She'd also begun to change. He'd noticed her chanting speed and resolution the first time he'd seen her in Susukino, but now her movements were even lighter. Unlike before, when her thoughts hadn't gone beyond recovery, she summoned nature spirits and sent them running every which way, and she didn't forget to use attack assistance spells to support the party.

She'd probably turn into a good healer.

And Minori.

It was likely that Minori had a completely different perspective from the rest of the group on the fight with the sahuagins. Just sensing the premonition that was visible inside Minori gave Naotsugu goose bumps.

At Minori's orders, the party changed formations, reconstructing combinations as a team.

"Rudy, cut down your output."

"Understood, Mademoiselle Minori."

"Serara. Recovery switch. Go join the attack, please."

"Icicle Ripper into the far left! Firing!"

Naotsugu knew what she was doing.

He knew because he'd spent a long time teaming up with Shiroe.

She was probably trying to keep track of the MP consumption of everyone in her party. Naturally, in order to do that, she had to have a solid grasp of all her companions' special skills, not just her own, and that grasp had to include not only the MP they consumed, but their performances and the situations in which they were used.

In addition, she had to keep track of the teamwork between her companions and the positional relationships between them and the enemy, the encounter sequence, and the order in which they were destroyed.

In other words, she was turning the "sentences" of destroying enemies into the "text" known as battle. Then, as she restructured the battle "text" into the "story" of tactics, she "read" it. That was exactly what it was.

Of course, battles were a series of unexpected events that unfolded in real time. In this situation, "reading" didn't mean immobilizing the battle as if it were a static text; it meant acknowledging all possible futures and reading it as a highly improvised story.

Although she was still awkward, Minori was trying to imitate Shiroe's full control encounters. That little girl was chasing after Shiroe's back.

One percent increments, and thirty seconds in advance, I think.
That was what Shiroe had said about the matter once.

He'd probably meant fighting thirty seconds ahead. The "1 percent increments" had been his grasp of his companions' remaining MP.

Of course, understanding the surrounding environment was fundamental to high-level battles as well. Even Naotsugu understood that. When he was fighting on the front line, even without checking his party status screen, he had a vague grasp of his friends' remaining MP. At most, though, there were only about six levels: "full tank," "still plenty left," "about half," "getting dicey," "low," and "flat broke." It was likely that most middle-class Adventurers only based their decisions on two levels or so: "still good for a while" and "better rest soon." It was just that hard to grasp the MP of a friend who belonged to a different class, even if you could keep a handle on your own MP.

Elder Tales had been a game, and because that was so, in extreme terms, only certain things could happen in it. If you got sufficiently used to it, you could even predict how monsters would move.

Shiroe's full control encounters didn't stop at grasping the party's remaining MP. It meant having an understanding of all their remaining resources as a matter of course, as well as the enemies' remaining resources, and standing up above it all and making everything unfold according to your plan.

Now that *Elder Tales* had become a different world, the chance battle occurrence rate was far higher than it had been when it was a game. Even Shiroe couldn't possibly have the power to see thirty seconds ahead at this point. However, on the other hand, he had the hope that if it *was* Shiroe, he just might. The "one percent increments, thirty seconds in advance" line hadn't been due to talent or a bluff. Shiroe had murmured those words after lots and lots of hard training.

Naotsugu knew about controlled encounters only because he'd heard things like that during his long friendship with Shiroe. Even though he knew Shiroe had acquired the ability through hard work, to Naotsugu, who was on the front line concentrating on the enemy in front of him, that "sense" seemed almost like a superpower. Even if he could read the "sentences" of defeating the enemies he was facing, he couldn't link them together into "text."

But Minori, right in front of him, was chasing Shiroe's back.

I wonder how many seconds ahead Minori's seeing... What increments does she have her group pegged at? Twenty percent? Or can she already read them at ten percent, at her level?

Just as Naotsugu stood, thinking that they needed to get back to the battlefield and let the newbies take turns resting, a sharp explosion echoed from Choushi's distant northern square. It was a special Druid attack spell, Shrieker Echo.

Naotsugu's reaction was delayed by a beat.

He didn't know why he'd heard a scream like that from the fields, far away from the Great Zantleaf River.

Behind the front line, the five members of Minori's party bore down on Naotsugu like the wind.

"We're on it, Master!"

"Thanks for your help here!"

"Ha-ha-ha! Just leave this to us! Sally forth!"

"U-um! You do your best, too, Nyanta!"

The five of them had beat a retreat from the coastline when he wasn't looking, and they dashed off to the north, as if leaving the rest to Naotsugu's group.

As they ran off in the summer sunlight, their backs seemed like migrating birds, making straight for the sky.

As Shouryuu and Lezarik responded, knowing they needed to fill the hole Minori and the others had left behind, Minori turned back to face them and the perplexed Naotsugu. The young girl was soaked with sweat, but a strong will shone in her eyes.

"It's a spirit reaction; I had Serara set it up to use as an alarm. The goblins have probably invaded from the mountains again. If it's only goblins, we can handle them. Since we've got a Bard and continuous combat abilities, we're better suited to this battle... And so, please take care of the coast, Naotsugu!"

"Minori!" Naotsugu called to her.

Minori waved a hand vigorously.

Then she and the others ran off, disappearing into the village of Choushi.

▶ 6

Rundelhaus was running at the head of the group.

He'd been focusing ferociously ever since that morning, and it seemed to him as though the force of his spells had increased slightly.

They'd had a high-level player take a look at the item they'd acquired in the deepest part of Forest Ragranda. Apparently it was a magic item called Magician's Gauntlets. Since it was the sort of item that level-25 characters could equip, in terms of the entire server, it was probably a very commonplace article. Still, it was the first magic item Isuzu and the other four had managed to win on their own.

It was a pair of slightly scratched gauntlets that gleamed dull silver and had magic circles engraved on them. Isuzu and the others had gazed at them as if they were looking at treasure. Since there was only one of the item, they couldn't all equip it at once. That said, the idea of selling the magic item they'd found after all that trouble and splitting the proceeds made them terribly sad.

As a result, they'd discussed it among themselves and decided to have Rundelhaus use this piece of battle gear. The item seemed to be specifically for the Magic Attack classes, and he was the only magic user in their group.

Rundelhaus had hesitated just a bit, but he must have been interested, after all. When they pressed him, he put them on, looking pleased.

As Rundelhaus ran ahead of Isuzu, he had those gauntlets on his hands.

They were a magic item that increased maximum MP by just a few percentage points of the maximum. The amount was only enough for a single magic attack, but by this point, Isuzu and the others all understood that the accumulation of that small percentage would have a great influence on battles. The red crystals set in the center of the gauntlets shone as if hinting at the flame magic Rundelhaus used, and his determination.

Isuzu switched her continuous support songs to Nocturne of Meditation and Fawn's March. The first song increased MP recovery efficiency, and the second was a special support skill that increased the whole party's movement speed.

"My thanks, Mademoiselle Isuzu."

"You slow down a bit, Rudy," Isuzu remonstrated, as Rundelhaus expressed his gratitude. It was fine to be energetic, but nothing good could come of having a paper-armored magic user at the head of the line.

"Mm. Sorry."

Rundelhaus slackened his pace as he spoke, and Isuzu handed him a canteen she'd taken out of her pack. She'd had the innkeeper's daughter fill it with water for her that morning. It had a little orange juice squeezed into it, and even now that it was all warm, it was still a bit refreshing to drink.

"…Um, are you okay?"

"Why wouldn't I be? I, Rundelhaus Code, am doing perfectly, of course. I feel as if I had no enemies in the world at all. Ah-ha-ha-ha-ha!" Rundelhaus answered after gulping down the contents of the canteen.

He really must have been fundamentally well bred: Even though he was doing something rude—rehydrating while walking fast (and laughing loudly on top of that)—it didn't make him seem vulgar.

Large eyes that tilted down slightly at the corners and smooth, soft, golden hair. *It's probably because he comes off a bit like a golden retriever*, Isuzu thought, laughing a little.

"You two get along well, don't you?"

Serara teased them, giggling, but Isuzu only shrugged her shoulders and answered lightly: "Sure we do!" To Isuzu, Rundelhaus was just a friendly dog.

A handsome, pedigreed dog kept at the house of the local rich family. A golden retriever with long, abundant hair who showed up at Isuzu's house all the time, simply because their gardens happened to be next to each other.

Naturally, because of his pedigree, he was so handsome he practically shone. His features were refined as well, and his behavior was courteous, with nothing coarse about it. However, once you got used to him, you realized he was dumb. The sort of "dumb" that got dead serious about catching the ball and ran around until he was worn out, and wagging his tail so hard the base hurt.

Was he stupid, or was he a natural-born airhead? The arrogant, excessively self-conscious lines he sometimes came up with were just another result of his dumbness surfacing, but they didn't annoy her in the least.

Isuzu and this dumb dog were already friends. They'd become friends the moment he'd licked her outstretched fingers. As a result, she was able to agree easily with Serara's banter.

"Done? Nn."

...To the point where she could take the canteen back from Rundelhaus, wipe it down, and return it to her bag as if that was completely natural.

"I'm sorry."

"Keh-heh-heh! Geez, Rudy, you're apologizing all over the place."

"That isn't true, is it, Mademoiselle Isuzu?"

Rundelhaus retored as Touya teased him from the head of the line, but Isuzu took no notice of him.

"You're a magic user, Rudy, so it's better if you act a little full of yourself. It makes you look nice and dumb," she shot back.

"What are you saying?! What do you mean, 'dumb'?! Did you actually have the gall to call me dumb?!"

It was incredibly strange.

She—a freckled, skinny, country high-school girl sorely lacking in feminine charms—was dealing with Rundelhaus, a princely type who might have stepped out of a picture book, as if he were a neighborhood puppy dog… Or, if that was too mean, a slightly airheaded, rich and pampered middle schooler.

Viewed objectively, it was outrageous, and something she probably should have felt badly about, but Isuzu couldn't think of it that way at all. Playing around with Rundelhaus this way was an incredibly care-free, absent-minded pleasure.

Just as Isuzu was about to open her mouth, intending to tease him one more time, it happened: Somewhere not very far away, a second Shrieker Echo went off.

Isuzu and the others looked at one another. Then they turned the corner, quickening their pace.

The shape of the village of Choushi was unique. Having been built along the Great Zantleaf River, it was long and thin, and one broad avenue ran down its center. There were side streets and crossroads as well, but they were all secondary and short.

This meant that, once they turned the corner of the avenue and headed north, they found themselves in a rural landscape of spreading fields. In this season, eggplants and tomatoes grew thickly on top of low ridges, swaying in the wind, and spring wheat showed its green.

Running through those fields were three—no, four shadows.

Immediately, Isuzu chanted Ballad of the Slowpoke Snail. The goblins slowed as if the strength had suddenly gone out of their legs. That slight chance was all Isuzu's trusty companions needed to launch a preemptive strike.

"Sorry, Rudy!"

As Touya yelled, he crouched extremely low, twisting his body drastically. It was a more aggressive stance than the one he used to draw enemies in by taunting.

His special Samurai taunting skills were inefficient against targets this scattered. Running around and getting the enemy together in one place would be a job all on its own.

"Leave it to me, Touya! Witness the melody of my glorious magic! Serpent Bolt!"

As its name hinted, the sheaf of bluish-purple lightning that leapt from Rundelhaus's staff raced every which way across the field, like ribbons. It was what general theory would have called a bad move: a preemptive strike by a magic user.

Eight goblins came running from all over the field. That was more than they'd expected, but Minori, who was hanging back at the very end of the line, calmly cast a Damage Interception spell. ...Not on Touya, but on Rundelhaus.

Rundelhaus was enveloped in a light blue, mirrorlike barrier, with his staff at the ready. The first goblin attacked him, and then a second goblin raised its ax high and charged. However, both attacks were blocked by the Damage Interception spell Minori had set.

Damage Interception spells were one form of the special recovery spell unique to Kannagi. When set on a character in advance, they could protect that character from a certain amount of damage.

The most famous example was Purification Barrier, but there were several other types, and the one she'd used this time was a spell called Defense of Doctrine Barrier. Its distinguishing feature was its large capacity for absorbing damage. It was a powerful spell that could negate more than four times as much as Purification Barrier could, but naturally its recast time was long, and it wasn't the sort of skill you could use casually.

Still...

Isuzu thought as she threw down a rapid series of notes.

Minori had made the right call. Thanks to that spell, right now, Rundelhaus's defense was even higher than Touya's. On top of that, the goblins had been angered by Rundelhaus's magic attacks, which had a far longer range than Touya's attacks, and they were being drawn right out in front of Isuzu and the other Adventurers.

The moment the goblins were assembled, Touya's Whirlwind Izuna struck home. Most of the goblins stood paralyzed, as if they'd been disconnected, and then Rundelhaus, Touya and Isuzu dispatched them one by one.

In the midst of these repeated battles, Isuzu and the others were learning not only basic team plays but irregular ones as well. Irregular plays were, as you'd expect, irregular, and they weren't tactics that could be used on a regular basis, but in specific situations, they could be used to great effect. You could say the group had acquired more problem-solving techniques.

That, and this—

"Well, Mademoiselle Isuzu?! Did you see my magnificent magic?!"

—were all the result of being yanked around by this dumb young man.

Isuzu smiled and smacked Rundelhaus's head.

That earlier spell had been amazing. The fact that he'd scored an accurate hit even with a range like that one was as much due to Rundelhaus's training as it was to the spell's capabilities.

Everyone was getting stronger. That meant Isuzu couldn't let herself fall behind, either.

▶ **7**

The confused fight continued.

The sun was already sinking in the western sky.

The five of them were the only ones in sight who were continuing to fight with the town in the balance. Minori's group was an isolated defense corps. Their midnight strikes on the goblins had done significant damage, and the fighting power of the midsized unit that had been dispatched to Choushi was believed to have been nearly wiped out. At the very least, their chain of command had to have been shredded.

The effect was visible in this sporadic attack as well.

This wasn't an organized effort on the goblins' part. Now that Choushi had been thrown off-balance by the sahuagin attack, they simply wanted to devastate and plunder the village at no risk to themselves.

Raising rough, repulsive voices, the short little demons attacked out of nowhere. Minori and the others lay in wait for them in the center of the farming road that ran toward the fields in the hill country and kept on defeating them.

Shrieker Echo, the settable Druid spell Serara used, was proving to be very useful. Setting several of these spells to act as alarms helped Minori's group cover for their small numbers.

"Sorry, Minori. Got anything to drink?"

Minori handed the groaning Touya a third canteen. She'd seen this much coming, and had been prepared. She chanted Instant Heal over

Touya, who had plopped down at the base of a tree by the side of the road.

Resilience was probably at work, since the battle had ended: The scratches on his armor, the ones that weren't very serious, were mending before her very eyes. So were Touya's wounds. However, he was so soaked with sweat it was as if he'd poured water over his head, and the sweat wasn't going anywhere. His body was probably still hot from the long, fierce battle. Maybe that was why his breathing was taking a while to calm down.

Minori was worried about him, but she didn't say anything aloud.

No matter what she said, she wouldn't be able to get Touya a few days of restful vacation. Besides, Touya probably wouldn't want something like that. Like Minori, what Touya wanted was this defense operation.

All Minori could do was hand him a well-wrung-out handkerchief.

"Thanks."

As she nodded, acknowledging Touya's words, Minori realized that she felt hot as well as she looked around at her companions. Most of them were trying to recover as much mental energy as they possibly could while they caught their breath.

Minori's job was field monitor. During this fight, she'd gone one step further and taken over the role of operator for the party as well. Because Minori had taken over Serara's task of keeping an eye on MP, the speed of Serara's reactions with regard to recovery and support had risen significantly.

In exchange, this meant that Minori was single-handedly performing the roles of paying attention to their surroundings and to her friends' condition; in other words, to battle information. At first glance, it looked as though she was slightly removed from the combat, but the burden of the role was a large one.

I'm still not that good, though...

As Minori took mental notes on the difference between her companions' remaining MP, she checked their degree of recovery. During battle, Minori grasped the trends in her companions' MP in 5 percent increments. Using that information and the shifts in the battle, she estimated consumption and "read" the battle, piecing together the future five or ten seconds in advance. She couldn't trust her accuracy yet, but it was a fact that this forecasting ability was helping them avoid unnecessary MP consumption.

They were defending a base in this continuous battle. Unlike normal dungeon expeditions, they were never able to let their guard down, and Minori's combat management abilities were constantly being refined.

Minori's own assessment of her control was that it was like a child's game compared to what Shiroe did, but if Naotsugu had heard those words, he would probably have been speechless.

Five percent increments meant making predictions about the frequency of other players' magic use on a concrete level, such as "She should be able to cast two more midsized recovery spells." That was far beyond the insight that most adventurers around level 30 could hope for based on what they were shown regarding other players' statuses. No one in the party had realized it yet, not even Minori herself, but she had quietly begun to develop a talent.

"Listen, everyone. During that last battle, Marielle contacted us."

Collecting herself, Minori made her report.

Because she was controlling the battle, Minori often went on standby, hanging back as a reserve. While she choked back the spells she wanted to cast in rapid succession, she monitored their surroundings.

Thanks to that, she'd noticed the telechat.

"According to Marielle, a special unit is on its way here from Akiba by ship. She said it should be here this evening."

"Evening? It's already almost evening..."

"You're right."

"Hmm. Maybe they're running a little late?"

Minori thought hard. The summer sky was still bright, but as far as the hour was concerned, it was already late in the afternoon. It would have been fine to call the time evening.

"From what I heard, they'll arrive by ship and come ashore. If they get reinforcements at the coast, alternates will come out to us as well, so... If we hang on for three more hours at the very longest..."

Isuzu and Serara's faces brightened. From Rundelhaus's and Touya's expressions, they seemed to be steeling themselves, as if they were determined not to get careless, even now. Still, it was true that they had relaxed slightly, as if a weight had been lifted from their shoulders.

During a battle that had lasted about half a day, they'd defeated nearly thirty goblins.

The total number wasn't all that large, but the combat was very stressful. They had a wide range to cover, and there was no telling where the goblins would attack; it felt as though they were playing whack-a-mole with only the Shrieker Echoes to rely on, and there were no opportunities to relax.

As sensors, the Shrieker Echoes were convenient, but they weren't perfect. On the contrary: They were incredibly worried that something might get through the holes in the net and make it to the village. As a matter of fact, there had been cases where a few Goblins had slipped through and headed for the village, and Minori and the others had had to hastily go back and subdue them.

As they fought, they were patrolling the area around the village out of consideration for the distance they'd have to travel to defend the center of Choushi if something broke through their line of defense, and in that sense, they weren't able to push up that line of defense.

It was fortunate that the Goblins had lost their chain of command. If they'd had a good commander, they probably would have used disturbance tactics like burning the field. Minori's group had been apprehensive about this, but so far, they'd managed to hold out somehow.

"You're right. When the ship arrives, people will come out to us, too."

Serara nodded in agreement.

It was clear that the root of their current distress was the way this double-fronted operation dispersed their forces. At present, when no large magical beasts had been sent into combat, neither goblins nor sahuagins were all that tough as individual enemies.

"Not much longer now. Let's all get out there and do our best."

On that note, Touya stood up energetically.

The afternoon wind was still as hot as if it had been sautéed in a frying pan, but the news that reinforcements would arrive if they hung on just a little longer was enough to bring life back to their faces.

It happened about fifteen minutes after they'd started patrolling again.

Minori and the others had hoped the time would pass without incident, but of course their hopes were betrayed.

Behind them, from the village's wide avenue, they heard an enormous crash. When the party turned back, wondering how they'd managed to let something make it that far in, they came face-to-face with a squad of goblins radiating an aura of violence, accompanied by two Dire Wolves.

▶ 8

The turn the fight had taken put them at an overwhelming disadvantage.

"Not gonna happen!!"

Touya charged again, blocking a Dire Wolf that had been about to leap at Isuzu. However, inevitably, the charge freed up the Hobgoblin he'd been holding back.

The repeated battles had exhausted nearly all of the members' big techniques with long recast times. Although they had MP reserves, courtesy of Isuzu the Bard, that alone wasn't enough decisive power to let them break out of the situation.

The Hobgoblin was holding a big hammer with both hands. Taking a full swing with it as if it were a baseball bat, the goblin slammed it right into Touya's defenseless side.

It won't be enough!

With a smashing sound you'd never hear in baseball, the attack crashed into Purification Barrier. The single-player barrier shone light blue, and the weird noise—as if thick glass were shattering all at once—was wearing away at its durability.

Damage Interception spells were a special type of recovery spell that was set in advance and negated a certain amount of damage. They could completely negate all damage, provided the damage was below the amount they could absorb. However, if it was over their threshold, they would fall away, no matter how long they were supposed to last.

As she saw the light of the barrier spidering like glass, Minori knew instinctively that it wasn't fully canceling the damage.

"Four Quarters Prayer!!"

Immediately, Minori cast her emergency Damage Interception spell. As befitted a spell in the Emergency category, it was extremely effective: On top of costing almost no MP, it was quick to chant, and it protected all of Minori's companions in the area with a defense that was nearly as strong as Purification Barrier.

However, the situation wouldn't be resolved that easily.

...And now I can't use that one again.

Minori bit her lip. Her face was pale.

As the name indicated, emergency spells were meant to get players through emergencies. Their recast times were long, and she wouldn't be able to use the same spell again for twenty-four hours.

"Stop! Sto-o-op!!"

Serara activated Willow Spirits. As though drawn by a spell, vines that had been clinging to the wall of a nearby warehouse wrapped around the Dire Wolf. The Dire Wolf gave an irritated bellow, then dug its claws into the ground and began to struggle, trying to work itself free of its bonds.

This was the third time Serara had used it. With the Dire Wolf's huge body and matching strength, it would be able to tear plant bindings to shreds. But was the restraint pointless? No: Because Serara had managed to check at least one of the Dire Wolves with this spell, if even for only a short time, Touya and the rest of the group were able to concentrate on the other enemies.

However, since Serara was occupied with the Dire Wolf, this also meant that Minori had to handle recovery spells, the area Serara was in charge of.

"I told you! It ain't gonna happen!"

Touya brought down his raised katana with all his might.

It wasn't a technique or anything, just a brute-force strike, but it sent one goblin flying, and a Hobgoblin who'd been in its path got pulled in as well.

The Hobgoblin used its superior build to shove the Goblin out of the way, then started toward Touya again.

Hobgoblins were a goblin subspecies. That said, although they were a subspecies, their abilities were higher than those of their parent race. For instance, goblins banded together and lived in groups, but even the most diplomatic couldn't have called their lives "well-ordered." Recently they'd just happened to crown a king and they had formed a plunder army, too, but the reality was that they were a tribal society, a chaotic and violent demihuman species that stole others' property.

And compared to the orcs (another wicked type of demihuman that lived in the south), who preferred military organization and nation building, the goblin race was lawless.

Yet while Hobgoblins had inherited the goblin temperament, they also had a strong desire to subdue others, which the regular goblins did not have. They were often more intelligent than goblins, too, and they mastered the weapons they took from humans.

This Hobgoblin was quite a formidable enemy: It was awkwardly wearing pieces of plate armor, probably stolen from some knight, and it used a metal sledgehammer. Its level might have been as high as 30. To be honest, at this point, that enemy alone could easily have been a bit too much for Minori's group.

That Hobgoblin was accompanied by two Dire Wolves and four goblins. Minori and the others were managing to oppose them right now only because they knew the topography of the village's main avenue, because they'd taken up a position where they couldn't be surrounded and were protecting the rear rank as they fought, and because they'd polished their teamwork during their recent special training. Minori's group had clearly gotten involved in a fight that was beyond what they could handle.

"Touya, switch! Pin down the wolf and the boss!"

However, determination that surpassed actual strength wouldn't last long. The battle was wavering on a precarious balance. In that case, they needed to take a gamble that would make maximum use of the benefits of the emergency spell she'd cast.

Making up her mind, Minori dashed out onto the front line.

Four Quarters Prayer had deployed Purification Barrier–class damage interception over all party members, and it had thirty-two seconds left. Minori may have been healer, but even she should be able to hold out against the goblins' attacks during those thirty-two seconds.

She'd made up her mind and leapt, but her legs were shaking, and the strength seemed about to drain out of them. The summer road, with its clouds of dust, felt soft and fluffy to her, as if it were made of cushions. Still, in an attempt to shake off the feeling of unreality, Minori unleashed a front kick at the closest goblin from an altitude that wasn't at all ladylike.

"Understood! Let's go, Mademoiselle Isuzu!!"

"Roger that, Rudy!"

As if they'd just woken up, yells of support rose from the rear ranks. Just hearing the first verse of Rundelhaus's chant told Minori that they'd accurately read her intent.

The goblin leapt at her, laughing maniacally, and Minori took its attack from a defensive stance. Relying on her own Damage Interception spell, she evaded only the attacks that were aimed at her vital spots, letting the hardened areas of her leather armor handle the rest. She wasn't dodging: Whenever an attack flew at her, she'd jump into its path, stopping it with her body before the weapon came down completely.

I'm scared! I'm scared! I'm scared— But!!

Watching his sister act as though she'd gone insane out of the corner of his eye, Touya did the exact same thing against the higher-level enemies: the Hobgoblin and the Dire Wolf.

Even if Damage Interception was in place, it had been a long time since they began fighting. The twins had patches of dried blood all over, but they built the front line together, now stopping goblin knives that looked like meat cleavers, now exposing themselves to the fangs of the fierce, demonic wolf.

The time the twins bought was used up by a ringing chant.

It was the most powerful of all Rundelhaus's ranged attack spells. The freezing spell had a long chant, but if it hit, it couldn't fail to do considerable damage. Isuzu's special support skill followed after, leaving a high-pitched echo in its wake.

As Rundelhaus shouted "Frigid Window," his voice was ornamented by Isuzu's singing voice, exactly one octave higher. The spell, which was now a round, froze all the goblins, turning them into statues.

As Minori retreated from the front line, which was abruptly dominated by cold air, she checked her companions' statuses. What was the situation? Even as she absent-mindedly chanted a new Damage Interception spell, her color wasn't good.

Rundelhaus's powerful attack had taken out the minor goblins at a stroke. However, in order to buy that time, Minori had stepped onto the front line, and during the time they'd lost there, Touya had continued to take damage.

Minori chanted a new Purification Barrier for Touya, but Damage Interception spells wouldn't recover lost HP. Kannagi used special recovery spells, and that was their fatal weakness—they exerted control such that damage was not inflicted, but they weren't good with normal recovery spells, the type that recovered the damage itself.

Minori herself had lost many options, including that earlier emergency spell.

The situation wasn't good.

Still, the fact that the goblins' numbers were down was great news. The enemy's advantage had been in the number of members who could make direct attacks. Now that they'd done away with that advantage, a slightly higher level of balance had been achieved on the battlefield. As Minori cast her own inferior recovery spells and damage absorption spells at Touya, she issued orders to Rundelhaus and Isuzu. Following those instructions, the two of them began concentrating their attacks on the Dire Wolf.

"When you've encountered multiple tough enemies, there are several possible strategies. If you're mounting a surprise attack, it's effective to take out the strongest enemy and damage their morale. If you do it well, the lesser enemies will run from you. But for other situations, in battles that take the best of both sides' ability, the key to victory lies in cutting down the enemy's numbers, starting with the weaker ones. You should firm up your damage control by reducing the number of enemies who participate in attacks."

What Shiroe had taught her came back to her.

Touya was still bleeding. Minori's precious little brother, the brother she was so proud of, was wounded, his face twisted in pain. However, precisely because that was true, they needed to concentrate on reducing the enemy's numbers right now.

While Touya supported the front line in exchange for his own blood, Rundelhaus and the rest needed to finish off the Dire Wolf. That was how they'd be able to reward Touya for holding the front line.

Minori was faithfully following Shiroe's advice, and just then, she had truly "read" the battle.

She grasped her friends' HP and MP, gave orders, supported, helped to boost each of them up—she saw all there was to see of the terrain of the battle, became the wind over the battlefield itself. Minori was living with everything she had.

However, even Minori's foresight couldn't predict everything.

The one thing talent couldn't make up for was combat experience.

A moment's accident was enough to bring the balance crashing down.

The second Dire Wolf shook off Serara's binding spell and joined the attack on Touya.

Two Dire Wolves and a powerful Hobgoblin. Against those three, the barrier Minori had cast shattered in a heartbeat.

In an instant, Minori took in the new information that had flown her way and ran calculations, half on instinct alone.

Nine seconds. —Yes. In nine seconds, Touya would die.

Minori stared frantically at her spell chant icon. Eight seconds left until the recast time for Purification Barrier was up. However, as she'd just seen, a Damage Interception spell in that class wouldn't be able to stop the attacks of the three enemies in front of them.

"Not yet!!"

Serara's scream rang out. The spell she cast was Pulse Recovery. This was a special recovery skill unique to Druids. The spell continuously recovered damage, and Touya's HP should have been gradually climbing, but it wasn't.

It was being lost faster than it was being recovered. Even Serara's Pulse Recovery did no more than prolong the time until his death.

Recalculate.

Recalculate.

Recalculate.

As she desperately twined feeble recovery spells together, Minori calculated. Even when she combined all the recovery spells she had and all the recovery spells Serara had, she couldn't push back the time when Touya would fall by more than thirty-five seconds.

Both her emergency recovery spells and her large recovery spells were exhausted. Recast time rendered more than half of the recovery spells available Minori and Serara unusable.

If this keeps up...

A nasty taste filled her mouth, and a nauseating shiver raced down her spine.

Touya was the cornerstone of the vanguard. If Touya fell, the odds of their being annihilated would skyrocket.

That wasn't all.

An instinctive revulsion—Minori sensed the smell of death.

It was hard to breathe.

It was as though the air had become a liquid, and she couldn't get it into her lungs. Time grew heavy, viscous, and all that filled Minori was a drawn-out sense of helpless, desperate impatience.

She wouldn't make it in time.

She wouldn't make it in time.

Minori stood, locked in cold air in midsummer, the blood pounding in her ears. All she could do was stare at Touya's HP as it fell every tenth of a second.

As though something had burst, time sped up again.

Rundelhaus, who had dashed past Minori, rammed into the Dire Wolf and thrust both arms into its mouth.

"Rudy?!"

"Leave this to me, Mademoiselle Isuzu!! I am... I am an Adventurer! As if I'd allow a petty mongrel like this to defeat me!!"

The wolf was enormous, the size of an ox. Its jaws were lined with fangs that looked as though they could bite off his entire upper body, and Rundelhaus had shoved his arms in up to the shoulder. But the Dire Wolf planted its feet, which might as well have been made of steel. It swung its head around, destroying the wall of a building and taking Rundelhaus along with it.

"Rudy!!"

Isuzu's shout was almost a scream. With the heavyweight spear she gripped in her hands, she struck out at the Dire Wolf, but its body was covered in bristles that deflected the blow.

"Calm down, Mademoiselle Isuzu. A gentleman...must always act noble..."

Rundelhaus had been dragged down onto the road, and over him, demonic flames blazed in the Dire Wolf's eyes. The air it exhaled as it tried to spit Rundelhaus out stank like wild beasts, but, even crumpled and smeared with sweat and mud as he was, Rundelhaus clung to the Dire Wolf's fangs, staying right in front of its face.

Every time the fangs gnashed, spraying the dull smell of blood around the area, Isuzu struck it with her spear, over and over, but Rundelhaus stopped her.

"If I run, this...thing will go af...ter Touya...again. Even Touya can't...handle three..."

He was right.

Because Rundelhaus was sacrificing himself, Touya would be able to escape death. The pressure of the attack damage had eased, and the situation seemed to be taking a turn for the better.

"But Rudy, you'll–!"

"Isuzu! We are attackers!!"

Rundelhaus shoved his arms even deeper into the wolf's mouth, as though saying he'd give them to it. Wolves were canines, after all: Because of their sharp teeth, when something was pushed deep into their mouths, it was difficult for them to attack another target until they spit it out.

"But–"

"Defeat the enemy!!" Rundelhaus yelled, and then, as if he felt more words would be a waste, he began to chant. His arms were already shredded, no more than lumps of meat attached to his shoulders. Even so, as he forced them into the Dire Wolf's mouth, he concentrated his flame energy. The magma spell Rundelhaus was shouting at the top of his lungs began to burn the Dire Wolf's insides before he fired it.

He didn't even need to fire it.

Rundelhaus's spell was being generated inside the Dire Wolf's mouth.

Unable to take the agony, the Dire Wolf tried to tear Rundelhaus off, but he clung like a man possessed, refusing to let the wolf go.

No: The fibers of the robe Rundelhaus wore were already tangled in the sawlike rows of fangs, and pieces of the elbow-length magic gauntlets were caught firmly in the teeth. It would have been hard for him to pull himself free.

"Do not underestimate me. I am—!!"

His hoarse voice echoed over the street, where the sunset was beginning to fade.

"I am Rundelhaus Code!! I am an Adventurer!!"

▶9

A scorched smell filled the area.

Rundelhaus had set the magic of the Magician's Gauntlets on a rampage. As he'd planned, it had burned away the Dire Wolf's insides, and then turned the right half of the Hobgoblin's body to cinders on momentum.

The battle had ended in victory for Isuzu and the others.

However, Rundelhaus, who had been the key figure in that victory and who should have been laughing a conceited, empty-headed laugh, was lying in front of Isuzu, covered in mud.

"Nature Revive!!"

Serara's resurrection spell had no effect.

Of course it didn't. As he lay there, his face was already pale, and it was practically smothered in blood. His eyelids—which, even dirty, looked like a prince's—were smooth, and he seemed just like a child of the nobility who'd fallen asleep, but…

…he was a Person of the Earth.

"…I'm sorry."

Something hot was dripping into the palm of Isuzu's hand.

"Why can't you bring him back? Hey, Minori, do it again!" Touya yelled. He didn't understand the situation.

Minori nodded and chanted Soul-Calling Prayer, but as expected, Rundelhaus didn't regain consciousness.

That was only natural.

"I'm sorry… Touya. Rudy is a…Person of…the…Earth…"

Isuzu spoke slowly.

It felt as though, if she admitted it, she'd be letting him go, and the words tangled up in her throat, refusing to come out. Out of the corner of her eye, she saw Minori clench her fists tightly, and she heard Serara murmur, "No…," but Isuzu couldn't care about any of it.

"—Rudy is a Person of the Earth. …He formed a party with us, adventured with us, ate with us, but… Rudy is a Person of the Earth, so…if he…dies…"

—If he had to…

Isuzu's chest hurt so much it felt as if the pain would crush it.

It wasn't as though she'd never imagined something like this.

It was why she hadn't wanted him to fight, and why she'd thought that, if she couldn't object completely, she'd protect Rundelhaus; she wouldn't let him do anything reckless.

…But she hadn't been able to stop him.

If she'd stopped him that first time…

If she'd flatly refused, back at Forest Ragranda, when she'd caught on. No, even if she hadn't done that, if she'd only been open and told everyone, things might not have turned out this way, but…

In order to make Rundelhaus's dream come true, Isuzu had cooperated with his lie.

When Rundelhaus had said, "I'm going to be an Adventurer," his face had been so much like a little kid's.

Adventurers and People of the Earth were different.

They were completely different beings.

He couldn't possibly "become" one, and yet…

Of course. Hadn't Rundelhaus been worried and hurt by it? He'd complained that no matter how much they fought, his experience points only rose at a snail's pace. He wasn't able to grow even half of half as much as Isuzu and the others, and he was irritated by the fact that his level wasn't rising. That was why he'd trained as hard and as furiously as he had.

Isuzu had never seen Rundelhaus lazing around in the tent. Whenever he'd had even a little spare time, he'd been out training hard or meditating. Rudy himself said it was "a noble's natural obligation," or "a man's long-cherished ambition," but there had to have been impatience and irritation there as well, and even so…

Isuzu had known, and she'd let it slide.

I'm sorry. Rudy…I'm so sorry…

The way Rundelhaus had wanted it had been so childlike and innocent that Isuzu had seen his dream, too. The dream that a Person of the Earth could become an Adventurer.

"Rudy...is a Person of the Earth...?"

Isuzu nodded, responding to Touya. When she nodded, the tears that were rolling down her cheeks fell from her chin in large drops, but she didn't care. This was Isuzu's punishment.

Rundelhaus had been so kind.

She was just a skinny country bumpkin, but Rundelhaus had treated her like a girl.

She worried about her freckles, and she wasn't the least bit sophisticated, but Rundelhaus had always called her "Mademoiselle."

...And yet, to the very end, she hadn't stopped him properly, had done nothing but get in his way, and she'd said he was dumb and doggish and had treated him just as she pleased.

She'd liked it when he talked to her.

She'd liked it when he complimented her.

She'd liked the way he treated her like a lady.

Isuzu couldn't make the words flood out; it was as if they'd gone mad. They lodged in her throat, pushing up tears and a tiny, moaning voice.

Every single warm, gentle, awkward memory was her punishment for driving Rundelhaus into the jaws of death.

"Oh..." Serara murmured softly.

She cast Instant Heal, then put her ear to his chest. Her expression clouded, and she performed another recovery.

"Huh? Don't tell me..."

Catching sight of an impossible hope, Isuzu pressed Serara for answers.

"I don't know. His pulse is almost gone, but when I heal him, it feels as if there's a very slight response... But I'm sorry. If resurrection won't work, then..."

Isuzu felt the hope she'd only just managed to reclaim crumble to bits. However, there was one girl who'd firmly latched on to those words.

"Not yet."

"Huh?"

"...Please help us. Please. We need your strength, *Shiroe*."

CHAPTER.

5

CONTRACT

▶ NAME: MISA TAKAYAMA

▶ LEVEL: **90**

▶ RACE: **WOLF-FANG TRIBE**

▶ CLASS: **BARD**

▶ HP: **8040**

▶ MP: **12237**

▶ ITEM 1:

[CALAMITY HURTS]

DEATH'S GREAT SCYTHE, SAID TO BRING ABOUT ALL
SORTS OF DISASTERS WITH ONE
SWING. A VICIOUS WEAPON
WITH A HIGH CRITICAL RATE
AND ADDED EFFECTS FOR
MULTIPLE ATTACKS. A RARE ITEM
THAT'S VERY POPULAR AMONG
PLAYERS, NOT ONLY FOR ITS
PERFORMANCE, BUT ALSO FOR ITS
OMINOUS YET AWE-INSPIRING
DESIGN.

▶ ITEM 2:

[DRAGON HORN]

A BATON MADE FROM THE HORN OF A RED
DRAGON. A HIGH-LEVEL PRODUCTION-CLASS
ITEM FOR BARDS. IT
INCREASES THE EFFECT
OF THE SUPPORT SONGS
USED BY MEMBERS OF THE
SAME RAID. ALTHOUGH DIFFICULT
TO USE IN NORMAL PARTY BATTLES,
IT SHOWS ITS TRUE WORTH IN
LARGE BATTLES.

▶ ITEM 3:

[SILVER THREAD–WOVEN GAMBESON]

PRODUCTION-CLASS DEFENSIVE GEAR
MANUFACTURED BY A TAILOR USING CELESTIAL
CORAL BUTTERFLY SILK THREAD MADE BY
ARTIFICERS AND FINE SILVER
THREAD MADE BY BLACKSMITHS.
THIS ITEM REQUIRES RARE
MATERIALS AND HAS A
COMPLICATED PRODUCTION
PROCESS, BUT IN EXCHANGE,
IT'S A MASTERPIECE: LIGHT, STURDY,
AND HIGHLY RESISTANT TO MAGIC.

<Tuxedo>
Wear it well, and you're a gentleman.
Wear just the bowtie, and you're a
gentlemanly pervert.

► **1**

"…Please help us. *We need your strength, Shiroe.*"

At that voice, which was forcing down pain to the point that it was heart-wrenchingly transparent, Shiroe's intuition told him there'd been a disaster.

Minori wasn't the sort of girl who would use a voice like that as a joke. She was serious and kind, stubborn and strong willed. She strove to emulate him.

Precisely because Minori tried to remember everything Shiroe did on the battlefield, right down to his casual habits and the way he walked, Shiroe wanted to teach her everything he knew.

And Minori always returned everything he taught her with effort that was worth more than full marks.

Shiroe didn't know what sort of life Minori had lived back on Earth. He'd never asked. He had no way to measure the feelings of a middle schooler who'd been dropped into a strange land with no one but her little brother.

However, even in this strange land, Minori's straightforwardness didn't seem to have decreased in the slightest.

That was a virtue Shiroe didn't possess. He'd been running away—running from making himself a place to belong.

An earnest girl who wasn't afraid of dealing with strangers…

Minori seemed to idolize him, but Shiroe thought he was the one who was constantly saved by her certainty.

He couldn't remember Minori ever actively asking him for a favor. She'd relied on him, she probably trusted him, and she tried to learn from him; but he didn't think she'd ever openly asked him for help.

It was probably her way of showing pride. Even that was included in Shiroe's respect for Minori.

The fact that she had contacted him by telechat in a voice that seemed to be desperately holding back tears that threatened to spill over at any moment, and the fact that she was relying on him over anyone else, shook Shiroe badly.

The view he saw through the tent flap was that of evening, already shading into purple.

"We've had a casualty. It's Rundelhaus. He's…"

In the telechat, behind Minori's voice, he could hear ragged breathing and shouting.

The telechat function was a bit like a low-quality cell phone. When you were on the receiving end, the audio was replayed near your eardrums and there was no worry that the sound would leak to those around you, but when you were sending, you had to talk aloud, and the surrounding sounds were picked up as well.

Apparently Minori was either still on the battlefield or close to it. Her surroundings seemed turbulent, and he could hear women's voices.

"He's—"

"Rudy is…a Person of the Earth."

Abruptly, another voice cut in.

Shiroe guessed that the voice belonged to Isuzu, the young female Bard Minori had told him about. In order for her to get her voice across this clearly on someone else's telechat, she had to be speaking with her lips practically touching Minori's.

At those few words, Shiroe understood everything.

He stood with enough force to kick the desk away, shouldered one of the magic bags that had been sitting nearby, and dashed out of the tent. He blew the pipe twice, then headed for the open space in the center of the Equestrian Garden without bothering to wait for the griffin's arrival.

"Give me a situation report, Minori."

Three big strides were enough to take him into the open area; he caught a telechat operator who was nearby and shouted for him to call Calasin.

"A fierce battle broke out during the defense of Choushi village. We won, but in the process, Rundelhaus was mortally wounded. Resurrection spells failed, but his body is still warm, and he has a pulse... Only he isn't waking up."

—The resurrection spells had failed.

Enormous wings came sailing across the sky, and Shiroe jumped on, moving more than half unconsciously. Akatsuki had followed him as closely as a shadow, but he barely noticed when she slipped into his arms. The magical beast's girth had been tightened, and he gave it a small sign.

On the strength of that slight sign alone, the huge, well-trained mount leapt into the sky, which was beginning to darken into night.

"His pulse is getting weaker...we think."

"Chant another resurrection spell."

"We've done it twice. He won't wake up..."

Resurrection spells were used to revive fallen comrades. They sounded miraculous, but the difficulty of the spells wasn't that high. In terms of level, all Recovery classes over level 20 knew them. In fact, resurrection spells also had ranks. With low-level spells, although the resurrection would succeed, experience points would be lost.

This was probably why Minori had contacted Shiroe after trying it twice.

No, even more than that...

People of the Earth weren't Adventurers. If they died, their deaths were absolute, and they would not resurrect in the temple. On the other end of the telechat, he could hear stifled sobs and voices talking in the background.

"Tell me your location and who's there."

"Me, Touya. Isuzu. Serara. And Rundelhaus, who isn't reviving. We're near the center of Choushi, at the big intersection."

"Are you safe?"

"There's no sign of the enemy in this area. However, the battle along the embankment is probably still going on. Goblins might attack here at any moment, too..."

—It was over.

A Person of the Earth had sustained damage in battle and was about to lose his life as a result. As far as the situation was concerned, one could very well say it was over. True, according to what Li Gan had said, during the short time before the yin and yang energy separated, resurrection spells could work on People of the Earth as well. However, if the resurrection spells weren't working, things had already reached the degradation phase.

"Shiroe, please save 'im! Save Rudy!"

Suddenly, he heard a strong voice right in his ear.

"Listen, Rudy's—he's dumb, and a moron, but he's strong and cool. Rudy was trying to save us!"

"I'm the one who brought him along. No, I mean, it wasn't exactly me, but Rudy wanted to come, and I didn't stop him. Shiro...e. If there's anything you can do, then—"

A tear-filled voice sounded on the other end of the telechat.

"We need you."

Minori's words echoed in his ears.

Those words were rapidly cooling Shiroe's mind.

He visualized a winter's night, and asphalt that looked ready to develop frost. He lay on that asphalt, his body heat leeching away. It was ominous, but it couldn't have been more serene. It was the image of Shiroe's release.

With all restrictions removed, his thoughts began to run wild. The visualization, which had split up in order to search all courses, examined a matrix of possibilities.

If Minori's counting on me, I have to help.

That wasn't his will. It was already a given.

In order to fulfill that prerequisite, Shiroe kept thinking at high speed.

"Tell Serara to chant a resurrection spell."

"Yes, sir!"

Minori's answer came back instantly.

She didn't challenge him with *Why?* or *But that didn't work.* Minori had placed complete trust in Shiroe. She'd contacted him because she believed that Shiroe would do something.

That was just a wishful assumption, of course.

There were some things even Shiroe couldn't do. Rather, there was an *overwhelming* number of things he couldn't do. In this incomprehensible, unreasonable other world, it was probably fair to say he couldn't do anything.

However, that was neither here nor there. If he couldn't do something, he couldn't do it. He could think about that *after* he'd tried and failed. What was important just now was that Minori had believed "Shiroe can do it," and in that case, there was only one answer Shiroe could give.

He had to try to believe he could succeed.

The feeling of believing rebuilt the matrix inside Shiroe. He shone light on the static—possibilities he'd discarded as impossible—from a new angle.

"I think his pulse got stronger... But he hasn't woken up."

"Wait 150 seconds. Have Touya guard the area. Tell Isuzu to set an MP recovery song. In 150 seconds, you cast a resurrection spell, Minori."

"Yes, sir."

Shiroe remembered what Li Gan had said.

Rundelhaus had died.

Person of the Earth or Adventurer, death was death.

Death in this other world began when all physical activity ceased. First, the body stopped moving, and body and spirit were separated.

The spirit would then be trapped in darkness.

This phenomenon occurred because the communication between yin and yang energy was severed.

Before long, the yin energy began to disperse.

Yin energy was the basic energy of the body, its life-force, and this process was known as degradation. The sturdier the body and the higher its level, the greater this energy was. In other words, degradation took longer.

Rundelhaus was a physically fragile Magic Attack class, and on top of that, he apparently hadn't reached the middle levels yet. Degradation would probably move quickly for him.

It was likely... Not definite, but likely, that the resurrection spell had come too late.

The resurrection magic used by the Recovery classes replenished the yin energy of a body in the process of degradation and rejoined it to the yang energy.

The spell caster gathered the yin energy that had dispersed into the surrounding atmosphere, supplemented any missing life-force with their own life-force, and returned it to the body.

The fact that his body was still warm and had a pulse probably meant that the physical reconstruction had worked to a certain extent. His mind wasn't returning, because the reunification with the yang energy wasn't going well.

If that was the situation, then it was likely…

It was likely that the dispersal of yang energy—soul rot—had begun. Yang energy was mental energy, and the carrier for the spirit. Yang energy that had lost its body began to disperse. A spirit that had lost its yang energy vanished, unable to maintain its identity.

There was no doubt that while Rundelhaus, a low-level player, was still in the process of degradation, soul rot had set in as well.

An Adventurer would have been sent to the temple, their body automatically repaired, and their yang energy linked to their body. Because the body was reconstructed, soul rot didn't occur. In other words, even though physical death occurred, spiritual death did not. They were resurrected in new bodies—aka, immortal.

"It's been a hundred and fifty seconds. I'm casting the resurrection spell now."

"In another hundred and fifty seconds, have Serara cast another resurrection spell. I'm on my way to you now. Keep chanting by turns that way and hold on for eight minutes."

He could hear Minori's report. The resurrection spells used by Minori and other players around level 20 were primitive. Since chanting them took time and left the caster defenseless, they were practically impossible to use in combat, and the recast times were a full three hundred seconds.

However, although they were just starting out, there were two Recovery magic users with Rundelhaus: Serara and Minori.

By having them cast their resurrection spells by turns, that three-hundred-second recast time was cut to 150 seconds. Resurrection spells devoured MP, and at the moment, Shiroe didn't know how long they could be used back-to-back, but there was nothing for it but to let them handle it on site.

The direct trigger of soul rot was the advance of physical degradation. The lack of a body to return to caused the spiritual energy to disperse; howso far it was possible to stop soul rot that had already begun depended on Minori's party's resurrection spells.

After that—

"Akatsuki, don't let me slip."

At Shiroe's words, Akatsuki, who'd been settled in his arms, twisted around, turning to face him. His fellow passenger, who hadn't said a single word for the past few minutes, carefully turned on the griffin's back—a terror-inducing environment—and, in the midst of a night wind that seemed to flay their skin, hugged Shiroe tightly.

Shiroe closed his eyes gently, imagined the items in his bag, and put his hand into it. He didn't know what item he'd need. He didn't even know if it would work.

However, even so, he found an item that was suited to the magic he was about to perform:

An ink Shiroe had painstakingly compounded.

It was the only bottle of its kind in the world: A fragment of soul.

▶2

In the midst of the sunset, Raynesia arrived on the battlefield, attended by the female knight.

This area of the steep-walled valley was under the control of Krusty's strike unit, and they'd been notified that it was secure.

"Ugh..."

"Are you all right?"

The female knight, who was holding a sheaf of documents, didn't look all that sympathetic, but she asked anyway.

In this world, very few people had ever experienced the atmosphere of a battlefield. Death came quickly to demihumans and People of the Earth, and if left alone, their bodies disappeared in less than half a day. No matter what sort of a battle it had been, once the corpses vanished, it was just a wilderness littered with weapons.

However, this particular battlefield had just been created.

The stench of blood was intense, and it affected Raynesia powerfully. Fortunately, the summer wind blew toward them through the greenery and kept it from being quite as bad as she'd anticipated, but even so, she wasn't able to look at the ground.

The female knight walked on.

They were on their way to meet up with Krusty, who was up ahead, to report in and to confirm the details of the operation, or so Raynesia had heard.

The female knight, who had introduced herself as Misa Takayama, had told Raynesia that they were the field monitor squad.

During combat, particularly during raids and battles in places where visibility was bad, it was extremely difficult to grasp the overall situation while fighting in the vanguard.

For that reason, in addition to the raid force that did the actual fighting, D.D.D. set up a field monitor team that ranged in size from a squad to a company. The field monitor team's main duty was to use optical instruments and magic to watch the entire battlefield from a distance and sequentially report battle information to the commander on the frontline.

Raynesia thought Misa Takayama must be a high-ranking officer in D.D.D., because of the way the people around them acted toward her.

Because they'd scouted a route beforehand that wouldn't force them to push through groves of trees, it took less time than she'd expected to descend to the valley floor. Attended by guardian knights, Raynesia reached a broad, stony, mostly dry riverbed that had a swift mountain stream running down its center.

This place seemed to be upstream from the battlefield she'd seen from the heights, and there were no Goblin corpses or traces of battle. The clear, light sound of the stream seemed to chase away the summer heat.

Around them, the Adventurers were taking a break, each of them relaxing any way they pleased. There were all kinds: Some had stripped to the waist and were bathing, while others were tending to their weapons.

They were right in the middle of the battlefield, but at the moment, no enemy units had been deployed nearby, so everyone except for the scout unit was resting in shifts.

Naturally, as a princess, Raynesia had inspected chivalric orders before.

However, in most cases, this had been performed from a balcony, or she had said a few words of greeting from a stage that had been set up for the purpose. Sometimes she'd gone to the parade grounds and spoken to the knights as she walked, but at those times, the knights of Maihama had been standing in rows with their spears neatly lined up.

That meant she'd never walked among knights that were this unreserved, and—in terms of the sensibilities of aristocratic society—impolite.

Of course, Raynesia was a Person of the Earth and a daughter of Maihama. Even if the town of Akiba had joined the League of Free Cities, the Adventurers weren't in a direct master-servant relationship with Raynesia, and so they weren't obligated to pay their respects to her. Raynesia had no intention of feeling put out by that, and she was also becoming more and more accustomed to the idea that they *were* Adventurers, and that their culture was different.

Raynesia had expected their lack of manners, and she hadn't planned to let it startle her or to take them to task for it.

What did surprise Raynesia was the fact that they didn't ignore her.

As her group passed by, the Adventurers called to her, loudly.

"Don't you worry, Princess. We'll get this war mopped up for you ASAP."

"That's a bona-fide Scandinavian angel right there."

"Our advance unit could take care of that pack of wussy goblins all by its lonesome."

"*Dude.* I just saw, like, the actual princess. I need a photo, anybody got a phone?!"

"Hey, Princess, you sure you should be out here? …Oh, Miz Takayama's with you, huh? Scary, scary."

"Ha-ha-ha! Princess, the Chief's up thattaway."

"Whoaaa! Whoaaa!"

"You be real careful you don't get hit by any stray arrows, a'right?"

Their words were rough enough to make her think, *This is what the mercenaries I've heard stories about must be like*, but strangely, they didn't make her feel out of sorts. It was probably because she understood that the Adventurers weren't making light of her or having fun with her. This was the way they normally talked, and when they spoke to her, they meant to be friendly.

Raynesia, however, was a recluse.

As a rule, she wasn't good at communicating or conversing with others.

Until now, she'd handled this sort of event by using her "Perfect Young Lady" mask, the one she'd acquired during her strict training. However, she was already learning that it didn't seem to work well on Adventurers.

Adventurers weren't familiar with aristocratic culture, and they wouldn't jump to the wrong conclusions and do things for her if she only fell silent and looked troubled, or nodded gently, or let her brow cloud over with sorrow.

For that reason, after giving it unusually serious—for her—thought, in order to strictly avoid bringing shame on the House of Cowen and yet match the Adventurers' simple etiquette to the greatest extent possible, Raynesia had come up with her own unique way of doing things.

Specifically, she smiled, raised her right hand to approximately the level of her chest, and gave a little wave.

When Adventurers spoke to her or gave her advice about something, she'd listen attentively to what they said, and then say, simply, "Thank you very much." After all, every last Adventurer was part of the same tribe as the mind-reading menace known as Krusty. Even if she tried to keep up appearances and gloss things over, they'd see through it. Besides, even if she showed them a face that was slightly unladylike, they weren't nobles, and they probably wouldn't care. ...This was the conclusion Raynesia had come to.

By the standards of the fashionable circles in which Raynesia had been rigorously trained, her current attitude and greetings were rude, very nearly those of a common town girl. Still, as she silently excused herself to her grandfather, she was dealing with Adventurers, and this was a battlefield.

However, although Raynesia completely failed to notice because she was trembling at the way she was overstepping her own common sense, her sweet gestures and open smile were incredibly well received by the Adventurers of the strike unit.

Because this mixed strike unit was under Krusty's command, it had been organized around the D.D.D. unit so that his orders would travel all the way through it. However, that alone would have made D.D.D. and Krusty too influential with the Round Table Council. For that reason, and because it was thought that the organization should display the unity of the Round Table Council, it was a mixed army, and about half its troops were veteran players who didn't belong to D.D.D.

Because its members included players affiliated with the Knights of the Black Sword and Honesty, their mantles and insignia were all different. As a result, it looked like a very strange chivalric order indeed to Raynesia, who, with aristocratic sensibilities, had assumed that *guild* meant something like "clan."

In noble society, clans and the relations between them were quite complex. Because kinship and profit intermingled, it couldn't be summed up in a word, but in general terms, the relationships between powerful clans were filled with enmity. This was one of the reasons behind the fact that the League of Free Cities still hadn't been unified.

However, on this battlefield, she didn't see any of that kind of friction.

Of course, from what she could tell from mantle color and insignia, they seemed to have broken into smaller clan groups to relax, but some were taking a light meal with the mixed unit, and some had handed their weapons to others and were having them check the condition. Was the group that was walking around briskly a transport corps?

Raynesia suddenly became aware of another reason for the strangeness she felt:

Even with this many knights in one place, she didn't see any servants or squires. Misa Takayama had explained to her that the unit was composed of the extreme elite, and in a unit like that, she thought the weak might only get in the way. Still, what could it mean to have so very many knights and not a single servant?

The Adventurers do seem to be free of the class system as well, but...

She understood that they were free, but when it showed up as reality, in their actions, Raynesia was taken aback by how unexpected it was, every single time.

"Right. Understood. Keep that up."

Beyond the rocky riverbed, in an open space where the stream meandered and formed a deep pool, Krusty was bathing. He'd stripped off all armor above his waist and was toweling his sweat away.

Even as he did this, he kept muttering; he was probably using the Adventurers' unique long-range communications spell to talk to someone. However, when he saw Misa Takayama and Raynesia's group, he turned back slightly.

Without rushing at all, Krusty wiped down his hard body with a tightly wrung-out cloth. Misa Takayama—who must have been used to Krusty's relaxed composure, or, perhaps it was best to simply call it "calm"—went up to him, report in hand, and began to deliver it orally, speaking rapidly.

Krusty listened, keeping his back turned to her.

He has quite an impressive build, doesn't he...

When he'd been at the Ancient Court, dressed in elegant clothes, she hadn't noticed it all that much. However, when she looked at his naked back like this, his body exuded an aura of overwhelming physical strength. There was a certain wild, animalistic beauty about his heavily muscled back, and in spite of herself, Raynesia stared.

What in the world am I looking at?

Raynesia shook her head, feeling daunted.

Being with Krusty always, always, threw her off.

She missed her peaceful room in Maihama. Raynesia really was a hermit, and the life she preferred was an idle, vegetative existence of eating and sleeping. Her greatest interest was basking in the sun, to the point that she was looking forward to getting old, and quickly, so that she could enjoy the life of a retiree to the fullest.

Raynesia thought that if her recent actions earned her criticism for treachery or corruption of her principles and position, there would really be no arguing with it.

"Understood. In that case, starting with the next location, we'll increase our peripheral monitoring system..."

By the time Misa Takayama's report ended, Krusty had also finished changing. His armor was the same as ever, but he seemed to have changed what he wore under it. His perfectly composed expression was no different from the one he'd shown at the Ancient Court of Eternal Ice, to the point that it actually annoyed her.

"What do you think of the battlefield?" Krusty asked, when he'd come up to her.

The difference in their heights meant that Raynesia was compelled to look up at him from below, and it made her feel disagreeable and dissatisfied. The way he was now, she couldn't find a trace of either the innocent, delighted expression he'd worn in the heat of battle, or its shadow side, that fading fragility.

All that stood before her was a mind-reading menace who was so polite and unconcerned that it made her wonder whether the other things had been an illusion.

"Were you frightened?"

Raynesia, lost in thought, had been late in answering, and Krusty had spoken in a tone of teasing jest.

"Not in the least. I was sure you would protect me, Master Krusty."

If Krusty was going to wear his palace mask, she was prepared to do the same. In any case, when it came to aristocratic turns of phrase, Raynesia's career was far, far longer than his.

"—You seem to have grown quite popular," Krusty added.

When Raynesia turned back, the group of Adventurers who were watching the two of them from a distance froze. The situation was incredibly awkward for Raynesia as well, so she gave them a smile and a little wave, and most of the Adventurers broke into smiles and went back to their duties.

"I don't believe that signifies in the slightest, Master Krusty."

Raynesia turned back to Krusty, loading her words with irritation at the fact that he'd changed the subject. Besides, since he always took this attitude, Raynesia was never sure whether she should use palace manners or Adventurer manners.

"And in any case—"

Just as Raynesia was about to take a step forward and hit him with a few more choice phrases, a howl echoed across the valley. The sound rang out from the eastern ridge, and although she could tell it was clearly far away, a cold wind blew into Raynesia's heart.

"What was that...?"

"A Dire Wolf. Must be quite a large one. From the sound of its voice, I'd say it's the Huge variety."

"...Is it...the Goblin King?"

"The Goblin King isn't on this battlefield. He isn't likely to leave Seventh Fall. This is the Goblin General's personal guard unit."

"His personal guard..."

Involuntarily, Raynesia clasped her hands tightly in front of her chest. She'd seen how bravely Krusty and the others had fought the night before, and she believed in their strength. However, Raynesia herself knew nothing about combat, and that made it scary. ...Not to mention the fragility she sensed in Krusty, as if he might melt away, into the battle.

She wasn't sure whether she should ask him to be careful or urge him on.

As Raynesia hesitated, wondering what she should say to him, the Dire Wolf's ferocious howl drifted down to them again. On hearing that voice, Krusty's lips twisted. Completely unaware of Raynesia's feelings, he broke into a cruel smile and murmured:

"I do believe we will leave cleaning out their nest for later. Shall we not begin by offering these Zantleaf trash as a blood sacrifice?"

▶ 3

Choushi's long central avenue made a perfect landing strip for the griffin. Using lift, the magical beast coasted in without moving its wings at all. On its back, Shiroe lightly touched Akatsuki's head and whispered: "Keep people clear of the area. You mustn't let anyone near, players or monsters."

Akatsuki nodded without saying a word.

Paying no heed to the fact that their ground speed was faster than a horse at full gallop, the two of them leapt down from the griffin, then parted ways. With movements that barely betrayed the influence of gravity, Akatsuki sprinted forward, darting like a swallow, and disappeared beyond the roofs of the stone edifices.

After confirming this, Shiroe ran toward Touya, who was waving at him.

Minori's group of four was gathered there, desperation clear in their expressions. According to a telechat he'd received earlier, although the *Ocypete* had arrived, resistance from the sahuagins was preventing them from going ashore. Naotsugu's group had relieved Minori's party and was fielding the goblins.

Well, that's more convenient for us, anyway.

He didn't know whether the "magic" he was about to attempt would succeed or not. It was based in theory, and Shiroe had carried out previous repeated experiments, but it was still a gamble. ...Even if it succeeded, considering what would follow, the fewer witnesses there were, the better.

The place might have been a shop, or maybe a tavern.

A young man lay in the shadows, under the wide eaves that opened onto the central avenue. The tear-stained girl who made no move to leave his side, a girl with charming freckles, was probably Isuzu.

They were surrounded by faces Shiroe knew well: Touya, who looked as if he was gritting his teeth against pain; Serara, her face worried; Minori, who seemed to be holding a sense of purpose locked away inside her.

Shiroe calmed his mind.

The temperature of the surrounding air was still high, but the inside of his head was as quiet as the sky on a winter's night.

"Minori, invite me to your party."

"Yes, sir."

Minori nodded, wasting no time on questions. Neither she nor Akatsuki did at times like this, and he was grateful for it. He examined the young man who was assumedly Rundelhaus. He certainly did have an air of refined nobility about him. His body was warm and he had a pulse, but as expected, he was unconscious. On the party menu, his "Dead" status blinked.

"Miss Isuzu, wasn't it? Keep singing Nocturne of Meditation, just like that. I'm about to cast a new spell. Don't speak of it to anyone."

Shiroe spoke to the new players in a tone that was almost harsh.

"If you can't agree to that, then either give up or leave this place."

None of the assembled players flinched at Shiroe's words. They all nodded.

"All right. Then I'll begin."

Shiroe selected a special magic skill from the icon. He was going to use Mana Channeling. It was a spell unique to Enchanters, and no one really seemed to know what to use it on.

It absorbed the MP of all members of a party, averaged it, and sent it back.

Right... Yang energy is the vehicle of the spirit, whose vehicle in turn is magic. In that case...

As the chant rang out, the MP was drawn out of every member of the party, collecting in Shiroe. Shiroe's level was far and away the highest in the group.

To Minori and the others, who hadn't yet reached level 30, the pull of the spell he was chanting must have felt like tremendous pressure.

Minori and Touya, and even Serara, grew paler and paler. Their MP was being siphoned away. Minori and the others seemed to be struggling to endure a sense of loss, like sudden dizziness. Only Isuzu continued to hold Rundelhaus's hand tightly, softly singing a mournful old folk ballad, although her face was pallid as well.

With his eyes half closed, Shiroe experienced the effect of the magic.

Right now, he was holding nearly all the MP that had been collected from the other members of his party. Although it was no more than a faint aura, Shiroe could feel the lingering fragrance of the others' spirits inside him. Touya's single-mindedness; the aura of Minori's earnest, serious magic... These were being deployed on the field of magic Shiroe controlled.

No doubt he held MP from Serara, from Isuzu, and from Rundelhaus himself as well.

The various MP, with their subtly different flavors, were blended into primordial "spirit energy." In accordance with Shiroe's guidance, magical circuits took shape and formed connections with his companions.

Shiroe divided the MP equally, then redistributed it.

Ghk.

The sudden outrush of MP filled Shiroe with a feeling like anemia.

His MP was greater than that of anyone else in the party. Enchanters were magic users to begin with, and they boasted one of the highest MP volumes in all the classes. On top of that, Shiroe was level 90. Joining a party of Adventurers with levels in the low 30s and redistributing MP was the same as using Shiroe to recover the others' MP at a stroke.

"Minori, use resurrection. Serara, cast back-to-back healing spells."

Everything until now had been the prelude. Shiroe kept issuing orders. They didn't have much time. They would probably have only one chance, just one word.

Rundelhaus was a Person of the Earth.

Because he wasn't an Adventurer, he wouldn't come back from the dead.

And Rundelhaus had died.

That meant he would not resurrect.

This was an absolute. There was no way to overrule it.

However, due to the Enchanter's mana redistribution spell, all members' MP had been recovered... In other words, their spirits and yang energy had been energized.

The mind's failure to return was a phenomenon that occurred because the circuits between yang and yin energy were broken. Technically, Rundelhaus was a vegetable. In that case, all they had to do was force those connections open again.

Shiroe took the second measure out of his bag.

"From this point on, we're racing against time."

While the echo of his words still hung in the air, he cast Revenant Incense.

It was a medicine that granted temporary life to fallen companions or creatures, bringing them back as special monsters: zombies to be used in battle. Its power was restoration, not resurrection. The effect was short, and after three minutes, certain death would follow. For Adventurers, it meant a mandatory trip back to the temple.

However, for Rundelhaus, whose only option under the circumstances was to let his yin energy disperse, the item held another possibility.

Either way, his body would be destroyed, along with the spirit and yang energy that clung to it.

Revenant Incense was a way to forcibly connect Rundelhaus's

recharged yang energy to his body. In exchange for unavoidable death in three minutes' time, for three minutes only...Rundelhaus would be pulled back to this world.

A false restoration...with a time limit. She must have known that.

As fat tears rolled down Isuzu's face, her hand tightened on the NPC's.

"Oh..."

Rundelhaus's eyes opened, very slightly, as if he were having a dream.

Isuzu cried, holding his hand. There was no telling whether Rundelhaus was conscious or not. He'd opened his eyes, but it might have been no more than a physical, conditioned reflex.

"Rudy...?"

"Mademoiselle Isuzu... Oh. My friends. I see... I suppose...I must have died."

Even after death, the connection that linked yin and yang energy was merely severed, and the mind remained. For Adventurers, the game screen went monochrome, and they watched their companions fighting. They didn't know what happened for People of the Earth, but Rundelhaus seemed to understand the current situation.

He gave a tiny laugh, then spoke to them in a voice that still held no strength:

"No, no, stop... Don't look like that. What could be more natural than to lay down one's life in battle?"

"—Natu...ral..."

At Touya's words, Shiroe felt a sharp pang in his chest.

A death this tremendously heavy, something that wouldn't even be a plausible joke in the game—this was "only natural" for People of the Earth.

"Even so, I wanted to become an Adventurer. I do hope you won't blame Mademoiselle Isuzu. It was I who begged her to allow it."

"No, I knew, too! I'd noticed, but I didn't do anything!"

A cry that was nearly a shriek escaped Minori. At her words, everyone abruptly understood: Even Minori, who had been conducting herself calmly until now, had privately been badly rattled.

"Ha-ha-ha! Yes, Mademoiselle Minori. Thank you. ...It's nothing to worry about."

"No, I'm worried about it," Shiroe broke in.

There was no time.

Shiroe thought about the magnitude of the terror of the thing he was about to attempt. It might be an enormous mistake. It was an act that could threaten the order of the world.

Even if it succeeded, there was no telling what effect the aftermath of this incident would have on the world.

In addition, he had no way to predict how the world would take this proposal.

Still, the young man in front of him who'd said his good-byes so philosophically had called himself an Adventurer.

That was no player's nickname. It was the name of Shiroe's companions, those who traveled this world and discovered sunrises no one had ever seen before.

If he called himself by that name, then he was a descendent of the tribe *She* had entrusted to him.

"No, I'm worried about it, Rundelhaus Code. I can't have someone who gives up over a thing like this calling himself an Adventurer. It's nowhere near enough. ...What did you learn in order to end in a backwater alley like this? What did you find in that dungeon? Not strategy or tactics. Wasn't it the determination to survive, and an unyielding spirit that would use any means available to do it?"

"Mister Shiroe..."

"Your determination is nowhere near enough, Rundelhaus."

"What am I supposed to do, then?! Tell me that!!"

Rundelhaus's eyes were brimming with frustration and chagrin. Even as he said there was no help for it, his heart wasn't entirely able to accept that, and was growing misty, was beginning to run.

And, for that very reason, Shiroe made up his mind to use the spell.

"Listen to me."

Shiroe took out a messily written document, something he'd drawn up on the back of the griffin, and thrust it out at Rundelhaus.

"That's..."

"It's...a contract?"

The paper Shiroe had taken from his bag was unmistakably a contract. It was written on Fairy King Paper, which was created from the best materials Shiroe could use, and penned with Aurora's Gaze Ink: a handmade item, the only one of its kind in the world.

"Contract— Shiroe, representative of Log Horizon, concludes the following contract with Rundelhaus Code. One: At the date and time on which Rundelhaus Code signs this document, Shiroe will accept him into the guild Log Horizon. Two: As a member of the guild Log Horizon, Rundelhaus Code will attend to his duties in a manner that befits his status and those duties. Three: Log Horizon will, based on mutual consultation and to the greatest extent possible, provide Rundelhaus with the support necessary to the successful completion of his duties. —This includes the identity of 'Adventurer.' Four: This contract is concluded through the agreement of both parties in a spirit of mutual respect, and, even in the event that the contract is rendered invalid, anything acquired by either party during the period of the contract will remain theirs. In conclusion, as proof of the establishment of this contract, two copies will be drawn up and signed by both parties, with one copy to be kept by each."

He heard a gasp.

"An Adventurer—?"

"But Shiroe, that's… That's…!"

The development of spells that had not existed in the *Elder Tales* game.

Shiroe had registered this possibility quite some time ago.

"In other words, if Chefs cook in the mewsual way, without mewsing the menu, the flavors of the ingredients will shine through in the resulting dish."

Nyanta had said this to Shiroe on their journey home from Susukino.

Then it had been demonstrated to be true.

However, the phenomenon wasn't limited to Chefs. Shiroe had persuaded the people around him of this fact at the Round Table Council.

If someone with an appropriate creative skill used appropriate personal abilities to make something—without relying on the item creation menu—it was possible to produce things that didn't exist in this other world.

That had been the true meaning of Nyanta's discovery.

It had been two months since then. Shiroe had researched the things he envisioned, continuing to experiment. This had been an idea he'd come up with to use as an ace up his sleeve during the Round Table

Council establishment uproar, but he'd accumulated further information through his subsequent research, and it had evolved.

He had taken inspiration from the Spirit Theory Li Gan had spoken of, and now his research was about to bear fruit.

Rundelhaus was a Person of the Earth.

Not only that, but in three minutes' time, without fail, he would die.

People of the Earth couldn't resurrect.

That meant Rundelhaus would vanish.

—In that case.

The answer was obvious: "During those three minutes, make Rundelhaus an Adventurer."

Through experiments, he'd established that Scribes could create simple contracts and various types of documents. With a sufficient Scribe level and magical materials, they could even create applications for quests, promissory notes, and other items that had magical or binding effects.

However, even in terms of special contracts like those, this one was of the highest rank.

A contract that admitted a Person of the Earth to a guild and gave them the identity of "Adventurer" sounded like fraud, even to Shiroe. However, precisely because that was the case, in order to fulfill those requirements, he'd used the skills of a level-90 Scribe and an ink created through unstinting use of ultraprime magical materials he'd collected during his *Elder Tales* days.

Shiroe held the contract right in front of Rundelhaus's nose.

"I've already signed it. Your signature is all that's needed."

"—ven...tu...rer..."

"If that's what you want."

The young, mud-spattered Sorcerer gave a hoarse, nearly involuntary murmur. Shiroe spoke to him:

"This contract carries risk. It will probably transform you somehow, turning you into a being completely unlike what you have been up till now. Adventurers are still newcomers to this world, and we don't know what sort of trouble we may be pulled into in the future. We probably don't possess as much glory as you think we do."

"What I want to become..."

The "dead" flag was still blinking on his status, and his HP was draining away before their very eyes, but Rundelhaus didn't even glance at it as he responded.

"...is an Adventurer. If I can save people in need, I won't trouble myself over trivialities. ...What I want isn't glory. It's to be...an Adventurer."

With shaking hands, Rundelhaus grasped the pen that had been held out to him, but he fumbled and dropped it. The effect of Revenant Incense was nearly spent. The link between Rundelhaus's yin and yang energy was fading.

"Rudy... It's okay."

Isuzu steadied his hand.

"I'll sign it with you."

Isuzu supported Rundelhaus as if she were hugging him from behind. Touya helped her. Minori and Serara continued to chant recovery spells. Everyone watched as Rundelhaus signed.

As his friends' encouragement warmed his trembling fingers, the magic ink took the shape of Rundelhaus's name. The signature flared up, blazing into golden light. Shiroe's trick was accepted by this other world, and became a new rule.

"Die once, Rundelhaus... You'll revive in the temple."

As Shiroe spoke, somewhere, he felt large gears begin to turn. The dispersing yin energy drifted up as particles, being sent to Akiba. In the midst of that fantastic scene, all the players except Shiroe stared with expressions of blank amazement.

This was the magic creation that would earn Shiroe a new byname: "Scrivener of the East."

▶4

Once again, a battle was being fought in the darkness.

In the heart of Zantleaf's central hills.

As before, the battle was taking place in a steep-walled valley. The only things that were not like the previous occasion were the width of the valley that served as the stage and the scale of the clash. When she asked Misa Takayama why valleys were chosen as battlefields, the answer was "Battalions need a fairly large, open space to assemble, and although units could be organized in the tree-covered mountains, it wouldn't be possible to set up headquarters."

When she thought about it that way, it made sense to Raynesia.

Even if they were demihumans, goblins had the bare minimum of intelligence. It stood to reason that when conducting military operations, they would naturally obey certain established tactics.

In addition, if the battle was staged in a mountain valley, there would naturally be several ridges that offered views down into that valley. This time, Misa Takayama and the rest of the observation squad had chosen one of these ridges. Unlike last time, only the bare minimum of furniture, such as the observation table, had been set out. This was partly due to the fact that they weren't sure whether or not they would have to move, and partly because Raynesia had firmly refused. Misa Takayama seemed subtly relieved, and from her attitude, Raynesia guessed that it really had been done out of consideration for her the previous time.

However, all these things were mere trifles.

Raynesia's interest was focused on the battle that was already in progress on the valley floor. The same was probably true of Misa Takayama and the others as well.

The unit was accompanied by countless Dire Wolves. According to Misa Takayama's explanation, they were goblin Tamers. The savage goblin tribes didn't have complex societies the way humans did, but they did have classes and primitive division of roles.

Most goblins were light infantry or soldiers with javelins, but she'd been told that some goblins had special roles. The best-known classes were Tamer and Shaman. Goblin Tamers sometimes bred and raised owlbears, hippogriffs, Dire Wolves, and the like.

Even from her vantage point, the unit deployed in the valley below seemed to have several hundred Dire Wolves with it. It was a scene straight out of a nightmare, as though the dark earth was writhing with a will of its own.

"Those seem to be a specially bred mutant strain," Misa Takayama continued, calmly.

"I fought them myself on a previous raid. They're Dire Wolves that are regularly exposed to undead miasma as they grow, and they have poisonous fangs. If this many of them are being used as a concentrated force, one of the tribes that followed the Goblin King must have included Tamers. ...How very interesting. I had no idea *Elder Tales* had such detailed background information."

"W-will they be all right...?"

"It's ridiculous even to worry."

Misa Takayama sounded completely disinterested, but Raynesia couldn't be so optimistic. The unit deployed in the valley really did seem to be several hundred strong, and the Goblin General was somewhere at its center, probably near the foreign tents and the mobile fortress on enormous wheels.

Even Raynesia wasn't worried about that monster of a knight, but his subordinates were knights as well. If they died in this battle... Well, no, they wouldn't *die*, but if they were grievously injured or in terrible pain, she would feel awful.

However, quite apart from Raynesia's concern, the hostilities commenced.

"That square... How lovely."

"It's called a quadrilateral formation. It's a military formation."

Misa Takayama must have been free just then; she came up beside Raynesia.

She continued, pointing at the nearly square ranks Krusty's strike unit had formed.

"It's a comparatively popular formation for raids. Since raid units are organized in multiples of four, quadrilateral formations are easy to put together from a command perspective as well. ...Because of the square's four sides, you see. In general terms, quadrilaterals are defensive formations. The front side is made up of personnel that can mount close-range attacks, with a focus on the Warrior classes; while the long-range attack classes behind them conduct mainly magic attacks. Since it's a closer formation, it's a poor choice when the enemy has members that can use powerful range attacks, but against enemies that are like packs of wild beasts, it has the defensive strength of an iron wall."

"Then…"

Raynesia's guess was correct.

The powerful front line easily repelled the Dire Wolves' attacks, while a barrage of arrows and spells flew from the rear ranks. Thanks to the night-vision balm, Raynesia could see even in the dark, but the pillars of flame that began to go up all over the battlefield were bright enough to render it unnecessary.

"They're about to make their move."

Misa Takayama pointed directly at the battlefield.

As if led by her fingertip, the entire square began to move. Even as its shape warped slightly, turning it into a trapezoid, the square territory advanced, steadily paring away the enemy's forces.

Misa had called it a defensive formation, but that assessment was completely misleading. It was the first large-scale battle Raynesia had ever seen, and since she'd never directly watched the castle knights fight a defensive battle, she had nothing to compare it to, but the scene in front of her was thoroughly unsuited to the word *defense*.

It was, in a manner of speaking, a square hole.

Krusty's raid army looked like a jet-black hole in the huge goblin army, and anything that touched it, goblin or Dire Wolf, was promptly dealt with. With a fastidiousness that bordered on lunacy, it was making the enemy forces as if they had never been.

"Now, watch carefully."

Just then, from the center of the square formation, four birds of flame soared up like an enormous bonfire. The gigantic birds, which scattered orange and deep crimson fire, were clearly summoned creatures. However, Raynesia had never heard of summoned creatures like these before. From what she knew of them, summoned creatures ranged from the size of a fist to the size of a puppy, and she'd never seen any creature with such ferocious grace.

"They're phoenixes. Players at or above level eighty-six can make contracts with them. They're high-level spirits with flame attributes, sacred and elegant beasts that qualified Summoners who have cleared a significantly difficult quest are able to contract with. …What is it?"

What was it? What else could it be?

Those creatures were on fire.

Wh-wha... What sort of beings do these Adventurers think they're summoning?! How can that possibly not be against the rules?!

Finally, and very nearly too late, Raynesia understood.

Krusty's attitude was most certainly not a bluff. He was simply being himself.

No wonder Misa Takayama had said, *It's ridiculous even to worry.*

True, there was no telling what would happen on a battlefield. However, there were men in this world who would stand on these unpredictable battlefields for fun. Men of that breed ruled the battlefield with an astronomical amount of experience that others had no hope of matching.

The people under his command were Adventurers who'd put in the same overwhelming training. Common sense regarding knights should never have been brought into it.

Raynesia felt it from the bottom of her heart:

The Adventurers were completely beyond her.

With an explosive roar, the Goblin General's huge, armed vehicle broke apart. A heavily armored bodyguard detail and a gigantic, stern goblin leapt from the shattered tank, but Krusty's army only pressed forward.

Raynesia's ears caught a voice they shouldn't have been able to hear:

Now, then. Let's rip them to pieces.

The voice was a whisper, calm, yet accompanied by a joy like honey on the lips, and it definitely belonged to Krusty.

Raynesia didn't have the ability to telechat, and there was no way she could have heard what Krusty said at this distance. Even so, she had certainly heard it.

Krusty's huge, double-bladed ax came down, pointing out the enemy, and an attack unit sprang out of the quadrilateral formation like a jet-black spear. A group of warriors with twin swords began to slash through the hoard of Goblins as easily as if they'd been thin fabric.

The Goblin General brandished an overdecorated spear and howled with rage, but Krusty stood as if to blot out the moon, and his display lasted only until Krusty's shadow swallowed him up.

"That ends the main course. ...Let's leave the rest for the General Staff Office's nets."

Misa Takayama shut her report with a light *thump*. Her voice was calm, as if she was delivering perfectly obvious information.

▶ **5**

The rendezvous happened before dawn.

The sahuagins' resistance had been stronger than anticipated, and it had taken time to get ashore from the *Ocypete*. As an experimental ship, the *Ocypete* had been given all sorts of different functions, but fundamentally, after all, it was a transport ship.

It wasn't a military assault and landing vessel.

It was also true that they'd been unsure of their ability to bring monsters that moved effortlessly in the water under their control, and this had made it difficult for them to conduct any bold maneuvers.

However, by the middle of the night, Naotsugu and Nyanta had summoned their griffins and ferried over a small number of Adventurers through the air, and these had begun to replenish the fighting power on the Choushi side. With Summoners on both banks, it was only a matter of time before they drove the sahuagins from a certain area.

"Well, kiddo! I wasn't expectin' *you* to turn up here."

Marielle grinned broadly.

There was no telling when he'd arrived, but as the sun set, Shiroe came walking out of the town, reassigned the limited number of personnel, and then began building a line of defense in the fields to the north of the village as well.

Shiroe was the leader of Log Horizon.

In other words, he was one of the eleven guild masters on the Round Table Council. That said, in comparison with that title, his name recognition was very low.

Of course, the particulars and internal circumstances of the establishment of the Round Table Council weren't at all secret. As a result, among well-informed Adventurers, Shiroe's name carried weight. However, compared to Krusty and Isaac, who were leaders of major guilds, or to Marielle, who had a vast circle of acquaintances, his face wasn't well-known.

True, once you talked to him, you found he was an agreeable, compassionate young man, but at first he was just a *biiiiit* tough to approach… Or so Marielle thought, at any rate.

He's a good kid, sure, but…! That face! Those eyes! They're scary!

Coming to this conclusion on her own, Marielle nodded vigorously, but Henrietta would probably have told her, "After you get to them, Marielle, most Adventurers are good kids."

For those reasons, Shiroe's appearance wasn't widely known (and he got called "a good kid" by Marielle!), but the impact of his arrival certainly wasn't a small one.

His reputation for courage might have been inferior, but Shiroe was the expeditionary army's counselor. Reinforcements directly from headquarters boosted morale naturally.

Shiroe had appeared in town quite suddenly, and the *Ocypete* unit had appeared at nearly the same time. This gave the bone-tired defense unit the impression that he'd come leading the *Ocypete* troops.

Marielle used that effect to the max.

She cheered on the defense unit at the top of her lungs, for one. The defense unit had been exhausted by the sahuagins' mass tactics, but the news of the arrival of reinforcements and Marielle's cheers restored their fighting spirit at a stroke. As spirits and summoned animals conjured from the *Ocypete* performed super-long-range support, every player, newbies included, worked hard enough for several people each and expelled the sahuagins.

The corpses of sahuagins that had fallen at the water's edge were taken by the waves with the tide, or else vanished after a set time had elapsed. In the midst of it all, the fierce battle continued far into the night.

Late at night, after the Adventurers had somehow managed to end the battle with a victory:

Completely worn out, the Adventurers who'd participated in the summer camp collapsed any way they pleased around the port between the Great Zantleaf River and the coastal beach.

The newly arrived unit, which still had strength to spare, had taken over the defense of the town for them and guard duty as well. The only ones gathered in this open area were the members of the summer camp, who'd fought full-time through defensive battles with both the goblins and the sahuagins.

Even as she thought that she should probably adopt an attitude that would set a better example, Marielle had also spread out her mantle and thrown herself onto it, facedown.

Haaaaaah... Somehow or other, we did it...

The Crescent Moon League had never participated in any large-scale conflicts or battles. Marielle had never taken command of such complicated battle lines in her life.

They were total amateurs. If this defensive battle had succeeded, Marielle thought, it was all due to the height of the new Adventurers' motivation and the support they'd received from Naotsugu and the other veteran players.

"You okay, Miss Mari?"

A voice spoke from above her, much closer than she'd expected.

It belonged to Naotsugu, the guy she'd just been thinking about.

"Dy'eek?!"

As Marielle sprang up, Naotsugu sat down beside her. He'd changed clothes at some point, and he was currently wearing a cool summer tunic shirt and loose trousers.

"What the heck kind of voice was that, Miss Mari?"

"Wow, hon, that's no fair. Why'd you change?!"

At Marielle's question, Naotsugu looked away uncomfortably.

"Well... Armor's heavy, yeah? Somebody else is on duty tonight, so why not?"

When she looked around the area, her bone-weary friends were also sitting up—although they moved sluggishly, like zombies—and seemed to be thinking about at least attempting to change clothes.

"Uuuu. Me, too?"

"You okay?"

"Erg. Not *real* okay..."

Marielle pressed her hands to her temples. The inside of her head felt numb and heavy from repeated spell use.

Clerics were recovery spell experts. In addition to their unique recovery spells, they could use spells in a wide range of configurations, and in terms of defensive ability and recovery performance alone, they boasted variation that was head and shoulders above the other Recovery classes.

During this group battle, Marielle hadn't joined a party. Instead, she'd dashed around the combat area as a lone leader. She'd gone around casting recovery spells from the outside, adopting a strategy known as street-corner healing.

She didn't think that strategy had necessarily been wrong, but the work had been a lot harder than she'd expected. Marielle had never completely drained her MP more than ten times in one day before, and the result had been a crushing headache.

"Maybe you should rest up a bit more, huh?"

"Uuuuuu…"

To be honest, Marielle didn't really want to move.

"The baths are probably full up, anyway."

"They've got baths?"

Baths were cutting-edge facilities, something that had only recently appeared in Akiba. The idea that there were state-of-the-art facilities in Choushi startled Marielle.

"Well, yeah. The only reason we didn't have baths in Akiba was because tubs weren't one of the pieces of furniture Adventurers could make. Or actually, technically, we had *tubs*, but they were just modeled shapes. They wouldn't fill up or heat water. Still, that was all, remember? Back when this was *Elder Tales*, we didn't need to take baths. The People of the Earth have always wanted baths, and they've got the facilities for it."

"Th-they do, huh?!"

Marielle held her head and let herself fall on her face.

In that case, even in Akiba, if they'd gone to the houses of the handful of People of the Earth who lived there, would they have found baths?

Marielle remembered the time she'd stealthily heated water in the guild kitchen in the middle of the night. She'd been rinsing off in a small washtub when she'd been discovered by Henrietta, and it had almost turned into a huge uproar. Henrietta had been real scary that time. Just remembering it made her expression turn gloomy.

"Anyway, it sounds like they're full up. We're crashing the baths at the inn and the village chief's house. And, by the way, the bath at the inn is guys only, and the village chief's house is for the ladies."

"Uh-huh. Gotcha. …I'm gonna cool down here a bit more."

"Yeah, yeah."

Naotsugu sat cross-legged, settling in.

Marielle slumped on her mantle, which was spread out on the grass. Pale moonlight shone down on them both.

When a cool breeze caressed her cheek, Marielle glanced over at Naotsugu, moving only her eyes.

As he gazed up at that white moon, Naotsugu was using a big, tropical-looking leaf to fan Marielle.

Oh…

Marielle felt as though her blood, which still glowed and buzzed with the residual heat of the battle, had finally regained a little of its calm. Thanks to this young clown who simply stayed beside her without saying a word, her rattled feelings were growing tranquil.

"Say, hon?"

"What?"

Naotsugu's laid-back voice brought home to Marielle the fact that the battle was truly over. They'd fought. They'd survived. And they'd managed to successfully defend this town. During the battle, enemy attacks had sent some Adventurers back to the temple in Akiba, but only a few of them.

"We did good, right?"

"Sure we did. We kept the town safe, right to the end."

Marielle was aware that, right now, she was smiling an even bigger, less controlled smile than normal. It was probably a smile so sickly sweet it didn't bear looking at. …But she didn't care about that, either.

Just for now, she wanted to bask in Naotsugu's consideration as it stroked her cheek under the moonlight.

▶ **6**

Somewhere, he heard the sound of a distant bell.

The area was filled with a refreshing fragrance and gleaming specks of light.

On top of an elaborately carved marble bier, Rundelhaus sat up.

This is...

Through the window, he could see a starry sky. Apparently it was night.

However, the ornamental plants placed here and there around this stone room gave off a substance like butterfly scales that emitted a strange light and brightly illuminated the space.

I see. This must be...the temple...

Rundelhaus understood. He'd heard rumors about it, but of course he'd never been inside it before. In any case, unlike Adventurers, People of the Earth didn't worship at the temple. ...Even if they *did* pray at the church.

The temple was one of the special facilities associated with the Adventurers, and it was more of a magical ruin than a religious building. Like the other People of the Earth, Rundelhaus had never used a facility like this one before.

For now... Good, I think I can move.

Still sitting on the bier, he tried carefully moving his body.

Right hand, left hand, both legs, shoulders—nothing seemed to be wrong anywhere. He felt a lingering fatigue in the marrow of his bones, but that was probably an aftereffect of being sent back here and revived.

He'd heard that being resurrected by the temple reduced your experience points. Rundelhaus opened his status screen, and he was startled by how much information it held.

The detail of the status screen for Adventurers was beyond anything he'd imagined: It showed everything from adjusted values for various abilities to subtle equipment bonuses, and detailed bars for MP and HP displayed their values in increments of one-tenth of a percent.

Even as the information dazzled him, he looked at the experience points column. As expected, it had gone down considerably. There was no help for that. Not only had he been sent back and revived, they'd used multiple resurrection spells on him earlier. This drop in experience points was a natural price.

But he hadn't died.

That alone filled Rundelhaus's heart to the brim.

He hadn't particularly longed for the identity or position of an Adventurer. What he'd admired was the way they lived. To

Rundelhaus, who'd been born as the third son of a corrupt noble family, the Adventurers' freedom and their justice that saved people had been dazzling enough to pierce his heart.

Abruptly, something caught his eye. Rundelhaus flipped between tabs on the status screen. What he found there was the word "Adventurer."

Name: Rundelhaus Code
Main Class: Sorcerer
Subclass: Adventurer

For a little while, Rundelhaus gazed at the letters in blank amazement.

I see. I didn't have a subclass, did I... That contract put me into a new subclass. If that's Adventurer, then...

Hastily, Rundelhaus checked the subclass abilities. The ones he saw were unfamiliar, but he'd heard about them in rumors: They were the Adventurers' abilities. "The ability to return to the temple and resurrect," "Telechat ability," "Acquisition and adjustment of experience points," "Bank safe deposit box," "Detailed status." In addition, all sorts of other bonuses were listed as abilities, although Rundelhaus didn't even know what they did.

There's so much here... With this much power, I could...

His lost time wouldn't return. Rundelhaus's past wouldn't change. But, from now on, he might not spend any more endless nights ruing his lack of power.

And, best of all, he'd be able to live in Akiba without hiding who he really was, alongside the companions with whom he'd bonded so deeply at the summer camp, who now seemed closer to him than anyone. He might be able to build a home once again. A place where he could be himself.

Rundelhaus remembered.

He remembered an Adventurer who had traveled through, conquering all the dissolute aristocrats.

He had wished he could have been like that person, and at the same time, he had cursed them, thinking he never wanted to be like that. But if he were granted another chance, he would become an Adventurer.

Then, Rundelhaus had vowed, he could measure the value of the miracle he had wished for.

This small burial chamber was the spot from which he'd make his second start. The young man with glasses and that serious face had also been an Adventurer. He was someone Rundelhaus's friends Minori and Touya respected: Their guild master.

I wonder if that Shiroe fellow knows of vistas I do not...

As Rundelhaus basked in the deep emotion of his resurrection, from a distance, loud footsteps approached.

"Rudy!"

The stone door to the room with the altar was flung open with nearly enough force to pulverize it, and Isuzu appeared. From the doorway, she glared at Rundelhaus with a complicated expression on her face, as if she was angry and troubled at the same time.

"Hello, Mademoiselle Isuzu. ...Erm, what's the matter?"

"'Wh-what's...the matter'...? No..."

Isuzu strode over to him, then drew herself up to her full height. Since Rundelhaus was sitting on the low bier, her head was higher than his, and when she stood like that, even if he looked up, it was hard to make out her expression. He heard something that sounded like a damp sniffle, but Isuzu's voice was definitely angry.

"What were you thinking, pushing yourself like that? What if you'd died? Stupid Rudy!"

"That 'stupid' was uncalled for. Some justice is worth carrying through to the end, Mademoiselle Isuzu, even if it means risking your life. Just as it is impossible to set a yoke on Adventurers' free souls, no one can halt my fight!"

"When I say 'Wait,' you wait!!"

"That's ridiculous—"

"You *wait*!!"

Isuzu's voice was dictatorial, and even Rundelhaus got annoyed. That said, when he thought about why Isuzu was there, he realized something.

Isuzu was the only one of his companions who'd realized that Rundelhaus was a Person of the Earth. In hindsight, Minori seemed to have known as well, but Isuzu was the only one who'd asked Rundelhaus himself, had pressed him with questions, and had cooperated with his wish to become an Adventurer.

Besides, the fact that she was here right now meant she'd used Call of Home to follow him all the way back to Akiba when he'd resurrected.

"I'm, um, sorry… I feel I may have worried you."

The instant Rundelhaus, who was still seated, spoke those words, a blow hard enough to bring tears to his eyes landed on his head.

Rundelhaus didn't know why he'd been hit, but he'd lived to be the age he was with the blood of nobles in his veins. He knew very well that when a lady was in this state, there was nothing to do but to fall all over yourself apologizing.

"My apologies. I shouldn't have done that, Mademoiselle Isuzu." "I-I'm sorry. I won't do anything like it again, so…" "Would you at least tell me why you're—"

Every word he spoke brought two or three more blows down on him. Rudy's head had been struck so often it was hot, and his mind was growing hazy.

"All right. I'll do as you say, Mademoiselle Isuzu."

"Really?"

"Really. I swear on the gods."

"You're going to tell me about when you were little, too."

"Why would you want… —?! A-all right. I'll tell you."

"If you do crazy things like that, no matter how many lives you've got, it'll never be enough."

"I have seen the error of my ways."

"Okay, then. Shake."

Huh…?

At those words, Rundelhaus looked up at Isuzu.

Isuzu's sweet, freckled face was sullen and angry; only her eyes were bashful as she softly put out her hand.

How am I supposed to resist if she looks at me like that?

In response, Rundelhaus gently placed his hand in hers.

Naturally, it was a gesture from another world, one that didn't exist here. To Rundelhaus, it looked for all the world like the gesture a knight used to escort a lady, only with the roles reversed, and it made him feel terribly embarrassed.

Later on, Isuzu told him it was a gesture dogs used to show their devotion to their masters, and he was furious, but circumstance had him by the scruff of the neck just then, and he was in no position to vent his anger.

Apparently, Rundelhaus was fated to be unable to oppose this freckled girl.

▶ 7

Akiba's first expedition force, which returned home in triumph, would later be called the Conquering Army of the East. This was linked to the fact that the Suzaku Gate Demon Festival incident in Western Yamato, which had been conducted at the same time, was called the Conquering Army of the West.

To be completely accurate, the expeditionary force hadn't defeated the Goblin King. It had only sealed his plunder army into the Zantleaf Peninsula and annihilated it. Roughly a week after Krusty and his infiltration strike battalion defeated the Goblin General, the entire operation was over.

During that time, Shiroe and Krusty's group stayed on their guard, half-expecting reinforcements from Seventh Fall, the goblins' main stronghold, but these never materialized.

They had Seventh Fall under surveillance, just to be on the safe side, and it was thought that an army of several thousand was probably hiding there. That number was about a fifth the size of the goblin plunder army, and if they only paid attention to the numbers, it wasn't a big threat.

However, speaking only in terms of the troop numbers was a mindset for considering battle potential back in the old world. In this other world, where the wide vertical distribution in individual fighting abilities ranged from the level of a single foot soldier to the equivalent of a tank, the number of individuals or troops could never be an absolute assessment of war potential. You could say that the recent Akiba expeditionary force had successfully proven this.

The Goblin King was still alive and well in Seventh Fall, and they predicted there were still many large magical beasts as well. The goblin

Shamans, who hadn't participated in the plunder army, were probably also lying in wait.

They had to assume that Seventh Fall still held a threat even greater than troop numbers.

However, they hadn't left Seventh Fall alone because it seemed difficult to capture. Even if there were a few formidable enemies left, with the Adventurers' strength, the Round Table Council assumed that subjugation was only a matter of time.

One of the reasons the subjugation of the Goblin King had been postponed was the decision that they ought to conclude treaties with Eastal beforehand.

A few members of the Round Table Council had something else in mind as well.

The Round Table Council had set bounties and issued numerous quests that involved patrolling the hamlets and villages in northeastern Yamato and putting down rogue goblins.

While it was one thing when they were in groups the size of the recent army, when they were in squads, the monsters known as goblins weren't much of a threat. Although they had put together a strategy in advance, the fact that Minori's group of players, whose levels were in the low 30s, had been able to fight them on equal terms was good proof.

To that end, these subjugation quests were aimed more at beginning or midlevel players than at high-level Adventurers, and the players were so extraordinarily glad to have them that scores of Adventurers rushed out of Akiba. They ran through the forests, fields, and mountains of northeastern Yamato, impressing upon the People of the Earth the fact that the Adventurers were back.

As they whittled away at the minor forces outside the stronghold, Seventh Fall would tighten its defenses even further. If they defeated the Goblin King in advance, by himself, it was likely that the goblin tribes would lose all discipline.

Having lost their sovereign, the goblins might disperse and cause problems they couldn't predict. In the abstract, this was how Shiroe had persuaded the Round Table Council. In other words, by sealing them away, they were laying the groundwork for their impending assault on Seventh Falls.

Shiroe had used the circumstances only because things had

happened to turn out that way, but the people around him kept calling him "black, black," and it made him feel rather glum. *As if there's any black or white in military strategy...* This was what Shiroe had to say, but that self-assessment managed to overlook several points.

Shiroe didn't know it, but the average Adventurer in Akiba thought that Shiroe had been the mastermind behind the Princess Raynesia campaign. In other words, they considered him a man who'd schemed to win over a sheltered, beautiful, naïve princess with clever words, then send her to the battlefield. As Raynesia's pure beauty won her increasing goodwill mixed with sympathy, the general estimation of Shiroe's character was on its way down.

Unaware of this, Shiroe was vaguely concerned that he seemed to be getting more flak than usual, and Henrietta cheered him on: "This is nowhere near the extent of your true blackness, Master Shiroe!" Shiroe had very mixed feelings about this.

During the grace period they'd won from their military campaign, three contracts were concluded between the Round Table Council and Eastal, the League of Free Cities: a basic relations treaty, a treaty of mutual traffic and commerce, and a peace treaty.

One month after the encirclement battle at Zantleaf...

A festival in honor of the conclusion of the treaties was in progress in Maihama.

Many nobles from all across northeastern Yamato had gathered in Maihama's beautiful, dazzling streets. The Lords' Council had been temporarily adjourned, and the lords who'd returned to their territories turned right around again and gathered in Maihama. Of course, unlike the Lords' Council, participation wasn't mandatory, which meant that a few faces were absent, but most of the noble lords and merchants were in attendance.

The town of Akiba was currently in a period of unprecedented economic development.

The great banquet held in honor of the treaties' signing was a rare opportunity to make acquaintances among the Adventurers. To the lords, it was a huge chance to push their territories' specialties and to conclude preferential contracts; their determination not to lose out to other lords combined with the heat of the festival to whip up a cutthroat negotiations war.

Meanwhile, however, it was the same for Akiba's various guilds: Production and commercial outfits and—if you considered guard duty and transportation—even the combat guilds alike, had looked forward to this banquet as a chance to win all sorts of business opportunities.

In any event, Yamato was presently short on practically every commodity there was, to the point where its collective head was almost spinning.

All the inns in Maihama's castle town were full, and many private houses had temporarily transformed themselves into guesthouses. The majority of guilds that held business talks here were small or midsized commercial guilds, as well as small guilds that had undertaken guard duty. Add in the peddlers who had come running from Akiba—bringing all the foodstuffs, swords, armor, and anything else they could sell off with the intent of making a windfall profit—and Maihama's population seemed to have doubled.

The royal palace had thrown itself open and was receiving guests, not only in its rooms for honored visitors and in its guest rooms, but even in the knights' palace. There, the lords were struggling desperately to conclude exclusive contracts with the major guilds.

Of course, in Earth terms, most of the *Elder Tales* players were far too young to be truly crafty, and the nobles had the advantage in the negotiations. Even so, the nobles were People of the Earth and weren't well acquainted with the Adventurers' demands and inner workings, and this caused frequent confusion.

Since both parties knew they were negotiating with someone they weren't used to, they tended to think, *That's probably good enough for now,* and compromised early. As a result, most of the negotiations ended on a pleasant note.

It was the sort of enormous festival that only happened once in a century.

The People of the Earth ate at all sorts of dining halls; street vendors and restaurants served the ballooning population until they were red in the face. Adventurers were so busy making items—or diligently selling them—that they had no time to sleep. Because everyone was able to make at least a little extra money at the celebration, and because the day's earnings were spent on drinking or meals that were fancier than usual or clothes that were finer than normal, both consumption and demand were skyrocketing.

The servants at the Court, some of whom were temporary workers, were flying around busily, following the steward's orders as he attempted to make all preparations to perfection. That said, as was only natural during an uproar like this, it was impossible to provide perfect hospitality, and the ever-serious man in charge of it all seemed ready to faint.

However, it was true that, in that sense, the Adventurers were quite an easy breed to deal with. Most Adventurers were the type who lived by the creed of taking care of themselves, and many were such self-effacing characters that even the simple act of being served at mealtimes made them uncomfortable.

If all the Adventurers had said, like the nobles, that they needed a minimum of three servants or maids just to take meals, change clothes, or bathe, even the Court of Maihama, the largest in the League of Free Cities, would have had to give up.

However, to the aristocrats, the Adventurers were almost shockingly simple, and splendid lifestyles seemed quite foreign to them. As they saw this, the more intelligent the noble, the further they tried to simplify their own lifestyles, at least during the negotiations. As a result, for the duration of the festival, even the self-indulgent, luxury-loving nobles became comparatively reasonable, and the attendants and ladies-in-waiting of the palace of Maihama breathed sighs of relief.

And now the festival to celebrate the conclusion of the treaties, which had pulled in everyone from the royal family to the townspeople—including seasonal workers, artisans, and farmers—had reached its climax.

Riding on a majestic melody played by an orchestra, a grand ball was about to begin in the great hall of Castle Cinderella, at the heart of Maihama.

This great hall was even larger than the one at the Ancient Court of Eternal Ice, and it was illuminated with the glimmer of countless candles and conjured lights. Invitations to the ball had been sent to nobles, the city's prominent merchants, and the Adventurers, and more than two hundred participants had gathered.

When their host, Duke Sergiad Cowen, announced the commencement of the ball to the guests, who were trembling in anticipation, the music swelled and grew clearer, welcoming the dancers.

But the ball was made abnormal by the presence of the Adventurers, and so the young knights and princesses alike shrank back. In the end, the first pair to step from their ranks was Krusty and Raynesia.

Krusty was the young hero from Akiba who'd saved the League of Free Cities from the threat of the goblins, and the mere combination of his name with that of the granddaughter of Maihama's House of Cowen—which headed the League of Free Cities—was enough to provoke curiosity. On top of that, this expedition was graced by a story that sounded like a heroic saga: Princess Raynesia had gone alone to the town of Akiba to plead with them, and the Adventurers, touched by her sincerity, had lent her their strength in the spirit of chivalry.

Krusty was a knight of such prowess that he was rumored to have fought the general of the goblin tribes one-on-one and defeated him, but the young man's quiet, intellectual looks belied that reputation. Behind his glasses, his profile was calm and completely unruffled. His height alone was suited to his profession: He was very tall, but the stolid image that accompanied the words "enormous knight" was nowhere to be seen. Krusty, who wore formal wear with sophistication, was the very picture of a young nobleman.

Meanwhile, Raynesia was said to be the most beautiful young princess in Eastal, the League of Free Cities. Today, she was wearing a comparatively reserved dress. Its satin fabric shaded from pale blue into violet and was delicately embroidered with silver thread. The puffed silhouette that completely covered her shoulders was conservative, but the neckline and the cut of the back were quite enough to capture the eyes of the gentlemen, and they highlighted the grace of her slender, swanlike neck.

The pair had advanced to the center of the floor, and a murmur that could have been praise or a sigh slipped from the people around them. They really did make an extraordinarily attractive sight, as if they'd stepped out of a picture.

"Aren't you going, my liege?"

Shiroe was in a dark, second-story space that overlooked the great hall, moistening his throat with Black Rose Tea. He glanced to the side.

There was Akatsuki, wearing the lovely dress he'd seen at the Ancient Court of Eternal Ice. (Henrietta had probably put her into it.)

While the pearl-colored dress was the same as it had been before, she was wearing a translucent, royal purple wrap with it today. Against the pale, layered colors of the dress, Akatsuki's silky black hair looked stunning.

"I'll pass this time. The leading role belongs to Krusty today. Even if I went, I wouldn't be much use. ...And anyway, it would tire me out."

As Shiroe spoke, Akatsuki came closer and sat down beside him, wordlessly.

The balcony held a small table and several chairs, and it felt rather deserted. Ordinarily, it would have served as a place for high-ranking nobles to rest, but the presence of Adventurer guests made the day's ball a boisterous one, and the court servants probably wouldn't make it all the way up here.

From their high vantage point, they had a good view of what was happening in the great hall below:

The orchestra, in matching uniforms, focused on performing. Business magnates and old aristocrats taken up in various corners, determined to thoroughly enjoy themselves. Adventurers who seemed a bit nervous. Brave, composed People of the Earth who were talking with knights and merchants.

As a wide variety of human-relation patterns played out, Krusty and Raynesia, having arrived at the center of the great hall, began to dance, their steps as captivating as a riot of blossoms.

"..."

Akatsuki, who had been watching intently, turned back to Shiroe, and their eyes met. Akatsuki opened her mouth. She seemed to be about to ask something, but then, as if she'd given up, she closed it tightly again. She looked completely at a loss, and it made Shiroe feel very gentle.

"Why are you laughing, my liege?"

"I'm not laughing."

"No, you laughed."

As Shiroe continued to say that he hadn't, Akatsuki bore down obstinately. However, abruptly, her tone softened and she apologized.

"I wasn't much use. Except for during battles, I only held you back, I think."

"That's not true, Akatsuki."

Akatsuki's words startled Shiroe. The incident had lasted a month from the time they were summoned to the Lords' Council, and Akatsuki had stayed by Shiroe's side for the duration, in public and behind the scenes, gathering intel and acting as his bodyguard. Hadn't they gone to Li Gan's study together, just the two of them, and come into contact with a corner of the mysteries of this world?

He told her as much, but Akatsuki's expression was still dejected.

I guess the fact that I'm grateful isn't really getting through to her...

Shiroe had only been trying to make a place for himself, and then to protect it, and yet this quiet girl had supported his wish the entire time. As Shiroe belatedly realized this, he stood up from his seat, almost without thinking.

"Shall we dance?"

"Huh?"

Shiroe stood, holding out a hand to the startled girl who was staring up at him from her chair. Just at that moment, from the great hall on the floor below, they began to hear rousing applause and the beginning of the second piece.

Light from the brilliantly illuminated hall shone into their dim, second-story balcony from below.

"My liege. I, um... Dancing isn't really..."

"You were practicing, weren't you?"

Shiroe took Akatsuki's hand and drew her to her feet.

He remembered Akatsuki rehearsing footwork in the courtyard that night, at the Ancient Court. That complicated footwork, unlike anything in martial arts, had been the exact set of dance steps Henrietta had taught Shiroe.

His taciturn companion, who seemed like a little girl even though they were the same age, had been secretly practicing dancing, out in the cool air that night. Over and over again: The motions she'd repeated often enough to make them a part of her had been exactly like Akatsuki's uncompromising character.

Even in this world, the only one who knew about it was Shiroe.

"My liege... Don't laugh."

"I'm an amateur at this myself. I won't laugh."

On the dark, narrow, second-story balcony, the two Log Horizon members took their first uncertain steps into the waltz that drifted up to reach them.

It was a faltering dance, in which each was hesitant toward the other.

▶ 8

The two who danced that same waltz in the midst of great brilliance were Krusty and Raynesia.

To Raynesia, Krusty looked like a huge tiger.

Krusty, who loomed right in front of her like a gigantic wall, was escorting her with steps so magnificent and orderly that they betrayed the image of his title as the general who'd commanded Akiba's expeditionary army.

His reputation at the court seemed to have settled into that of a handsome, gentle young man (Raynesia had learned as much from the rumors her maids brought her). Raynesia, who knew what he'd looked like on that battlefield, wanted to tell them, "Your eyes are X-marks drawn on with ink."

He's a tiger. This person is a monstrous tiger-human!

Some had also commented, *For a knight, he's quite slim, isn't he...* However, this was only because, from a distance, his height made him look comparatively slender. Seen right up close like this, with his arm around her waist, everything from the thickness of his arm to the depth of his chest made her feel very keenly that he was a completely different human—or rather, a completely different creature—from herself.

"What's wrong, Princess?"

"Nothing at all, Master Krusty."

Pasting on an expression that would look like a smile to the nobles and Adventurers around them, Raynesia whispered back crossly.

Krusty had lowered his voice as well, and in this great hall, filled as it was with orchestral music and the hum of voices, their whispers would fail to reach those around them.

Some might realize from the movement of their lips that they were whispering about something to each other as they danced, but their expressions and the situation would probably lead them to decide that the conversation was a friendly one.

Raynesia knew the romance-starved court ladies would turn their conversation into whispered sweet nothings in no time. She was actually hearing that sort of thing at that very moment.

"—It's maddening."

"What is?"

The most maddening part of it was the attitude Krusty was taking toward the rumors. He didn't deny them at all. Of course, if he had denied them, his laid-back attitude might have irritated her anyway, but she couldn't handle having that composure waved in front of her, either.

"It's nothing."

"Something seems to have offended you."

At his words, Raynesia mentally muttered, *Yes, you,* but the moment she did so, he answered with, "Well, surely it was me," and left her speechless.

Honestly! Imagine having your own private thoughts responded to! In any case, he doesn't even sound apologetic.

Thinking of the future, Raynesia sighed.

Her grandfather had shown a marked coolness regarding this whole affair. Eastal, the League of Free Cities, and the Round Table Council had concluded the treaties on the understanding that their relationship was an equal one. In this matter, neither owed a debt to the other.

On the other hand, when the goblins were on the point of devastating eastern Yamato, it was Raynesia, acting as an individual, who had asked for the Adventurers' help in their time of need. While the League felt the utmost gratitude and respect for their actions, they did not consider themselves to be in the Adventurers' debt.

Raynesia's grandfather had told her so, quite plainly.

Put simply, I am to pay back the debt to the Adventurers all by myself...

During this celebration and the festival that would follow, the Adventurers were being treated as guests of honor, but there was apparently no intent to repay them for their war expenditures. That alone was enough to make Raynesia turn pale.

Apart from what she'd said during her speech in Akiba, she'd thought the League of Free Cities would provide at least a little funding or a reward. If this was how things were, she couldn't pay a single condolence visit to the Adventurers who'd been injured during the expedition.

Even though she was remembering gloomy circumstances like these, possibly as a result of long years of training, Raynesia's body continued to execute elegant steps half automatically.

One step right. Two more steps right.

Quarter-turn. Step left. She raised her hand, gently touching Krusty's fingertips.

A flute like a flowing stream. Raynesia and Krusty danced on the sweet, melancholy tones of violins and melting ecstasy.

"Do you hate the idea so much?"

"It isn't that…"

The compromise her grandfather and the House of Cowen had proposed was to install Raynesia as an ambassador. Fundamentally, in the lords' aristocratic culture, ladies were symbolic figures. Although their beauty might be used in politics, it was unthinkable to expect political talents or business abilities from the ladies themselves.

However, according to her grandfather, "Raynesia has climbed out of that protective enclosure of her own accord," and so, in the future, such consideration would be unnecessary. She had then been ordered to take up the position of responsibility for the embassy that was being established in Akiba. Apparently, from now on, Raynesia would live shuttling back and forth between a villa that had been built in Akiba and Castle Cinderella in Maihama.

You are the one who created this debt, so it's only good form for you to stay nearby, humbling yourself before the Adventurers from time to time, don't you think?

Although her grandfather, Duke Sergiad, had spoken those words with a stern face, his eyes had been smiling. It was an unusual expression for him, but he was probably thinking this served Raynesia right.

That thought made her feel more than a little daunted.

"It comes with three meals and naps."

"Pardon?"

"Three meals and naps are included," Krusty muttered, in a weary, resigned tone. "The ambassador to Akiba, I mean. Of course Akiba is expected to continue to develop, and the lords will want facilities to handle their business trips, and bases for negotiations. We're aware that Maihama has gotten in first by putting a villa in Akiba. It will probably have some sort of effect… Still, we are Adventurers, you know. We don't care as much as aristocrats do about the aristocratic routines of aristocrats. I doubt there will be many tea parties or soirées. Since that's the sort of town you'll be coming to, Princess, I imagine you'll be able to revel in the life of a hermit, with three meals a day and naps."

At Krusty's abrupt statement, hope filled Raynesia's heart.

Was it possible that this was a state of affairs to be welcomed?

Now that she thought about it, leaving her parents' home meant escaping their watchful eyes as well. If things were like this, she could probably implement the plan she'd dreamed of for years: Lazing around for three whole days without even taking a bath.

"Well, three days or so is probably within the permissible range."

As Krusty spoke, having read her mind yet again, Raynesia's cheeks instantly flushed bright red. This nasty human menace was truly impossible to deal with. In a fit of anger, she squeezed his hand hard, but it probably did less damage to Krusty than if a songbird had alighted on it.

To the eyes of those around them, the people who knew nothing, it might have looked as though a young knight who boasted legendary military fame was escorting a beautiful princess, and that the pastel love between the two of them was causing the princess, who was filled with melancholy, to blush.

However, the rumors of bystanders often fail to match reality. Even if they do happen to match, it's simply hindsight being twenty-twenty, and no one but the people involved know the finer details.

"Now I'll finally be able to return to a life of untidiness. Won't I, Master Krusty?"

"Hmm, I wonder about that. You seem rather prone to shooting yourself in the foot, Princess."

As the rumored pair fought a whispered feud with one another, as they laid plans, like sworn enemies, or possibly like accomplices… For now, they simply rode the music of this ball held in celebration of peace, continuing to dance with elegant steps.

<Log Horizon, Volume 4: Game's End, Part 2—The End>

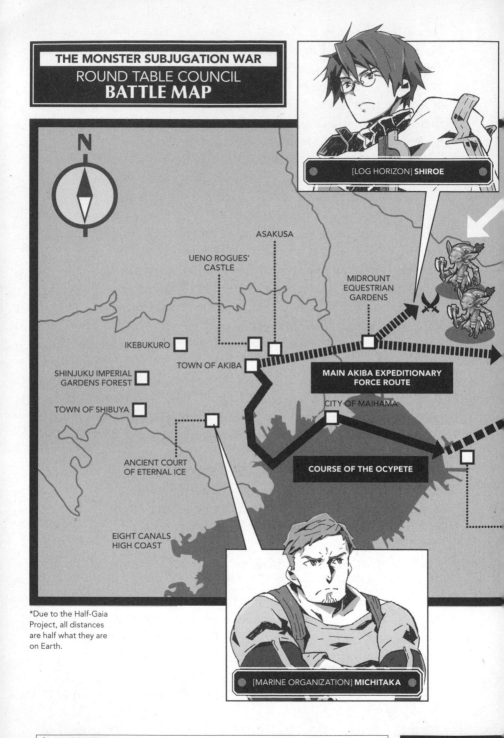

THE MONSTER SUBJUGATION WAR
ROUND TABLE COUNCIL
BATTLE MAP

N

[LOG HORIZON] **SHIROE**

ASAKUSA

UENO ROGUES'
CASTLE

MIDROUNT
EQUESTRIAN
GARDENS

IKEBUKURO

TOWN OF AKIBA

**MAIN AKIBA EXPEDITIONARY
FORCE ROUTE**

SHINJUKU IMPERIAL
GARDENS FOREST

CITY OF MAIHAMA

TOWN OF SHIBUYA

ANCIENT COURT
OF ETERNAL ICE

COURSE OF THE OCYPETE

EIGHT CANALS
HIGH COAST

*Due to the Half-Gaia
Project, all distances
are half what they are
on Earth.

[MARINE ORGANIZATION] **MICHITAKA**

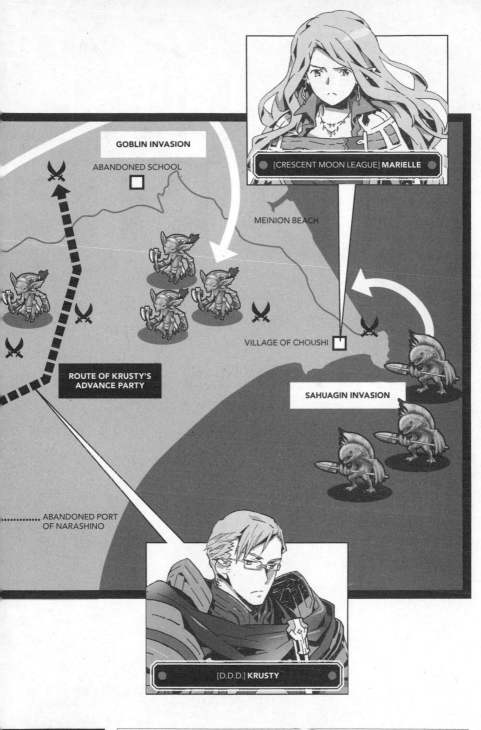

GOBLIN INVASION

ABANDONED SCHOOL

[CRESCENT MOON LEAGUE] MARIELLE

MEINION BEACH

ROUTE OF KRUSTY'S ADVANCE PARTY

VILLAGE OF CHOUSHI

SAHUAGIN INVASION

ABANDONED PORT OF NARASHINO

[D.D.D.] KRUSTY

[ELDER TALES]

MONSTE

AN IN-DEPTH INTRODUCTION TO MONSTERS,
THE SHADOW PROTAGONISTS OF *ELDER TALES*!!

Illustration: Mochichi Hashimoto

600

500

400

300

200

100

0

▲ SHIROE

▲ RAT MAN

▲ GOBLIN

▲ GOBLIN SHAMAN

▲ LAPIS FLY

R FILE 2

DIRE WOLF &
GOBLIN TAMER

UNDINE

GOBLIN
GENERAL

RUSEATO OF THE
SEVENTH PRISON

RAT MAN

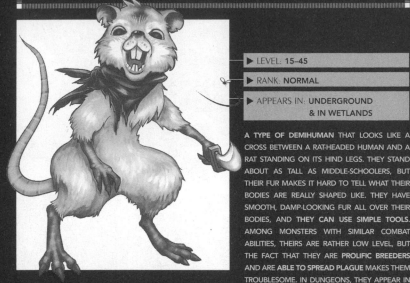

▶ LEVEL: **15–45**

▶ RANK: **NORMAL**

▶ APPEARS IN: **UNDERGROUND & IN WETLANDS**

A TYPE OF DEMIHUMAN THAT LOOKS LIKE A CROSS BETWEEN A RAT-HEADED HUMAN AND A RAT STANDING ON ITS HIND LEGS. THEY STAND ABOUT AS TALL AS MIDDLE-SCHOOLERS, BUT THEIR FUR MAKES IT HARD TO TELL WHAT THEIR BODIES ARE REALLY SHAPED LIKE. THEY HAVE SMOOTH, DAMP-LOOKING FUR ALL OVER THEIR BODIES, AND **THEY CAN USE SIMPLE TOOLS**. AMONG MONSTERS WITH SIMILAR COMBAT ABILITIES, THEIRS ARE RATHER LOW LEVEL, BUT THE FACT THAT THEY ARE **PROLIFIC BREEDERS** AND ARE **ABLE TO SPREAD PLAGUE** MAKES THEM TROUBLESOME. IN DUNGEONS, THEY APPEAR IN SWARMS.

GOBLIN

▶ LEVEL: **5–46**

▶ RANK: **NORMAL**

▶ APPEARS IN: **MOUNTAINS & DUNGEONS**

A TYPICAL VARIETY OF DEMIHUMAN, WITH A SHORT, UGLY, SKINNY, WARPED BODY. THEY STAND ABOUT ONE HUNDRED AND FIFTY CENTIMETERS TALL, AND THEY ARE THE MAIN EVIL FORCE IN THE NORTHEASTERN YAMATO ARCHIPELAGO. THEY ARE STUBBORN, CRUEL AND VICIOUS, AND THEY BREED VIGOROUSLY. WAR-LOVING. THEY HAVE A SIMPLIFIED TRIBAL SOCIETY WHOSE INHABITANTS LIVE DIVIDED AMONG SEVERAL FUNCTIONS, AND SOMETIMES THEY ADD MEMBERS OF OTHER RACES TO THEIR TRIBES AS SLAVES. THE MAJORITY LIVE IN SMALL SQUADS, BUT ON RARE OCCASIONS, A KING WITH A FORTIFIED MAIN STRONGHOLD WILL APPEAR.

▶ LEVEL: **29–33**

▶ RANK: **NORMAL**

▶ APPEARS IN: **MOUNTAINS & DUNGEONS**

MEMBERS OF GOBLIN TRIBES WHO ARE EXCEPTIONALLY SKILLED WITH MAGIC AND CAN USE SEVERAL SPELLS. MOST OF THEIR SPELLS ARE LOW LEVEL, BUT THEY CAN BE LETHAL TO BEGINNERS, WHO HAVE FEW WAYS TO COPE WITH MAGIC ATTACKS. THE TERROR OF GOBLINS LIES IN THE VARIATION OF THEIR TROOPS. WHEN GOBLIN SHAMANS START TO COOPERATE WITH MEMBERS WHO HOLD OTHER FUNCTIONS, THEY BECOME TOUGH ENEMIES.

LAPIS FLY

▶ LEVEL: **73–89**

▶ RANK: **PARTY**

▶ APPEARS IN: **MOUNTAINS & NEAR MOUNTAIN STREAMS**

A FORMIDABLE LARGE DRAGONFLY, AN INSECT MONSTER. IT HAS A BEAUTIFUL BLUE CARAPACE THAT'S OFTEN COMPARED TO LAPIS LAZULI AND TRANSPARENT, IRIDESCENT WINGS. BOTH ARE USED AS MATERIAL IN A FEW RECIPES. AS A RESULT, MANY ADVENTURERS TRY TO HUNT THEM, BUT THE HIGH EVASIVE ABILITY UNIQUE TO FLYING MONSTERS AND THEIR ACTION PATTERN OF FLEEING QUICKLY WHEN THINGS GET ROUGH MEANS IT'S HARD FOR EVEN A HIGH-LEVEL ADVENTURER TO RETRIEVE DROPPED ITEMS FROM THEM. OF COURSE, IF YOU PUT THESE ON THE MARKET, YOU'LL MAKE A FORTUNE IN NO TIME.

▶ LEVEL: **19–46**

▶ RANK: **PARTY**

▶ APPEARS IN: **FORESTS & MOUNTAINS**

A PAIR THAT CONSISTS OF **A LARGE WOLF MADE CRAZED AND VICIOUS** BY MANA AND THE MAGIC OF THE MOON, AND A **GOBLIN TAMER** THAT CONTROLS IT. GOBLIN TAMERS ARE ABLE TO USE SPECIAL CURSES AND SKILLS TO RAISE THE DIRE WOLVES' FIGHTING ABILITIES AND TRAIN THEM. THESE ARE POWERFUL TROOPS WHO **CAN MOVE AT HIGH SPEED AND ATTACK MULTIPLE TIMES,** AND THEY **OFTEN BREAK THROUGH ADVENTURER VANGUARDS. THE STANDARD MOVE IS TO CONCENTRATE YOUR FIGHTING POWER TO DEFEAT ONE OF THE TWO,** BECAUSE IF YOU SEPARATE THEM, THEY'RE EASY TO VANQUISH.

▶ LEVEL: **62**

▶ RANK: **RAID 1**

▶ APPEARS IN: **FORTRESSES & DUNGEONS**

MEMBERS OF THE GOBLIN TRIBES WHO HAVE HIGH INDIVIDUAL COMBAT ABILITIES AND THE SKILL TO COMMAND. THE KING OF THE GOBLIN TRIBES IS SERVED BY SEVERAL OF THESE GENERALS. ALTHOUGH THEY'RE COMMANDERS, THEY'RE STILL ONLY GOBLINS: THEY'RE UNABLE TO USE HIGH-LEVEL STRATEGIES AND SO EXCLUSIVELY USE BRUTE-FORCE ATTACKS THAT RELY ON NUMBERS. HOWEVER, THEIR ABILITY TO SPUR THE ENTIRE ARMY ON AND INSPIRE THEM FROM THEIR TANKS IS TROUBLESOME, AND THEY RAISE THE STANDARD FIGHTING ABILITY OF GOBLINS IN A WIDE-STRETCHING VICINITY. THEY ALSO HAVE HEALTH AND PHYSICAL STRENGTH FAR BEYOND THAT OF ANY NORMAL GOBLIN.

▶ LEVEL: **19–43**

▶ RANK: **NORMAL & PARTY**

▶ APPEARS IN: **WATER'S EDGE**

A TYPE OF **SPIRIT THAT CONTROLS WATER**. IN THE WORLD OF *ELDER TALES*, WHICH IS OVERFLOWING WITH UNTAMED NATURE, UNDINES OFTEN MANIFEST TO EITHER **HELP OR HINDER ADVENTURERS**. THIS TYPE OF SPIRIT IS **A MONSTER THAT HARBORS THE THREAT OF NATURAL FORCES**, BUT SUMMONERS WHO HAVE COMPLETED CERTAIN QUESTS CAN CONTRACT WITH THEM AND PUT THEM TO WORK. UNDINES ARE A FAVORITE OF MANY SUMMONERS FOR THEIR MANAGEABLE POWERS AND, ABOVE ALL, THEIR **BEAUTIFUL FORMS**. SINCE THE CATASTROPHE, THEIR ABILITY TO CREATE WATER HAS ALSO COME IN HANDY.

▶ LEVEL: **95**

▶ RANK: **RAID 1**

▶ APPEARS IN: **DUNGEONS**

A POWERFUL RAID-CLASS MONSTER THAT APPEARS IN THE NINE GREAT PRISONS OF HALOS. THE SEAL CREST ON THE KNIGHTS' PRISON MAKES IT IMPOSSIBLE FOR RECOVERY OR MAGIC-ATTACK CLASS MEMBERS TO MOVE, AND BATTLE IS CONDUCTED UNDER THESE CONDITIONS. MANIPULATING THE MECHANISM AND RELEASING THE SEAL SETS THE MEMBERS FREE, BUT RUSEATO HIMSELF POWERS UP AS WELL, ENTERS WHITE KNIGHT MODE OR BLACK KNIGHT MODE, AND BEGINS TO USE MAGIC ATTACKS. A POWERFUL FOE THAT MAKES TACTICAL DECISIONS NECESSARY.

▶ELDER TALES

A "SWORD AND SORCERY"—THEMED ONLINE GAME AND ONE OF THE LARGEST IN THE WORLD. AN MMORPG FAVORED BY SERIOUS GAMERS, IT BOASTS A TWENTY-YEAR HISTORY.

▶THE CATASTROPHE

A TERM FOR THE INCIDENT IN WHICH USERS WERE TRAPPED INSIDE THE *ELDER TALES* GAME WORLD. IT AFFECTED THE THIRTY THOUSAND JAPANESE USERS WHO WERE ONLINE WHEN *HOMESTEADING THE NOOSPHERE*, THE GAME'S TWELFTH EXPANSION PACK, WAS INTRODUCED.

▶ADVENTURER

THE GENERAL TERM FOR A GAMER WHO IS PLAYING *ELDER TALES*. WHEN BEGINNING THE GAME, PLAYERS SELECT HEIGHT, CLASS, AND RACE FOR THESE IN-GAME DOUBLES. THE TERM IS MAINLY USED BY NON-PLAYER CHARACTERS TO REFER TO PLAYERS.

▶PEOPLE OF THE EARTH

THE NAME NON-PLAYER CHARACTERS USE FOR THEMSELVES. THE CATASTROPHE DRASTICALLY INCREASED THEIR NUMBERS FROM WHAT THEY WERE IN THE GAME. THEY NEED TO SLEEP AND EAT LIKE REGULAR PEOPLE, SO IT'S HARD TO TELL THEM APART FROM PLAYERS WITHOUT CHECKING THE STATUS SCREEN.

▶THE HALF-GAIA PROJECT

A PROJECT TO CREATE A HALF-SIZED EARTH INSIDE *ELDER TALES*. ALTHOUGH IT'S NEARLY THE SAME SHAPE AS EARTH, THE DISTANCES ARE HALVED AND IT HAS ONLY ONE-FOURTH THE AREA.

▶AGE OF MYTH

A GENERAL TERM FOR THE ERA SAID TO HAVE BEEN DESTROYED IN THE OFFICIAL BACKSTORY OF THE *ELDER TALES* ONLINE GAME. IT WAS BASED ON THE CULTURE AND CIVILIZATION OF THE REAL WORLD. SUBWAYS AND BUILDINGS ARE THE RUINED RELICS OF THIS ERA.

▶THE OLD WORLD

THE WORLD WHERE SHIROE AND THE OTHERS LIVED BEFORE *ELDER TALES* BECAME ANOTHER WORLD AND TRAPPED THEM. A TERM FOR EARTH, THE REAL WORLD, ETC.

▶GUILDS

TEAMS COMPOSED OF MULTIPLE PLAYERS. SINCE IT'S EASIER TO CONTACT AFFILIATED MEMBERS AND INVITE THEM ON ADVENTURES AND BECAUSE GUILDS ALSO PROVIDE CONVENIENT SERVICES (SUCH AS MAKING IT EASIER TO RECEIVE AND SEND ITEMS), MANY PLAYERS BELONG TO THEM.

THE ROUND TABLE COUNCIL

THE TOWN OF AKIBA'S SELF-GOVERNMENT ORGANIZATION, FORMED AT SHIROE'S PROPOSAL. COMPOSED OF ELEVEN GUILDS, INCLUDING MAJOR COMBAT AND PRODUCTION GUILDS AND GUILDS THAT COLLECTIVELY REPRESENT SMALL AND MIDSIZE GUILDS, IT'S IN A POSITION TO LEAD THE REFORMATION IN AKIBA.

LOG HORIZON

THE NAME OF THE GUILD SHIROE FORMED AFTER THE CATASTROPHE. ITS FOUNDING MEMBERS—AKATSUKI, NAOTSUGU, AND NYANTA—HAVE BEEN JOINED BY THE TWINS MINORI AND TOUYA. THEIR HEADQUARTERS IS IN A RUINED BUILDING PIERCED BY A GIANT ANCIENT TREE ON THE OUTSKIRTS OF AKIBA.

THE CRESCENT MOON LEAGUE

THE NAME OF THE GUILD MARI LEADS. ITS PRIMARY PURPOSE IS TO SUPPORT MIDLEVEL PLAYERS. HENRIETTA, MARI'S FRIEND SINCE THEIR DAYS AT A GIRLS' HIGH SCHOOL, ACTS AS ITS ACCOUNTANT.

THE DEBAUCHERY TEA PARTY

THE NAME OF A GROUP OF PLAYERS THAT SHIROE, NAOTSUGU, AND NYANTA BELONGED TO AT ONE TIME. IT WAS ACTIVE FOR ABOUT TWO YEARS, AND ALTHOUGH IT WASN'T A GUILD, IT'S STILL REMEMBERED IN *ELDER TALES* AS A LEGENDARY BAND OF PLAYERS.

FAIRY RINGS

TRANSPORTATION DEVICES LOCATED IN FIELDS. THE DESTINATIONS ARE TIED TO THE PHASES OF THE MOON, AND IF PLAYERS USE THEM AT THE WRONG TIME, THERE'S NO TELLING WHERE THEY'LL END UP. AFTER THE CATASTROPHE, SINCE STRATEGY WEBSITES ARE INACCESSIBLE, ALMOST NO ONE USES THEM

ZONE

A UNIT THAT DESCRIBES RANGE AND AREA IN *ELDER TALES*. IN ADDITION TO FIELDS, DUNGEONS, AND TOWNS, THERE ARE ZONES AS SMALL AS SINGLE HOTEL ROOMS. DEPENDING ON THE PRICE, IT'S SOMETIMES POSSIBLE TO BUY THEM.

THELDESIA

THE NAME FOR THE GAME WORLD CREATED BY THE HALF-GAIA PROJECT. A WORD THAT'S EQUIVALENT TO "EARTH" IN THE REAL WORLD.

SPECIAL SKILL

VARIOUS SKILLS USED BY ADVENTURERS. ACQUIRED BY LEVELING UP YOUR MAIN CLASS OR SUBCLASS. EVEN WITHIN THE SAME SKILL, THERE ARE FOUR RANKS— ELEMENTARY, INTERMEDIATE, ESOTERIC, AND SECRET—AND IT'S POSSIBLE TO MAKE THEM GROW BY INCREASING YOUR PROFICIENCY.

►MAIN CLASS

THESE GOVERN COMBAT ABILITIES IN *ELDER TALES*, AND PLAYERS CHOOSE ONE WHEN BEGINNING THE GAME. THERE ARE TWELVE TYPES, THREE EACH IN FOUR CATEGORIES: WARRIOR, WEAPON ATTACK, RECOVERY, AND MAGIC ATTACK.

►SUBCLASS

ABILITIES THAT AREN'T DIRECTLY INVOLVED IN COMBAT BUT COME IN HANDY DURING GAME PLAY. ALTHOUGH THERE ARE ONLY TWELVE MAIN CLASSES, THERE ARE OVER FIFTY SUBCLASSES, AND THEY'RE A JUMBLED MIX OF EVERYTHING FROM CONVENIENT SKILL SETS TO JOKE ELEMENTS.

►THE TOWN OF AKIBA

ONE OF THE MAIN ADVENTURER TOWNS IN THE YAMATO REGION. IT'S BUILT ON THE SITE THAT AKIHABARA OCCUPIES IN REAL-WORLD JAPAN.

►ARC-SHAPED ARCHIPELAGO YAMATO

THE WORLD OF THELDESIA IS DESIGNED BASED ON REAL-WORLD EARTH. THE ARC-SHAPED ARCHIPELAGO YAMATO IS THE REGION THAT MAPS TO JAPAN, AND IT'S DIVIDED INTO FIVE AREAS: THE EZZO EMPIRE; THE DUCHY OF FOURLAND; THE NINE-TAILS DOMINION; EASTAL, THE LEAGUE OF FREE CITIES; AND THE HOLY EMPIRE OF WESTLANDE.

►CAST TIME

THE PREPARATION TIME NEEDED WHEN USING A SPECIAL SKILL. THESE ARE SET FOR EACH SEPARATE SKILL, AND MORE POWERFUL SKILLS TEND TO HAVE LONGER CAST TIMES. WITH COMBAT-TYPE SPECIAL SKILLS, IT'S POSSIBLE TO MOVE DURING CAST TIME, BUT WITH MAGIC-BASED SKILLS, SIMPLY MOVING INTERRUPTS CASTING.

► MAIN CLASSES

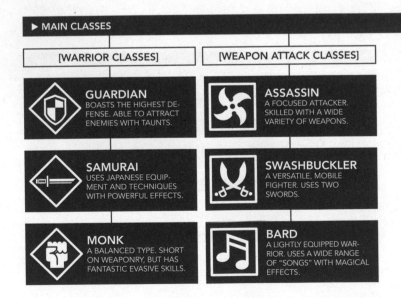

[WARRIOR CLASSES]	[WEAPON ATTACK CLASSES]
GUARDIAN BOASTS THE HIGHEST DEFENSE. ABLE TO ATTRACT ENEMIES WITH TAUNTS.	**ASSASSIN** A FOCUSED ATTACKER. SKILLED WITH A WIDE VARIETY OF WEAPONS.
SAMURAI USES JAPANESE EQUIPMENT AND TECHNIQUES WITH POWERFUL EFFECTS.	**SWASHBUCKLER** A VERSATILE, MOBILE FIGHTER. USES TWO SWORDS.
MONK A BALANCED TYPE. SHORT ON WEAPONRY, BUT HAS FANTASTIC EVASIVE SKILLS.	**BARD** A LIGHTLY EQUIPPED WARRIOR. USES A WIDE RANGE OF "SONGS" WITH MAGICAL EFFECTS.

▶MOTION BIND

REFERS TO THE WAY YOUR BODY FREEZES UP AFTER YOU'VE USED A SPECIAL SKILL. DURING MOTION BIND, ALL ACTIONS ARE IMPOSSIBLE, INCLUDING MOVEMENT.

▶RECAST TIME

THE AMOUNT OF TIME YOU HAVE TO WAIT AFTER YOU'VE USED A SPECIAL SKILL BEFORE YOU CAN USE IT AGAIN. THIS RESTRICTION MAKES IT VERY DIFFICULT TO USE A SPECIFIC SPECIAL SKILL SEVERAL TIMES IN A ROW. SOME SPECIAL SKILLS HAVE SUCH LONG RECAST TIMES THAT THEY CAN BE USED ONLY ONCE PER DAY.

▶CALL OF HOME

A BASIC TYPE OF SPECIAL SKILL THAT ALL ADVENTURERS LEARN. IT INSTANTLY RETURNS YOU TO THE LAST SAFE AREA WITH A TEMPLE THAT YOU VISITED, BUT ONCE YOU USE IT, YOU CAN'T USE IT AGAIN FOR TWENTY-FOUR HOURS.

▶RAID

THE TERM FOR A BATTLE FOUGHT BY NUMBERS LARGER THAN THE NORMAL SIX-MEMBER PARTIES ADVENTURERS USUALLY FORM. IT CAN ALSO BE USED TO REFER TO A UNIT MADE UP OF MANY PEOPLE. FAMOUS EXAMPLES INCLUDE TWENTY-FOUR-MEMBER FULL RAIDS AND NINETY-SIX-MEMBER LEGION RAIDS.

▶RACE

THERE ARE A VARIETY OF HUMANOID RACES IN THE WORLD OF THELDESIA. ADVENTURERS MAY CHOOSE TO PLAY AS ONE OF EIGHT RACES: HUMAN, ELF, DWARF, HALF ALV, FELINOID, WOLF-FANG, FOXTAIL, AND RITIAN. THESE ARE SOMETIMES CALLED BY THE GENERAL TERM, "THE 'GOOD' HUMAN RACES."

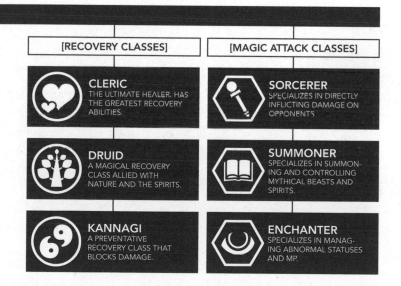

[RECOVERY CLASSES]

CLERIC
THE ULTIMATE HEALER. HAS THE GREATEST RECOVERY ABILITIES.

DRUID
A MAGICAL RECOVERY CLASS ALLIED WITH NATURE AND THE SPIRITS.

KANNAGI
A PREVENTATIVE RECOVERY CLASS THAT BLOCKS DAMAGE.

[MAGIC ATTACK CLASSES]

SORCERER
SPECIALIZES IN DIRECTLY INFLICTING DAMAGE ON OPPONENTS

SUMMONER
SPECIALIZES IN SUMMONING AND CONTROLLING MYTHICAL BEASTS AND SPIRITS.

ENCHANTER
SPECIALIZES IN MANAGING ABNORMAL STATUSES AND MP.

AFTERWORD

Hello for the first time since last month. Mamare Touno here.

Thank you very much for buying *Log Horizon, Vol. 4: Game's End, Part 2*. This is the direct sequel to *Log Horizon, Vol. 3: Game's End, Part 1*, which went on sale last month. Catch the punch line for everything that happened last month in this volume! As with the previous volume, there's a ton of content in this one, too.

In the average *Log Horizon* afterword, starting about here, the point is for me to run on and on about my little sister (the truth is out!), but this time it's going to be a bit more like a report.

As a matter of fact, I got outed to my relatives.

For the eight months since *Maoyuu*, I'd lived as though I hadn't had a book published, but now my entire family is wise to it.

"Hm. Did you get it released through Iwanami or one of those places?" said my uncle, and I just about keeled over. No, sir, I did not. I mean, it isn't academic or a thesis or anything. It's a much lighter book. Light, *raito*. And I don't mean it illuminates things, or that it's correct. And no, it cannot fly. And anyway, we're brother and sister, not two brothers.

I mean, really, it's *light*, and when I say light, consider that *lite*. It's not butter, it's margarine. The low-calorie, plant-based stuff.

I'd be grateful if you'd just let the content pass without remark. Not that it's anything embarrassing… I say, completely on the defensive.

Anyway, it all began with a direct comment straight out of left field from my middle-schooler nephew at our family meeting. Busted by Twitter, apparently. I guess it's only natural, after I blabbed all that local information, but still. As an alumnus of Saint Francis Preschool, I did consider administering education on becoming silent, but the fact that he's also a valued reader put me in a bit of a bind.

As I was dealing with that, the entire coalition of relatives stormed me with a public interview session.

"What sort of books are you writing?"

"Is it something they sell in bookstores?"

"You sure they're not pulling your leg?"

"I wonder if we should hand them out to the neighbors…"

"Go buy me some ice cream."

What awful abuse to inflict on a social recluse.

It wasn't as if I'd done anything wrong, so why was I meekly listening to sermons from relatives? Because I'd kept it a secret. Only it wasn't like I was actively trying to hide it…Th-th-they just didn't ask me, all right?! …I say, giving pointlessly *tsundere* responses, completely flustered.

The one who really surprised me was Sister Touno.

Get this: My sister stuck her tongue out and said, "I knew."

Why, little sister? Tell *me* these things, little sister.

I *did* ask, and apparently she had caught on when the complimentary copies were delivered. I just assumed she hadn't noticed.

And then, Sister Touno…

"The main character is a virgin, and it's about him making out with a lady with big boobs."

…laid down some covering fire for me, and I was terribly grateful. Thanks to that, the family meeting underwent a miraculous transformation from public Q&A to public execution. The skillful remodel moved me to tears.

Personally, the line I really can't forget is my uncle's "Don't tell me you still haven't…" Do they think I'm a magician? This is going to end in tears, you know.

Sister Touno's surprise attack landed me at death's door.

And so, after the family meeting ended, the two of us had words on our way home.

She really ripped me a new one: "You're stupid, stupid brother, and you have lousy taste in shoes" and "Hermit" and "Go buy a new refrigerator."

This even though Sister Touno loves red pickled ginger so much that she started eating it and—"Big brother! Big brother! This is really, really good!"—ate her way through the entire bag (a business-use pack we bought at Okachimachi Niki Sweets). Even though, up until just a little bit ago, she thought *psychology* meant "not very popular at all, to the point where you're really and truly alone." Even though she sings Doraemon songs in the bathroom.

But the cat was out of the bag anyway, so I asked her if she wanted a copy of *Log Horizon*. And she gave this great big sneer and said, "I already bought one, so I don't need it." So I'll forgive her.

Even though she's a seriously annoying little sister.

All right: Touno family meeting aside, this is *Log Horizon, Vol. 4*.

In this volume, I cover the battle against the goblins and sahuagins that are invading the Zantleaf Peninsula. Minori and Touya and the rest of the newbie party worked really hard in the last volume, and they're still at it! Master Shiroe was messing around dancing at balls with beautiful women, but he's active in this one, too.

The world is overflowing with "best-laid plans" that don't work out, but for that very reason, when you've made up your mind to do something, if you believe it's the right thing to do, then it's okay to go all out. That's what this volume is about. Even going all-out may not pay off in the end, but precisely because that's the case, the freedom to decide to give it everything you've got and take action belongs to you. In other words, it's all right to lay those plans. Both the newbies and the Akibans are giving it all they've got.

This has been *Volume 4*, during which I thought, *I'm going to have to give it everything I've got, too, or else.*

The items listed on the character status screens at the beginning of each chapter in this volume were collected on Twitter in July and August 2011. I used items from bad_blade, ebius1, ginnoougi, gontan_, hige_mg, hpsuke, iron007dd22, kuroyagi6, makotoTRPG, nekoanagi, roki_a, sawame_ja, sin_217, tepan00 and vaiso. Thank you very much!! I can't list all your names here, but I'm grateful to everyone who submitted entries. *Log Horizon* is created through your support.

Those of you who became *Log Horizon* fans through the printed editions, stop by the website, too! Visit http://mamare.net. You'll find the latest information there, including news about the series. Information on the comic adaptation is there as well. I'll also have a big announcement to make soon!

...And finally. Shoji Masuda, who produced this volume, too; Kazuhiro Hara, who poured his heart and soul into drawing that Krusty and Princess cover; Mochichi Hashimoto, who designed the monsters again; Tsubakiya Design, who handled the design work (lots of fiddly little jobs here!); and little F——ta of the editorial department! I'm sorry to have caused you trouble! And Oha, who always plays straight man to my idiot prose! Thank you very much!

Now all that's left is for you to savor this book. *Bon appétit!*

Mamare "I hate to admit it, but, if nothing else,
the stewed dishes at the main house are top-notch" Touno

WONDERFUL WORK.
SEE YOU NEXT VOLUME.
HARA

▶LOG HORIZON, VOLUME 4
MAMARE TOUNO
ILLUSTRATION BY KAZUHIRO HARA

▶TRANSLATION BY TAYLOR ENGEL

▶LOG HORIZON, VOLUME 4:
GAME'S END, PART II

▶YEN ON
1290 AVENUE OF THE AMERICAS
NEW YORK, NY 10104
WWW.YENPRESS.COM

▶YEN ON IS AN IMPRINT OF YEN PRESS, LLC.

▶THE YEN ON NAME AND LOGO ARE TRADEMARKS OF YEN PRESS, LLC.

▶FIRST YEN ON EDITION: MARCH 2016

▶LIBRARY OF CONGRESS CATALOGING-IN-PUBLICATION DATA

NAMES: TOUNO, MAMARE, AUTHOR. | HARA, KAZUHIRO, ILLUSTRATOR.
TITLE: LOG HORIZON. VOLUME 4, GAME'S END, PART 2 / MAMARE TOUNO ;
   ILLUSTRATION BY KAZUHIRO HARA.
OTHER TITLES: GAME'S END, PART 2
DESCRIPTION: NEW YORK, NY : YEN ON, [2016] | SUMMARY:
   "THE STRONGHOLD OF AKIBA FACES A NEW THREAT: A MIGHTY GOBLIN
   ARMY! IN THEIR EFFORTS TO REBUILD THE CITY, THE ADVENTURERS OF
   ELDER TALES HAD NEGLECTED IMPORTANT QUESTS, AND NOW THEY
   REAP THE CONSEQUENCES. WITH THE REVELATION THAT IN-GAME
   DEATH LEADS TO MEMORY LOSS OF THE REAL WORLD, THE STAKES
   HAVE NEVER BEEN HIGHER. AND WILL CUTTHROAT POLITICS DESTROY
   TENUOUS NEW ALLIANCES BEFORE THE REAL BATTLE EVEN BEGINS?"
   —PROVIDED BY PUBLISHER.
IDENTIFIERS: LCCN 2015038410 | ISBN 9780316263856 (PAPERBACK)
SUBJECTS: | CYAC: SCIENCE FICTION. | BISAC: FICTION / SCIENCE FICTION /
   ADVENTURE.
CLASSIFICATION: LCC PZ7.1.T67 LOJ 2016 | DDC [FIC]—DC23 LC RECORD
AVAILABLE AT HTTP://LCCN.LOC.GOV/2015038410

10 9 8 7 6 5

▶LSC-C

▶PRINTED IN THE UNITED STATES OF AMERICA

AUTHOR:
▶ **MAMARE TOUNO**

SUPERVISION:
▶ **SHOJI MASUDA**

ILLUSTRATION:
▶ **KAZUHIRO HARA**

▶AUTHOR: MAMARE TOUNO

A STRANGE LIFE-FORM THAT INHABITS THE TOKYO BOKUTOU SHITAMACHI AREA. IT'S BEEN TOSSING HALF-BAKED TEXT INTO A CORNER OF THE INTERNET SINCE THE YEAR 2000 OR SO. IT'S A FULLY AUTOMATIC, TEXT-LOVING MACRO THAT EATS AND DISCHARGES TEXT. IT DEBUTED AT THE END OF 2010 WITH *MAOYUU: MAOU YUUSHA* (*MAOYUU: DEMON KING AND HERO*). *LOG HORIZON* IS A RESTRUCTURED VERSION OF A NOVEL THAT RAN ON THE WEBSITE *SHOUSETSUKA NI NAROU* (*SO YOU WANT TO BE A NOVELIST*).

WEBSITE: HTTP://WWW.MAMARE.NET

▶SUPERVISION: SHOJI MASUDA

AS A GAME DESIGNER, HE'S WORKED ON *RINDA KYUUBU* (*RINDA CUBE*) AND *ORE NO SHIKABANE WO KOETE YUKE* (*STEP OVER MY DEAD BODY*), AMONG OTHERS. ALSO ACTIVE AS A NOVELIST, HE'S RELEASED THE *ONIGIRI NUEKO* (*ONI KILLER NUEKO*) SERIES, THE *HARUKA* SERIES, *JOHN & MARY: FUTARI HA SHOUKIN KASEGI* (*JOHN & MARY: BOUNTY HUNTERS*), *KIZUDARAKE NO BIINA* (*BEENA, COVERED IN WOUNDS*), AND MORE. HIS LATEST EFFORT IS HIS FIRST CHILDREN'S BOOK, *TOUMEI NO NEKO TO TOSHI UE NO IMOUTO* (*THE TRANSPARENT CAT AND THE OLDER LITTLE SISTER*). HE HAS ALSO WRITTEN *GEEMU DEZAIN NOU MASUDA SHINJI NO HASSOU TO WAZA* (*GAME DESIGN BRAIN: SHINJI MASUDA'S IDEAS AND TECHNIQUES*).

TWITTER ACCOUNT: SHOJIMASUDA

▶ILLUSTRATION: KAZUHIRO HARA

AN ILLUSTRATOR WHO LIVES IN ZUSHI. ORIGINALLY A HOME GAME DEVELOPER. IN ADDITION TO ILLUSTRATING BOOKS, HE'S ALSO ACTIVE IN MANGA AND DESIGN. LATELY, HE'S BEEN HAVING FUN FLYING A BIOKITE WHEN HE GOES ON WALKS.

WEBSITE: HTTP://WWW.NINEFIVE95.COM/IG/

Adventurer, you whose weight is borne by your winged soul! The mystical world of Theldesia is home to dragons and giants, magical beasts, and demihumans. Fragrant green winds blow across this new yet ancient land that opens before you like a blank page. Fill it with your life.

LOG HORIZON